AS YOU WERE

Also by Elaine Feeney

Poetry
Where's Katie?
The Radio Was Gospel
Rise

Elaine Feeney

AS YOU WERE

BIBLIOASIS
Windsor, Ontario

First published in North America by Biblioasis in 2021

FIRST EDITION
1 3 5 7 9 10 8 6 4 2

Library and Archives Canada Cataloguing in Publication

Title: As you were / Elaine Feeney.
Names: Feeney, Elaine, author.
Description: Originally published: London : Harvill Secker, 2020.
Identifiers: Canadiana (print) 20210215844
Canadiana (ebook) 20210215852
ISBN 9781771964432 (softcover) | ISBN 9781771964449 (ebook)
Classification: LCC PR6106.E36 A82 2021 | DDC 823/.92—dc23

Simultaneously published in a numbered hardcover limited edition of 300 copies, designed by Natalie Olsen and signed by the author.

Readied for the press by Daniel Wells
Softcover jacket designed by Zoe Norvell

Softcover jacket painting: Daisy Patton, *Untitled (Judy's 5 Jan '49)*
80"x60," Oil on archival print mounted to panel, 2017

PRINTED AND BOUND IN CANADA

For Jack and Finn

We do not know our own souls, let alone the souls of others.
Human beings do not go hand in hand the whole stretch of
the way. There is a virgin forest in each; a snowfield where
even the print of birds' feet is unknown. Here we go alone,
and like it better so. Always to have sympathy, always to be
accompanied, always to be understood would be intolerable.

Virginia Woolf – *On Being Ill*

I want to take my mind off my mind.

Mike McCormack – *Notes From a Coma*

Pisreógs|

I didn't tell a soul I was sick.

OK, I told a fat magpie.

She was the first beating heart I met after the oncology unit and she sat shiny and serious on the bonnet of the Volvo.

One for sorrow.

And I saluted her with that greeting you give when you find yourself alone and awkward with one magpie and she flew away, piercing her black arc through the sky blue.

An arrow points to You Are Here. This is OK.

Breathe.

You are just a dot. Swirly Space.

Breathe.

No one will ever find you.

Good. This is a good thing.

Thump.

onetwothreefourfivesixseveneightnineten

Thump.

After saluting Magpie, I sped at one hundred and thirty-nine kilometres per hour out along the M6; stone walls hurled past and end days of August conspired with night, letting a cold dusk down. Thirty-nine. Fitting. On the car's windscreen, a fog was creeping around my eldest son's initials, traced inside a fat heart.

But I was Fine.

Father always told me I was Fine. So as the years went by I grew increasingly mistrustful of bad-news bearers. Miss Sinéad Hynes was fine. Father said so. I was Fine. I am Fine.

I will be Fine.

By Jesus when I get my hands on her, I'll fucking kill her; I'll throttle her, that little cunt. She's fine, and she pretending to be sick. Truth is, there is absolutely nothing wrong with her a'tall, but I'll tell you what, there's a lot wrong with the old ewe twisted on her back all night, and she didn't even bother to check her, just even once, throw a quick eye on her. She wouldn't mind a china cup, that one. Where is she? Under here? Here? In the cupboard? Hot-press? Come out! Come out! Wherever you are! Feefifofum. I smell blood. Where in the name of good God is she? Leaving an old ewe all the night through on her back. Reading books somewhere, and she isn't sick, she's fine. There's not a thing wrong with her. Fine. Hiding is all she's at. Afraid of work, that bitch, well, she can tell that to the dead animal, so she can, reading books. I'll give her books when I get my hands on her.

My mother told me to have a hot bath or put on a nice hat if I was having a bad day. When I'd leave home, she'd stand in the doorway and knead the hollow space between my shoulder blades with her knuckles as I slipped past. She'd dip her index finger into the little hole at the feet of Jesus and flick droplets in my wake. He hung on a loose nail by the door, pasty and lean with bright red drips on his hands and feet, loincloth and blue eyes to die for.

3

In the name of the Father, and of the Son, and of the Holy Spirit.

Amen.

Growing up on the farm I kept bad news to myself, for going public with fortune or misfortune brings drama. I'd hide out underneath my single bed tucking the eiderdown flaps tight around me. Father'd bellow for things he needed urgently, hammer, ladder, cup of tea, plasters, jump-leads, pair of hands, mother, phone, vet. The phone for the vet was dragged in a rush out from the kitchen and my mother'd place the cream receiver into his large hand, dial for him, he'd have a palm on his forehead. Panic. Always panic.

I loved being outside with the animals, especially in the moments after they birthed; foals are the most incredible – how fast they rise and run with their mother. But I loved it best when I was completely alone with no one looking for me.

As I grew older and hair stung my armpits, spread between my legs, pimples erupting on my face, body betraying my early deftness, I borrowed more books from the library. I was clumpy and awkward and left the animals to themselves. I also stole some books from my mother's locker. Binchy or Cookson, some Wilde with witty phrases that made me laugh and had come free with Christmas cards. Books didn't see you. Stare at you. Notice your thick thighs that rubbed together as you moved.

Father despised all learning that came from books.

Later I read forbidden things. *Just Seventeen*. Judy Blume. McGahern. Edna. I longed for a Mr Gentleman to drive by, but people rarely came up our road unless they were lost or looking to buy an animal. When the house was empty, I liked to draw pictures sitting at the long kitchen table. Often birds, a fat robin landing in snow. Robins were my favourite, their blood breast and the unlikelihood of them being allowed to perch inside the house for the misfortune they'd bring on our family, all the pisreógs we hid from – putting new shoes on the table, walking under a ladder, cracking a mirror.

This power made them mysterious, cheeky outsiders. Like loner magpies.

Freeze.

My mother would cry out often about traumatic events or the threat of them. Father would say, *It is no use in the wide earthly world crying alone in a darkened room for yourself.*

All shock was shock, good or bad.

★

Before Magpie, I had been to Hospital a handful of times, three times to birth three boy children – the three kings. Once to have a thickened viscid appendix plucked off my bowel and once for an STD screening that turned out to be discharge from a burst ovarian cyst. Phew. You went to Hospital for a baby and it was a happy place. That's what my mother and the neighbours said. They shared packing advice, make-up bag, fluffy bed coat, Solpadeine, Epsom salts, prune juice, new flannels, XL disposable knickers, yellow or cream clothing for baby, cream blanket with breathing holes, mittens, babygro, hat, a change of clothes and some snacks for your husband. You reacted accordingly because you knew you should be happy, it was a happy time and you'd be happy with your baby because Hospital was a gift when you went there for a baby. Any misgivings or nerves were shushed. The happenings inside maternity wards were not up for discussion.

If you were heavy all over like a small silage bale, they'd say it was a boy; if you were neat and all forward to the front, slung low like a soccer ball stuffed under your jumper, they'd say it was a girl. But all that mattered was health and happiness (and to make a bowel movement

quickly and painlessly afterwards, that didn't rupture
your stitches).

Once or twice I went in secret with a drunk friend and
watched as they gawked up charcoal-laced vomit out
through a crow-yellow mouth, twisted ankle or a broken nose from falling over in stilettos that got trapped in
Galway's dodgy cobbles. As they spewed out sadness
they grasped hard on to the steel roll of the trolley,
knuckles pale and blue. I'd claw my foot along the floor
and haphazardly begin apologising.

No, she's not always like this, no, soz, I don't know her
date of birth, or soz, no, don't know her next of kin
either. Soz.

Soz.

Schuch. Schuch. Schuch.

I said over and over and overandoverandoverandtodover
wegooverandoveragain.

Schuch. Schuch. Schuch.

This was how I would herd sheep. Chanting. I use it
now to control the pain.

Count it. Chant. Bellow. Watch it. Observe your pain closely.

Then, equate it into a number.

Onetwothreefourfivesixseveneightnineten. End. All pain ends at ten.

I also went to Hospital to birth a daughter but we weren't far enough along to tell whether I was low down or carrying forward or if, perhaps, I was just fat with puffy feet.

She had no heartbeat.

Schuch. Schuch. Schuch.

★

After Magpie it was impossible to focus, everything was hostile – where to fall asleep or in what position, how to avoid having sex with Alex, where to watch TV and what to watch. I flicked aimlessly through Sky Planner. I couldn't watch the shit I had recorded on Series Link. Not now, gawping at another CSI, or some overfed guy shoving a million meat-feast sandwiches into his mouth in a tacky Omaha deli. I couldn't coordinate an outfit. Not one for sitting around the house. I couldn't just listen to the radio. I was unable to do anything with sustained interest or longevity apart from cracking open boiled apple sweets between my back teeth. Though even that had its consequences as the skin on the roof of my mouth had thinned and tasted rusty from sucking the green-and-red drops.

With everything unpalatable, I froze. Ostrich. Attempted to blend in. Chameleon.

And while I understand the wacky madness of ostriches and the complex threat chameleons are under from forced domestication and threadworms, after Magpie, emulating them was the best I could muster, and yes, it was somewhat considered, and yes, many times it was neglect, and yes, I may be judged harshly for my non-disclosure of my bodily activity, and yes, at other times it was downright cruel, hiding my terminal status from Alex, but mostly it just was what it was.

Dwelling in my body had become complicated, and negotiating language for its actions and more specifically the actions of my wayward cells was far from simple, even if now I know that everything has a point of simplification.

And it was utterly bewildering.

Abjectly terrified of the complications of social relationships, it suited me to go underground after Magpie, turn in on myself. This protected me from known drama-hacks, addicts, fuck-wits, mentalists, religious, super non-religious, egoists and lack-of-ego-sap-the-ego-outta-ya-ists that cling on around the sick.

Christmas came and went. Seasons here are reliable, the way they move along, constantly motored, and while people noticed how thin I was and commented on it, they also believed me when I said it was taking some time to shake a flu virus thing.

Spring arrived, shy and reserved, with a little frost spite. Daffodils popped, snow fell, winds came, lambs dropped, crocuses hung delicately above soil, wind howled, sun shone on cobwebs, and the few old ewes that survived the long harsh winter were applauded.

I stayed at home and worked from our bed. But really I was under my duvet, Googling, in case I suddenly dropped dead and needed a soft landing spot.

I desperately wanted to pick up a book as I ran my hand along their spines over and over. But I baulked.

Maybe you might help with the sheep herding and shir it'll take that pasty look off your face — is that infection back again?

Aren't you a lot weaker than your mother? And all those anti-biotics she's giving you. I keep telling her you're fine, and you have to fight it yourself. You can't keep falling in under sickness like this. Jesus Christ above in heaven, I don't know where we got you from. Well, you're certainly not following after my side. Fine strong people on my side, not pale city people. Weak they are, the city people, it's the smog, or the lack of work. Both probably. If you rubbed a bit of rouge onto your sour-dough puss, you know, I declare to Christ but you might look, indeed you definitely would look, a lot better. Men don't like to look at a pasty pale face, and you do want one at some stage I presume, because you'd hardly brave it all alone, you wouldn't last an hour. If the toaster broke, or you had to fix a plug, what good would that Moira Binchy be then? No fucking good a'tall. You should try to fight it, for fuck's sake, you should fight this better, with your fists or anything at all you have, you should claw your nails at it, pity you're still gnawing them off, the nails, but you need to fight it, you've no fight, with your puss all pasty, a cowardly girl. Did I really rear a coward? What age are you now? Hmmmm? Age? Twelve? Nearly twelve. You're nearly twelve? Twelve is a woman.

Fuck.

I grew meticulous in herding, obsessive, counted animals until I became dizzy and forgot the count. Start over. And over. I determined those I cared for from those beyond my responsibility. I fenced off the strays, ushered them into small verdant fields, leaving them to their sullen business deep in flaxen-yellowed ferns and beryl moss, dappled with hillocks and jaded flat thistles. There's bad land in the West of Ireland with its vertical drystone walls that criss-cross the fields.

I hate it. The rain-soaked greenness of the fields, glum Jenga-like walls. But I like order. I separated our neighbours' sheep from ours, identifying them by their deep ruby-red markings. H. Dark indigo-blue oily targets on their rumps. Sheep skimble/skamble unlike cattle and at times they'd run at me, big woeful eyes as though they were running to a cliff's edge or to the slaughterhouse.

As they cut all my clothes off in the ambulance I noted how very skinny I was. I was thrilled to see my hipbones. I wouldn't have to Google Tips on Losing Weight for the foreseeable future. But I'd continue to chat to Google under the duvet. For solace. How to Live the Pain-Free Life. Doing the Proper On-Line Will. How to Control your Dying. Safe ways to Euthanise. Last Death Rattles. Irish Health Care Cutbacks. The Rate of Incorrect Diagnostic Tests. Outsourcing of Diagnostic Tests and Positive Percentage Error. Kefir Grains. How-the-Average-Mid-Late-Thirty-Something-With-It-ALL-Feels. The Perfect Dinner: Cheap and Superfooded. How to Stand Comfortably in Heels All

Day Long. In-Hair Styles. Layers are Out. Structure In. Nail Polish Longevity. The Best Broth Recipe to Eat Cancer Cells. Chipped Your Tooth off Your Wine Glass? How to Fix It in an INSTANT. Best Fish and Chips in Galway. Why Galway is one of the Fastest Growing Foodie Heavens next to Glasgow. Why the Irish Love the Scottish but not (really) the British. How to Pronounce Quinoa. The Irish Treaty Commemoration Planned Parties and How We Feel About All of That Now We Often Shout for England in the World Cup. Dehydrating Your Nails to Help Your Varnish Stay in Place. Dehydrating Foods. UVA vs UVB Ratings on Suncreams. How Elephant-Breath is replacing Duck-Egg-Blue as the Hottest In-Life Room Colour. How You Become Antibiotic Resistant. Property Prices in Bulgaria. How to Enjoy Sex When You're Sick. How to Enjoy Sex after a Botched Episiotomy. Are Protein Power Balls Actually Any Good For You or Do They Contain Secret Sugar? How to Get the Thigh Gap. Why the Ugly Animals' Preservation Society is Legendary but the President for Life Element Uncovers the Dictatorial Fringes of Environmentalists. Doing an Online Will and How to Make it Toxic-Family-Proof. Doing an Online Memory Box. How the Sociopath can Manipulate the Elderly. Do Magpies Really Predict the Future? Are Magpies Prone to Sociopathic Behaviour? Detachment Theory. Is There a Way to Control the Anxiety of Thinking You're a Sociopath? Keeping

Secrets. How the Blobfish Mates. Cremation With Tooth Implants. Anxiety Testing Online.

Taking a Social Media Break.

How to Switch the Internet Off.

★

One January when I was around nine or ten, I went plucking green rushes to make my mother a St Bridget's cross. It's said the cross should hang in a house to ward off disease and protect it from burning down. I liked the sound of the stream near the rushes. Spluttering. Father had been threatening to burn the house to the ground due to our ungratefulness as his children, and I wanted to do something practical, for him and for the house, but mostly to cheer up my mother because she was terrified of fire. I hacked clean the first thin wild rushes, but soon began to distinguish hardy ones from lazy ones and with a gentle pinch to the exact middle of each, I heated the sap between my damp fingers, then began bending at the centre point, finally overlapping them. Limp rushes can't prop up a cross that's expected to save an entire family, but I was only learning. The base has to be more solid. My first attempt was sloppy, and fell apart a little, but it cheered up my mother and became the Hynes'

Family Cross. It hangs over the front door and upon returning home, I'm reminded of my failures.

I wouldn't fail now. I wouldn't tell a soul.

Palliative. Doctor. Time. Tick Tock Hynes. Tick Tock.

Chapter 1|

The Ward. Six-Bedded. Much Hospital Paraphernalia.

- Corticosteroids, intravenous. **Wired.**

- A white plastic pen from the bank that I use for cheques, not my journaling pen. **No use.**

- Two books. *New Selected Poems* by Heaney and *The Gift of Mindfulness*. **No use.**

- Heavy Astral night cream from a blue tub that I use on bikini line (not for face). **No use.**

- Vaseline that I use as an eyebrow dye barrier, strictly not for face. **No use.**

- Roger & Gallet soap. Fleur d'Osmanthus Eau Fraiche. Flowery, floral. (Way over the top, usually kept on show in downstairs loo.) **No use.**

- MAC Ruby Woo lipstick. **Perfect but a little drying.**

- Jo Malone Rose Oud perfume. **Good.**

- Three competing Get Well Mum cards. **Too much.**

- Blobfish slippers. **Aces.**

- iPhone 4G. **Useful but patchy.**

- Baby wipes. **Great.**

- A picture of us all at Santa's Grotto. **Fuck.**

Hospital is entirely recognisable if you are into Victorian dramas or *Prison Break*. In Hospital you are a) Kept In or b) Let Out. You're checked fastidiously, usually by the dinner-bringers. You're tagged. Your clothes are removed, cut off, packed away, lost, stolen, or, perhaps like me, you may arrive entirely naked off an ambulance with only a strapless Wonderbra in the shaking hands of your husband. You no longer have a title, or hardly a name, and all recognisable connection to the past (aka the outside) disappears and is replaced by bright lights, chicken-tikka-with-light-mayo sandwiches in plastic triangular boxes, dark-chocolate-chipped-cereal-bars-with-cranberries, life-saving-Goji-berry sprinkles on salads from the Hospital shop, visitors sipping out of coffee cups, blowing their pursed lips into the tiny hole, the liquid never seeming to cool down, lots of family fighting, lots of TV shows in the Visitors' Room doing loud Lie Detector tests on people with bad teeth, lots of brown bags full to their necks with pyjamas and impractical fluffy slippers, some ciggie breaks with copious amounts of bitching about doctors who gave the news too harshly, the doctors who gave the news too quickly, gave the news and left for coffee, and then, then worst of all, those doctors who didn't give news at all.

Conversations spun.

Now hello. Who do we have here? Are you on any medication? Have you anyone at home? Do you drink? How much on average? Ah now. Come now. A week? Liver enzymes. Sharp scratch. Deep breath. Have you slippers? A bag? Perhaps you'd like a glass of water? Oh, we are so sorry, we've no plastic glasses. Or water. No, no jugs either no, sorry. You can buy water bottles in the Hospital shop. No, sorry, no one has time to bring you there. It's only on the Ground Floor. Oh, yes, you're all lines. Well, maybe later.

'Morning,' said Michal Piwaski, as he walked briskly onto the Ward, cracking his pale knuckles into a thin fist. He checked his watch. Margaret Rose Sherlock was perched in the bed opposite me.

'Morning,' she replied to Michal and threw an eye over the cover of *HELLO!* magazine.

Michal Piwaski passed out my bed and busied himself fussing about Shane-no-one-caught-a-surname, my neighbour.

'Hullo,' Patrick Hegarty said.

'Morning, Mr Hegs,' Michal Piwaski replied, while tucking Shane's chin on top of his collarbone, using one bone off the other as leverage. Unfortunately this left Shane's narrow mouth wide open like a delicate orchid. Michal then busied himself with wiping Shane's gaunt face vigorously with a blue washcloth.

'Ah now, well, Good Morning, you see, isn't it early you're all up and about?' Jane Lohan said excitedly, to no one in particular, and stood out of bed, grabbing on to the window frame. A breeze billowed outside, and Jane Lohan begun a half-pirouette with her arse cocked upwards.

Claire Hegarty, the attentive daughter of Patrick 'Hegs' Hegarty, sat directly opposite Shane, on an elaborate leather visitor's chair, and yawned silently while scanning the middle pages of the *Irish Independent*. She read out yesterday's parliamentary proceedings in Dáil Eireann to her father who began shaking his head while making disapproving noises. He was an awkward rotund sort of man-boy, balding, particularly hard to age and with a most peculiar sheen to his face.

At first it had been difficult to be so close to other humans, the unreserved way of us, for the engineering of the human body is not, sadly, inclined to modesty during illness, contrary to my own best efforts. The rationale for not being given a private room, despite paying private health insurance, had been given to Alex upon my check-in, in many loud acronyms. Private rooms are only for the most seriously infectious, MRSA, GBA, GBH, HIV, Clap, Strep, A B C D, Z-eka Virus, ADD, EBD, DTs, ALP.

Margaret Rose Sherlock put down *HELLO!* and picked up her ebony rosary beads, glancing her good eye over Shane as she muttered some prayers, ending loudly with The Agony in the Garden.

Then she closed down her good eye to match the bad one.

Shane's Wi-Fi Connect?

Nice one. G'man Shane. April Fool's Day Headlines.

Hulu promises TV Abbreviated to match our shortening attention spans

Amazon launches Petlexa, guaranteed to read your cat's requests

Shane was recovering from a heart op, returning to the Ward after a couple of nights in ICU. He had shattering paralysis after dancing off his bike at high speed on the greasy Galway–Dublin M6 surface some years back, after it first opened. Everyone fussed around him, plugging in his MacBook, popping in his peg feeds. No visitors, just some Enable Ireland interns and a banana board with a smiley emoji face.

Now, now, we'll have you fixed in no time, Shane. Everyone lift and groan and again. Now. Fixed. In. No. Time. And did you hear? Lift. And down. Lift. And lift again. Count. Fixed in no time. And. Now, ah, you'll have to work with us, Shane. Want anything in the shop, love? No. K. G'man. Lift, and turn. And lift. Oooh. Ouch. And burst. Down, please. Sudocrem, please.

Margaret Rose Sherlock had had a stroke, most likely. Her bloods were a little wayward. She had further and more pressing complications from a wanker husband who had abandoned her and was now missing-in-action with Bernie, his long-time mistress. Usually, it was only a day or two at most, but Margaret Rose hadn't been able to locate the exact coordinates of Paddy for some weeks now and so she'd been unable to persuade him to return home. Ordinarily, she'd be relieved with the break, and had become used to it over the years of their marriage, adept at passing off his absence as family business, but her second youngest daughter, Niquita, was soon to be married, and getting tetchy about her father's absence. Niquita Sherlock was, in fact, beginning to panic, for her betrothed, Jonathan O' Keefe, was getting impatient and developing a habit of looking at young wans of the Lally family.

Margaret Rose Sherlock had a rose-gold Nokia on which she conducted her business. She couldn't make or take a call without a considered amount of pre-planning the bathroom's vacancy. Alternatively, for some peace and quiet, she'd dive under the Hospital's white bed sheet and chat away under there, where she could be still heard perfectly.

Jane Lohan appeared on the surface to be rather genteel. She had some form of dementia, peppered with the oddest moments of intense lucidity, followed by any manner of madness – often manifesting in bizarre physical moves. She was spritely and agile for a woman in her eighties, but seemed all alone in the world, despite claiming a large family of nine grown-up children, and a husband, Tom, for whom she appeared to care (on a practical level), and an unnamed dog that she loved most in the world.

Hospital is Street, with its odd old sumptuary laws, a place to score. You scavenge for razors, shower gel, coffee, a diagnosis that makes sense, and the most sought-after of all, a Care Plan. On the Ward you scored off the care assistant, Michal Piwaski.

'How's yar wife, Michal?' Margaret Rose asked.

'Oh, is tired ... tired,' Michal said, rushing about with a heavy load of soiled sheets. 'I need to give her tea and put her feet up and fix her before I leave, see.' He began lifting my lines, then stood me up, helping me out of my wet leggings.

I smelled his morning's coffee. Stale.

'And then she 'ees shouting –' Michal threw his thin arms to the air – 'she 'ees now all the time shouting at Michal ... Michal, I need help. Stay home, Michal, what if baby comes and I here alone and you in that big Hospital with people, giving them tea ... what about me, Michal, and your baby? Make tea for me, Michal Piwaski ...'

Jane Lohan began screeching as she pulled a cannula from her thin wrist. Blood sprayed upwards and forwards like my son's urine when he stood up for the first time in the garden and peed. Proudly. Michal abandoned me as I tried with some difficulty to pull a T-shirt over my head.

'What you gone and done, now, now, good Janey? Ah, all she wants is perhaps make baby come, quicker, quicker ... always wanting baby to come quicker,' he said over his shoulder. 'I mean what is the rush? Hmmm? Why would we rush baby? But Karolina is well, thank you, mind you very fat and swollen on the ankles.'

I licked up to Michal because Margaret Rose told me his cheap coffee worked to open the bowels and give you an energy surge. He also had an uncanny way with doctors, making them divulge things, as he was neither apologetic nor shy and he didn't read social cues very well, which gave him accidental power.

Welcome to the Ward. Named after a saint. Female. French. Five of us. And Claire.

★

Hysterical after Magpie, the next morning, I had driven into town, skidded on the pavement outside my office and left a wing mirror around a Children Crossing sign. I ran in and out, breathless. The offices were barely recognisable. I don't know if I met anyone. I think back and imagine that surely I must have passed out the receptionist, Martha, or the guy who does all the design and layout, and I don't know did I look in the frosted glass at my accountant, Liam, but I don't remember it, except that the walls seemed to hang down over the desks, or the ceiling had fallen in some feet. I filled my arm cradle with a map of Bulgaria, brown envelopes, an opened sheaf of A4 paper, two dried-up yellow highlighter pens, three pearl dark green tampons, a box of fruity tea, a protein bar (salted caramel), a ream of paper and a wasted tube of Clarins' handcream. In over ten years I'd never left the offices for longer than a hiatus to look at high-risk properties abroad and the obligatory annual ten-day all-inclusive, where my anxiety would reach peak Fucked Up.

Later that week, I let everyone know I was stepping aside for a while. Weekly updates, but I was to be left alone. Alex was thrilled. Finally. A break. Time out. Mindfulness. Me time. And we had some bubbly to celebrate that I threw down the loo. I didn't know how to tell him.

I didn't plan to go into private industry. I didn't dream about it as a kid lying awake at night listening to the pigs squealing outside, or the bitch whining when her pups were taken from her, or the cows cawing out for their calves. I don't know if I enjoyed buying properties or selling them more, but there was a certain rush, dividing rooms into smaller liveable options and it was what I knew. I understood something about organising bricks on land and it made me deeply satisfied. There was something ferocious in covering over the earth until you could no longer see it, forgetting it ever existed.

They're not making any more of it, land, Father'd say, cursing and muttering under his breath.

That's no job for a woman.

This made me more determined and wild in my decisions.

Eventually even Alex grumbled about it. At first, it was the lack of time I had for him, but then it was something worse, something more direct about my choices, and in turn, something more direct about me. You're not who I married, he'd go on, I thought you wanted to own a farm and make cheese or do something useful (for that was my original promise). When will it be enough? How much is enough?

Until the I-don't-even-know-who-you-are-any-more-exasperation set in.

Alex and I learned, in time, to stop asking awkward questions about each other's days. And if we did, in a tick-box way, we chose topics with neutral buoyancy. He'd fill me in on Jacob's spelling tests, doctor visits, braces. Nathan's cat obsession, dinosaur films, karate belts, Christmas lists. Joshua's play dates, swimming strokes and trampoline prowess. I'd fill him in on office politics. Chit-chat. Aside from the children, food and drink produce took a decent chunk of conversation time. Fit Bits. Weighing Scales. Vacuum Cleaners. Deep Freeze. Potted plants. Sunday lunch spots. Bathroom fixtures. Passive Housing; A Greener Way of Living. (Can a house ever be passive?) Car Services. Winter Coats. Winter Tyres. His Mother (though neither neutral nor buoyant). Netflix. Soccer Transfers. Almond Milk. Cutting down on bacon. Cutting down on dairy. Cutting down on sugar. Cutting down on one-use plastic. Taking up Yoga. Too slow. Taking up Bikram. Too hot. We need to make time for each other. We do. Tomorrow. Promise. Hotel. No. Awkward Hotel Sex. Printer ink. Apple trees.

★

Our daughter would be nine now, tucked in between Nathan and Jacob. Alex never speaks about her. Before landing on the Ward, I hinted about her the odd time, usually when I was drunk, but that rarely went anywhere, for he'd shut me out, mostly by leaving the room, or heading out on his bike. I tried dropping her name in here and there, but even I'd begun acting as if she hadn't existed either. Only ever inside of me and there's a tight rein on language we use for events that go on inside the body, especially inside your uterus, to the extent that sometimes I wonder did I imagine her, dream her all up, alone. Confinement is such a mad liminal place. Dreamlike. Nightmarish.

At the beginning of the week on the Ward, Alex was easily convinced I had respiratory failure caused by a nasty infection, which had lingered for months, hence all the nee-naw drama. Alex liked to believe what I told him, it was an efficient way to coexist and not go mad. He expressed most concern for the awful Hospital coffee and offered to rig up a Nespresso machine on my nightstand until we were all back to normal. He loved normal. He had packed my bag and also perched the photo of us all at Santa's grotto on the Hospital nightstand, a large laminate thing that beamed and was flimsy beside a wicker basket that once belonged to my mother. In the picture we look happy, holding plastic flutes of mulled wine and the children with paper pots of marshmallows and strawberries dribbled over with warm milk chocolate. And though he was upset at first that the children couldn't visit, I countered it by saying I'd be terrified they'd contract the same woeful hack as myself, and begrudgingly, he agreed.

Though I refused the coffee machine as I think Nespressos are for bell ends that drive Land Rovers in cities and eat avocados with poached eggs and turmeric.

New mail. Ping. Inbox.

Seven Ways to Boost your Metabolism

'You not getting out of bed, should lie down, lie down, good … good … do you want me to take you somewhere?' Michal asked me.

one - power up with protein

'Where?'

'Wherever you like, oh, but it's so rattling. So not good. You need sit up, or get some air? My, my, it would worry me if it was my chest rattling as yours.'

It did worry me.

two - fuel up with water

'Lave her be,' Margaret Rose said, 'she isn't even fit far a walk to the loo.' She motioned at me to lay back on my pillow as she took a few deep breaths, encouraging me to imitate her.

three - Go on top while having sex and work those abdominal muscles

Margaret Rose began another decade of the rosary as she picked up her phone and squinted at the screen, and then dropped it down hard on the table-tray, anxiously awaiting some communication. She repeated the action.

four - park away from your destination, walk a little, cardio surge, work the heart

When I was a kid I tied a grocery-shop plastic bag in a crude knot at the nape of my neck, tight. I held a pen in my hand to see how long I could withstand it, before I'd need to stab it and take in air quickly like the junkie scenes on *Casualty*, pen through windpipe.

Bang.

It grabbed my mother's attention for the day. She banned me from watching *Casualty*.

five - drink iced water every hour

I watched as our nurse, Molly Zane, changed incontinence pads and injected my Ward friends. Their shadowy grey hips stacked on top of each other, milk-udder catheters, black eyes, rasping chests, hollowed-out shoulders.

six - eat raw chillies (remember to wash your hands afterwards)

I crouched in the tiny bathroom with its infinite London Tube-like tiling and inspected myself all over, ravenous to find something, a sign that would show people my sickness without me having to explain, without having to case it in language, something outward and obvious, like a kid with a *Finding Nemo* Elastoplast on his knee. I found one resilient tiny V-shaped tea stain of fake tan on my right ankle. Otherwise I was a washed-watercolour hanging in a cheap hotel, all white and purple, the skin barely covering my bones. Streaks of new blue bruises from the lines ran up my arms. I wished I had put on a fresh layer of tan, even just run one of those wipes over me, like I do on my ankles and wrists in winter. That would have done.

seven - masturbate and build good muscle definition in upper arms (rigid)

I was delayed once, outside a gaudy apartment block, waiting for some Irish kids to wake up from their sun holiday piss-up. The white tour bus revved and choked on its fumes. A group of women were turning wank-tricks for loose coins before Ryanair could get them for charity or Lotto cards. The women ushered their prey behind a scattering of ugly Dragon trees. The men were lured by their own devilish blood sap – a promise – like how bright orange seedpods would burst open on the tree branches. They'd return to the cracked pink pavement, with weeds shooting up between the slabs, disorientated/relieved, zipping up their fly, in the way men do, lifting their torso up and exaggerating a double chin. Some ran out bewildered, catching their bollocks in the zipper. The women squeezed short darts of bottled mineral water over the arch of their hand, just where the thumb attaches itself to the pointy finger, and continued their chats with each other over the sound of crickets and wet skin being slapped like a chicken fillet before frying. I thought about returning soon, and so I did and I bought an old house there, gutted it, and rented it out as some tattoo parlours and a large nail bar.

★

A stethoscope lay in the basket, abandoned by a young intern in a bleeper hurry. I listened to my own chest. Heard my heartbeat (heart beat) beat. Wafting from the nightstand came the smell of lavender from the mouldy basket. My mother was always reusing things.

It started out as days, not telling Alex the news. At first the words didn't come, nor did I attempt to form them – I needed more time to figure out the language, but this had lingered to months, in the way time does.

Eight months since Magpie.

When I listened to my heart beating, pain shot through the soles of my feet, electrical energy sizzling up through my shins. It was like fish angrily nibbling my feet, Gara Rufas or the like, and then a few cheap Chinese foot-eaters started to savage me. You shouldn't listen to your heartbeat (beat), and especially not the heartbeat (beat) of your in-utero child. It sounds like the kid's on speed. My daughter made no sound at all. Not one. Not one small gallop stride babies make inside you. Nurse. Now. Cold jelly. All chat. Bit of cold. Now. There. No chat. Cold jelly. Wipe jelly. Silence. They warn you about the cold jelly more than any part of pregnancy or mother-hood, perhaps because we are awkward with truths or because we can put language on discomfort that's rather painless, cold jelly, sand in your socks. But of course, the worse the pain, the sparser language becomes, until eventually we pulverise it, language, and we are only left with our pain.

Alone.

The midwife moved the heart-beat prong around, push-ing down hard. I heard gurgling as I had eaten a bar of Turkish Delight. I hadn't been feeling movement and when I'd Googled it, it said to relax, try a little sugar. The baby should start to flap soon after with the energy surge. Like a butterfly inside, the nurse said at first, does it feel like a butterfly? Can you feel anything at all? And she was saying, oh now, come on, where are you hiding? When was the last time you felt something? Can you remember the time? Maybe last night, perhaps after din-ner? Or this morning? Anything? No. OK. That's OK. We'll double-check with a scan.

Double-check.

It feels like nothing. I can't feel anything. I screamed. It feels like fucking nothing.

NOTHING.

Next a radiographer arrived and moved another bigger prong around on my belly, over and back, tracing my fallopian tubes, in and out, pushing on my full bladder, the window to the baby, she said. Under her arms was getting wet, a creeping pattern crawling along her blue scrubs, making two navy patches. I remember she was Welsh because I love a Welsh accent and she said apolo-getically, now where are you hiding? And so I immediately began apologising for screaming, and then took to apologising for lots of things, eating the lovely chocolate, and apologising for reading my book, until there was very little left to apologise for except the dirty cubicle curtain, and she apologised for this, and we were all apologies. Until the prong was pushed down on my pubic bone, hard, and I apologised for the bone, and she apologised for hitting off it. Then a doctor arrived swiftly, and he took the prong up and off my belly, placing it back in the claw of the machine.

I'd failed. Again. And he didn't contradict me.

I wanted it out. Now. I begged Ms Welsh to please just get it out now. But she had lost her voice and was rubbing my forearm up and down. Please. I can't bear it. But then the doctor interrupted and muttered something about spontaneous and labour. As though, together, we would waterfall her out. It's dead, I screamed. But he wouldn't listen. 'All in its own good time', he said, as if I was ageing a barrel of whiskey. A cask. I picked up my book as the jelly was getting sticky on my belly and I thought of myself as an utter cunt; it was disgraceful to have eaten such a large bar of chocolate just moments before I knew my child was dead, the pink sweetness made its way back up my food pipe to goad me. I had thought the sugar would make her squirm and wriggle and wake her up and I would discharge myself from this fuck of a place once I felt some movement. I said something like this. But no one listened. Then I vomited.

And Ms Welsh said she was so very sorry for my vomiting. Or my vomit.

I think you're just a very weak child. And the nose running on you again. Wipe it up, you amadán.

My book was *James and the Giant Peach*, Joshua's copy. It was dog-eared and wet as he was far too young to read anything properly, preferring to suck pages. I was alone in the room then. You get an Alone Room with a couch and a telephone and no TV when you have a dead baby inside you. Just when you need a distraction, they leave you all alone, with a telephone. You can't call anyone at that moment because they'd shower you with advice about trying again, even with the dead inside you. God is Good. What's for you won't pass you. God is Good. God, I wonder what happened? Did you wash windows? That can sometimes kill them. Did you eat shellfish? God is Good. Did you rub a cat?

God is so overfuckingrated.

Myself and Contents and the two aunts, Spiker and Sponge, were all rolled up fetal in the bed. Howling.

That's what they called it now, Contents. And they didn't probe it or talk to it with their useless machine, now that the machine no longer answered back. How terrific it would be to escape to the middle of a peach, right into the core where a brown stone sits heavy, waiting to come out. Waiting. No heartbeat. Never listen. Nothing is real before you first hear its sound. And just like that, I lost my daughter. As though I weren't fit to mind her. As though I had left her down at the Salmon Weir Bridge or behind the barbeques in Woodie's or at a train station. Lost. I lost her.

The heart is for a doctor and a Valentine card.

Alex had a mouse-like heart murmur. Though, I must confess, I've never actually listened to the heart of a mouse with a stethoscope, but once, full to his fat chin on poison I'd laid down, one sat in my hot-press, ever so bloated, and I watched his big heart beating to the rhythm of his tiny breaths. He was perched on a white and silver *Just Engaged xxx* towel and he died like this, staring at me with his pretty beady eyes. I buried him in the towel underneath the Leylandii trees in the back garden, proficient as I was at killing and burying little things of great beauty.

Chapter 2|

Hospital evenings on the Ward brought a tea of green offerings, soggy scallion-streaks like solidified washing up liquid strewn across lumpy potato-salad and coleslaw dollops in low mountain ranges, knife marks slashed into the beige plates, vile green-pink tomato quarters, and a slice of ham rolled up, pumped with water. Its jelly eye stared at me.

'More soda bread?' said Michal.

The soda bread tasted good like my grandmother's baking. I remember nestling into her skin and the beads of sweat on her forehead in the tiny hot kitchen, back when I used to hang around her neck and lay my head into her warm freckled cleavage.

Margaret Rose Sherlock loved the soda bread. Hegs loved it too, though his daughter never allowed him to put butter on it, and consequently he found it difficult to swallow dry, coughing loudly and irritatingly as he ate. Jane refused Hospital food and searched her purple hold-all for half a beef burger patty that she had upon her entry to Accident and Emergency. She looked for it with such fervour and a fixed determination that I was certain if she could locate it, it would indeed save her life and give us all a boost.

Shane was nil-by-mouth.

The butter in Hospital was real and straight from a factory in teeny gold-foiled patties.

'More coffee?' Michal offered.

'I'd like some,' Margaret Rose said, but Michal ignored her, as he continued to pour for me in a highly exaggerated action. I was determined to keep Margaret Rose on side and offered her my cup. She declined with a gracious hand wave and turned her head away. The coffee came with an ivory plastic wand. No silver spoons, no chink-clink of cutlery. But it was, for all intents and purposes, a luxury item, and one of the last things I could stomach, so I didn't care. Or complain.

'They were stealing the teaspoons,' Michal said, reading me.

'Who? The patients?'

'Yeah,' he said, 'and they think Polish are stealing everything. They blame Polish for everything, y'know? But it's not just Polish, it's everyone, stealing, Irish stealing too ...' he said, glancing quickly at the floor. 'And in maternity they'd steal anything, yuss? It gets way more crazy up there. The hormones ... turning them into mad stealers.'

'Fuck,' I said, 'really ... d'you think the hormones turn them into kleptomaniacs? Nesting?'

Michal considered this. 'Hmm, maybe. Perhaps. I dunno.'

Jane began tightly rolling herself in my curtain, waving her long arms above her head, then she swan-dived forwards and clapped her own performance. I clapped too, like when a baby does something slightly dangerous but exciting.

'No sure why all the stealing ...' Michal said, still mulling it over, as he began unravelling Jane like a roll of new carpet. Jane Lohan hadn't had one single visitor during her time on the Ward and Margaret Rose said that this was very sad for a woman with nine children, a husband and a dog.

I received some cards and texts from the boys. Mostly lines of emojis. Turds, cherries, hearts, soccer balls, cats, laughing faces, pizzas at dinnertime. I sent back salad and fruit emojis. They'd return a green vomit face. And for as long as Alex remained innocent I could chat to him about silly things, emojis, nail varnish colours, Jane's dog.

I balanced/bargained my avoidance of opening up, being honest, with Google statistics on death, reckoning death most often comes as a shock, crossing the road, lighting the fire, swimming, getting on a train (getting off a train), slipping out of the bath, shower falls, airway obstruction from boiled sweets, allergies, drowning, taking selfies, feeding the cat, slipping out the back door, removing a wasp nest, dropping the boot of your car on your head, masturbating in an aeroplane toilet, glueing your nostrils shut. I figured, the way the world works, Alex could very well be gone before me.

I wasn't the type of person that could even consider writing letters to the children, or baring my soul to my husband like they do on shows like *Love Island*. It's so intense, that level of public declaration, intense and crazy. I loves ya, babes. Hun babes, I so do and I'm the luckiest girl alive to have found you here in this house with all the cameras and the dorms and all that, and hun babes, loves ya. Besties. Yeah. 4eva and eva.

Fuck that.

The longer we were together, the harder it had become to gush promises. A gathering resentment perhaps, or cynicism, exhaustion or protection? Never say for ever. It's very risky in any case, that kind of self-exposure. I can share my life story with a woman on a train journey but I can't repeat it to my mother. Even looking Alex in the eye had gotten quite difficult. I can't quite remember when this began, this oddity I feel when I look into his eyes. But to be frank, I had begun avoiding eye contact with people for some time now, long before Magpie.

We were 'strictly' curtailed to two visitors at Visiting Hours, until half past nine, and the most excitement I could hope for on the Ward was Margaret Rose's stay opposite me. Her visitors passed no heed on the poorly laminated Visitor Instructions sellotaped to the wall, and she enthusiastically encouraged the passing-of-no-heed. She had oddly olive skin, Mediterranean, and a substantially thick bob of platinum hair. The hollow rattle of her chest was not her main complaint. One eye dropped until it rested on the sharp edge of a prominent cheekbone and her forehead skin on that side was taut and unreactive, like a *Phantom of the Opera* mask. She spoke out of the side of her mouth in a raspy whisper. A blessed sacrament of Our Lord and the Most Blessed Virgin Mary and the ebony rosary beads hung like large caviar eggs on a frayed leather cord beside her head frame when not in use. A large charcoal Dell laptop sat on her meal table. Every night after her visitors, Margaret Rose watched the computer's screen until dawn, mostly photos of her family, playing hypnotically, large neon love hearts bursting out here and there. She spoke gently, in a curiously cautious manner, especially when speaking about herself or her children.

It was luring to watch her hold court and for now, the wedding of Jonathan O'Keefe with her daughter Niquita Sherlock required her full attention, as she ran the day and night of her family from the Hospital bed, simultaneously attempting to smoke out her husband, Paddy.

Margaret Rose Sherlock, finally, had had enough.

First the young men came. Early evening. Jovial, good-natured, full of energy, and energy drinks, pasty arms outstretched, limbs loosely held away from the body, bright colourful sports tops, baseball caps perched up on their heads, sometimes sitting like young giddy children moving up and down on a see-saw. Sitting or standing, they were constantly moving, while their feet remained rigid to the same spot like that giraffe toy where you squeezed the base and the animal's legs buckled in a heap. They were awkward but most earnest and over-eager to help, as though their presence on the Ward somehow depended on their behaviour, which it did. And they were inclined towards a deep interest in us all. They were interested as they filled Hegs's empty water jug, checked out my iPhone screen grab, made faces and sounds wearing my blobfish slippers on their hands, asked about the pictures of my kids, names, ages, interests. They'd take off on several trips to the loo, praying a decade of the rosary with Jane, mumbling prayers, nudged on by their mother but not quite remembering if they were the call or the response.

The young visitors brought some carnations, bright bottles of soda and a varied selection of biscuits, mostly Mikado, as these are easily digestible to the stroke victim. Chocolate Kimberlys and Ginger Nuts should only be attempted after a dunk-in-tea, or if you have all your own teeth, they warned. They were clumsy with the grocery bags until Margaret Rose ushered them this way and that and eventually after some coaxing, they shoved them in under her bed, with a sideways flick of an Adidas runner.

★

Hegs wasn't interested in them. Not in them filling his water jug, not in them looking at him, not in them trying to make polite and meaningless conversation. He'd make the most peculiar eye squints when Margaret Rose had visitors, especially when the young men called. He administered frosty hostility, though all the while remaining most cordial to Margaret Rose. The young men wiped clotted jam off Jane's fingers, stared at Shane and blessed themselves. I couldn't judge them for this, his peg feeds had become monotonous, as he lay awkward with his laptop opened all day and all night, nothing happening on it, no sound, just left on. I couldn't see the screen but there were no headphones sprouting from it, and if the charger came undone or fell, he'd cry out until it was fixed back and in its proper place, propped up by an ugly doughnut cushion from the maternity ward. I was sick of the brutality of his feeds, the repulsing falseness of it, the laptop on constant charge and the way he'd look at it all day with one eye open, drooling.

'What was it, Mammy?'

'Was it diabetes?'

'Yar father has diabetes, not me,' Margaret Rose said, correcting them.

'Did ya catch it off him?'

'Bet ya did, the fat fuck.'

'Haha.'

'Stop that. Ya canny catch diabetes. Ya have ta have it. Or ya can get it. But it's not contagious,' Margaret Rose said.

'Ya can catch it in Supermac's,' one boy said, and everyone laughed.

'Or if yar a fat cunt like him.' They laughed again, everyone except Margaret Rose.

'Don't speak like that 'bout your father,' she scolded, 'yar upsetting me.'

'Sorry ... well, what is it that ya have then, like? Everywan's asking about ya.'

'Ah now, they're sure I had a bad stroke, far wan minute I was sitting at the sink in the kitchen about to get up and make Nora a pot of tea, and we was chatting about your father and getting him to come home to get fitted far the wedding.'

And suddenly everyone became serious and quieter.

'A stroke. Jaysus.'

'Was Niquita there?'

'No,' Margaret Rose said. 'See, I just dropped off the side of the couch.'

'Jaysus.'

'You were lucky.'

'Did you go cold, with a bang like?'

'Will yar face stay like that far Niquita's wedding?'

Margaret Rose moved her hands up to her cheek with a CGI definition, certain of her actions, unlike Jane who was giddy and moved her hands all day long, even in her sleep, tugging at her hair, brushing her teeth, applying lipstick and forever fixing part of herself back into its original place, even if she couldn't quite remember where the original place was.

Hegs barely lifted his hands above their resting sweet spot, limply outside the thin Hospital quilt, just below his belly button.

Chapter 3|

The Ward's rattling windows framed the grey exterior shell of some of the Hospital's buildings, including the Special Care Baby Unit. Clouds were billowing fast above us. The shadows of parents bent over in the Unit, known locally as SCBU, said quickly down through the nose, Scabooooo. It haunted our view, with nurses bending over the incubators and Perspex cots. I had watched my boys in those little cot homes, moments after birthing them. I was so terrified – terrified to interrupt them, to touch them, to pick them up, to bend an arm into a tiny jumper, or even just look at them in case they disappeared, or left me, or saw through me and were disappointed.

Beyond the long windows memories of picturesque Galway flickered at me, taunting me, in the manner of a picture, fit-to-be-made-into-a-picture.

Michal hoped his wife's baby didn't end up in Scaboooo and Margaret Rose blessed herself, said God was good and God was so good that he would be especially good to his wife Karolina after such a long journey away from her mother to be with him. Jane let out a terrified shriek. Hegs was oblivious to SCBU. He wasn't entirely sure where he was born, couldn't remember when Margaret Rose asked him and he laughed, awkwardly.

'Well, that's a lie ... of course you know quite rightly where you were born,' Jane said. 'I, for one, was born at home,' she announced, folding her palms out forwards like a rose opening and willing us all to engage in follow-the-leader.

Margaret Rose played along. She was born at home too, somewhere near Clare, and her surname was Sherlock, after her husband, proper order, though there was something unconvincing about the way she said it, as though she were still testing out the name, trying it on herself.

I was born here in this Hospital, I told them, and my maiden name was Hynes, and still is my name, and always would be. They all said aw, as if it was a shameful thing, so I quickly explained that my mother had no pain relief during my birth, that she was a solid and rather silent woman, practical, and that she spent forty-two hours in labour with me without eating a morsel or muttering a word, and they said ah, as if this were a good and positive thing and made up for my faux pas.

Jane continued to chat about her own birth, as if present in faculties and not just body. She was told repeatedly by anyone who came near her, from dinner-bringers to consultants, that she was taking up a bed on the Ward and that she really needed to get one of her family in, to help her consider 'options'.

Nurse Molly Zane said she was born in Melbourne, and her mother was Irish or her mother's mother. She didn't have red hair or a love of the Irish or gift-of-the-gab according to her mother. Though Hegs and Margaret Rose most vocally insisted on the girl's Irishness as though this were a compliment, Molly was Australian. She had a marvellously uncivil swagger and a wide face. She was told, she said, that Ireland treats its nurses poorly, doesn't like its women too public, and takes them like tequila, quietly sharp, somewhat submissive, with a pinch of daft. So far, this theory had proved itself to be true.

Molly had visited the Molly Malone statue in Dublin when she first arrived in Ireland, the only touristy thing she did, though Bobby her wife loved touristy things. But Molly went along for Ms Malone, her namesake, had that song her mother would sing to her when she was a little pissed. She was unimpressed with the statue, and as she looked down on her large cold breasts and watched her push her cart, make a living, she couldn't help but wonder why Molly Malone was left out to the mob, day and night, why we could all ogle her fine cleavage from an open-top bus ride, why a nation had chosen to demean a woman like this? But did it worry her? No. Molly Zane considered a lot while worrying about very little.

'When I think about how the world just turns,' she said, jabbing my arm with a needle, 'and holds on, ya naw, I get very overwhelmed, darl. But I don't worry, waste of time.'

The yellow sun shone for everybody, and this, it seemed, pleased Molly Zane. Homes stayed standing, the moon did things to the tides, babies left on doorsteps were taken in and given out again, planes stayed in the air. And when you lay on the ground on a summer's day, it looked after you, held you in its earth hug as it gently turned. For the past twenty-seven years, Molly Zane's head had not risen above thirty-seven degrees.

'I always loved travelling,' Margaret Rose said.

'Rilly? Whereabouts, hun?'

'Ah, only England, few trips, yeah mostly England, lived behind Wembley far a few years, loved it, a big gang of us would head off to Horse Shows up narth, lots of family and always business to be done up ... ya knows the ways?' She nodded at her Nokia, and back at us. It wasn't a question. It was a statement of fact, we all returned nods in her direction, though in truth, none of us knew the way of Margaret Rose's business.

The day Molly said yes to travel with Bobby, was the first day she scalped a cadaver.

'Scientists,' she said, 'harvest cells from the scalps and brains of cadavers.'

Margaret Rose grew pale.

'Once I watched my anatomy teacher slice the forehead skin of a cadaver and peel it back. Eventually the brain was opened like an avocado sliced. Popular now, avocados,' she said. 'Miss the ones from home.'

I distracted myself.

What if

I didn't eat sugar for a year?

What if

all I really needed was air?

What if

there is a cure?

What if

I have wasted too much time?

What if

I could slow this down? Shit.

What if my children thought I had just disappeared, run off with another man, and I arranged someone to send them something every year for their birthday and Christmas, and though they hated me for running off, they never knew of my death? What if this were easier? For them.

'I reckoned ya need to see the body dead,' Molly said. 'It's no use hilping the living if you weren't willing to face up to the consequences of them dead. See, I have such respect for the dead.'

Margaret Rose retched as Jane nodded, her head high up and then her chin tipping on her sternum, top of the class for Jane.

'Washing the body, fixing it. It's so special. That's an honour, ya'naw?'

That was all she missed, avocados. When Molly spoke about her parents, she spoke rapidly in the third person. Molly's mam drinks, ya'naw? Molly's dad was always very busy, ya'naw? Yeah, sure, she Skyped her parents the odd time, her mother preferred phone calls so she could continue sipping nips of Sullivan's Cove, her bent over a moonbeam granite worktop, so that after an hour or two on the weather, the Hospital, old school friends, her daily routine, the arrogance of her father, her speech became so slurred that she was perfectly incoherent. The disclosures were embarrassing. So in an effort to balance the awkwardness, or perhaps due to the steroid concoction that made me buzzy, I told Molly and Margaret Rose about the time my grandfather drank a house. It was the first time I'd spoken about it – how he drank it brick by brick until nothing was left save for a child's rainbow spinning-top on the linoleum when they shut the door on it and a woman that never spoke to him again. Ever. Then, in free fall, he drank away the clod-wet site the house lay on. I understood how this could happen. I also understood that this was something to be both afraid and ashamed of.

'I've never taken ta the air, mind you,' Margaret Rose interrupted, changing the subject, but I felt she was protecting me, not berating me. 'Boat's as far as I could go, 'tis unnatural I always think, something so large in the sky. Drink's a terrible thing,' she added, acknowledging me almost as an afterthought, unable to avoid it. 'Just terrible. Has the country ruined and more countries too. Yar both not alone. Every family's affected. Does terrible damage, just terrible. They say they canny help it, mind you, but it's terrible, especially on children.'

It was dusk. The air was lumpy and heavy, and it was hard to get a decent breath in.

Or out.

'Oh no, hun, I think this is blocked, see if I can flush it through for ya, 'K?' Molly said, sitting on my bed, as she slapped hard the swollen watery back of my hand. 'Sorry. Shit. Shit. Sorry.' She slapped it again as she told us about the day she decided to travel to Ireland. She'd watched a man soak a hunk of pork in a big plastic bucket. He looked Irish, and that was the sign she needed. My mind was on the juicy pork joint, the crackling lid of hide left on top of the muscle, mother telling me to mind my teeth. The bolus flushed through me, fast gushes now, stinging the life out of my hot veins. The cannula was always angry.

'He reminded me of Ireland, the chef guy,' Molly said.

'Really, why?' I said.

'Don't naw, see he lift the shoulder steep overnight in a basin of lemons and ipples with some cinnamon sticks.' The Irishness wasn't jumping out at me. 'The water was dripping off the meat and it made me bloody horny. Irish men do that to me, see.'

'I love the crackling,' Margaret Rose said.

Molly squeezed through the end of the fluid that hung over me in a transparent plastic, her hands cupped possessively around the sack as her white top lifted to reveal the lace edging of a powder-blue bra.

'I always go by my gut when it comes to doing a line. Especially with a woman,' Jane said, pulling a pair of red fingerless gloves from her purple holdall and stretching the leather onto her fingers, then thumbs, onetwothreefourfivesixseveneightnineten. The gloves had knuckle holes so Jane's round bones bobbed like four pale heads in sleeping bags.

Molly Zane perched on the edge of the bed writing down my numbers, chewing on the furry troll of her pen, then sucking on its lime hair. My blood sugars, the speed blood was pressing through me, the amount of sugar leaking, protein in my piss, beats of my heart, systolic/diastolic, amounts of drugs taken, time given, numbers of drugs to be taken, if I'd pissed, if I'd shat. Then, finally, she shoved a clean jab of blood thinner into my wobbly stomach.

'Ya know, ya rilly need to start to think about some treatment, darl ... or at least chat 'bout it ... look, see, I'm here, any time. I've taken on so many shifts, ya'll see me all the time, 'K?' she said, leaning over me with a syringe.

I looked away, pretending not to hear her, and spaced out as Jane moonwalked across the tiles in her knickers and a scrub top, the red fingers fanning her face.

'Here to talk, 'K, hun?'

''K,' I said.

Jabs from the blood thinner shots left a nasty raw sting. I didn't feel them going in, but the pain on withdrawal is like a tomcat peacocking his dick needles and pulling out quickly.

Molly Zane and Bobby were weeks shy of their twenty-seventh birthdays and they would mourn Amy Winehouse for a copious amount of time, they loved her, ya'naw, like I had with Cobain and my mother with Elvis (though she hid it), until the moment came, as it always does, where they'd begin to doubt her and buy health insurance and liquorice tea for their bowels, and coconut oil for pulling the toxins out of their gums, and they would, like every other demented couple, begin arranging cushions to make diamonds out of squares on their narrow couch, buying toilet rolls in colours that matched their toilet suite and drawing open-mouthed fish stencils on the bathroom walls, spraying birdcage stencils on the kitchen walls beside pictures of them-selves-with-large-jugs-of-beer-and-bungee-jumping-off-cliffs. Molly Zane took all the extra Hospital shifts she could, mostly to avoid making any real-world deci-sions. I didn't share these secrets with her, these you have to learn for yourself.

'Anyway, drugs time for you, missy ... just have a little think,' and she tucked me in. Eek. And while I enjoyed watching her mouth move, making shapes, the vintage pink stain of her lips, lying there made me a prisoner to any chat anyone wanted to have.

Hospice is not an option. I can't be alone at night. The desperate hush-hush of weeping midnight terrifies me.

There weren't *options*. I'd started panicking in the middle of the night, the brutality darkness brings, and waking lathered in that sticky sweat that turns cold and feeling a warm hand pressing down hard on my throat. At home I'd try to scream but my tonsils would be swollen up like water balloons and nothing would come out. Alex would ask if I was OK. Yes. Fine. Just a bad dream. Another one? Yeah. Turn out. It's fine. Night. Spoon. Unspoon. Spoon. Night. I'd lay there long enough to talk to myself and try and talk myself down from it.

Arrow. You Are Here. It's OK. Remember.

Arriving in Hospital, everyone panicked. Tubes went up my nose, down my throat, next they'd need to put one up my urethra, like Shane, and I'd have a bag hanging off me too. I resisted this the most, tried to clean up my own accidents without them noticing. On the Ward they were trained to keep you alive, like vultures. I needed to go where they were trained not to.

Home.

Chapter 4|

Sunday rainfall was heavy and winds battled the dodgy windows as Molly pushed them open. The gusts knocked over some cards and kidney dishes on the windowsill near Jane. I watched as the fog cleared. The day was like a home-from-school-sick-day, when my mother would open the single-pane windows, mahogany frames, clearing away the condensation from the night's sleep. We'd listen to a radio drama, one set in a hotel near the seaside, hands around mugs of tea. We could hear the actors breathe, sneeze, the rustle of paper, supressed coughs, giggles, seagulls, rattling of cutlery, clink of crockery. Then she'd go back to her work, sweeping, wiping, lifting, folding, pushing, feeding, steaming, boiling, carrying, wiping again, placing, dragging, sewing, preparing, chopping, cutting, peeling, slicing, ironing, setting, washing, drying, lighting, sweeping again, ironing. Sometimes crying.

'I love Tom, you see,' Jane said, striding out, criss-crossing the Ward moving away from the draught. 'Have you seen him? He went up the yard under an hour ago because there's a cow calving. You know if he's not up soon I'll need to bring him down the calf-jack myself, none of you seem likely to stir out. Aren't you all a right lazy bunch? And signs on you all, you could all do with a breath of fresh air.'

Jane wasn't wrong.

By lunchtime Hegs was heaping red jelly from an ivory bowl into another ivory bowl of ivory ice cream with an ivory plastic spoon clutched in his fat ivory fingers. Claire was bolt upright on the chair beside him, pulling faces at the ritual that was being inflicted on the dessert.

'Ah, but it's a Sunday,' he muttered a few times, noting her discomfort.

Hegs had his share of soldiering Christian paraphernalia, scalpers, rosary beads, a bottle of Knock-Holy-Water, a photo of Padre Pio's mitten, and hanging over his head were a plethora of mass cards – A Mass for the Sick from Knock, A Trio of Masses, A Mass from Croagh Patrick and, pride of place, A Mass from Lourdes with a saying from the Romans. But Righteous One – By Means of

Faith He Will Live. Mass cards should be signed directly by a priest who adds the names of the sick to their mass intentions, but now they were often purchased in a local shop, stamped by the box-load by a savvy priest as he ate jelly beans in bed while watching *Sex and the City* repeats.

The gathering of religious icons made me a little envious.

'Did you get iny sleep, Mr Hegarty?' Molly said.

'Well, indeed now, Miss Molly, I most certainly did get myself a little sleep, not much indeed though,' said Hegs. 'Shir indeed and didn't I wake ever'hour, on the hour, but I declare to God, didn't I manage to settle meself again?' as he enthusiastically applauded his ability to rock himself back to sleep.

'Good. Happy ta hear that, hun.'

'I was, of course,' he added rather cautiously, '... often tempted to ring the belleen, but shir ...' he said, 'I couldn't place my hand on it ... and I hate to be a bother to ye. Is it here on my pyjamas, or where in the cursed Christ was it?' Molly found the bell, and attached it back onto his pyjamas with a large steel safety pin, like a medal of honour, all the while patting him.

All night through he had called out *Mammmmmmmmmy*.

'Daddy,' said Claire, 'you had a draught on you again last night.'

'I'm fine, please stop your fussing ...' Hegs said.

'Well, I will most certainly fuss. Wouldn't it be worse if no one were fussing? I told that young Molly girl that window was not to be left ajar,' she continued, nodding at Molly Zane. 'You know something, Daddy, you can't beat the Irish nurses. And I do not like them opening and shutting that window all the time, it's a death-trap, the putty is all disintegrated, if there was any putty to begin with. Disgusting, the whole place would need to be levelled and, well, to be quite frank, nothing for it but to be rebuilt.'

Molly turned and left.

'Ah now, you see, you should quieten down, in fact, it would be better if you shut up,' Jane said as she applied Margaret Rose's blue mascara to her lower lashes with a large hairbrush in one hand and a tiny wand in the other.

Claire roused herself and lifted up to tackle Jane, but Hegs thrust his hands out to grab and coax his daughter back downwards into her chair. He managed to grab a small crease of material on the back of her dress and pulled hard. 'She's gone astray, Claire, please ... leave her be,' he whispered, pulling at her again. 'Besides she's so very ... well, look, really we don't need to rattle her, please leave it.' He stopped abruptly. Claire sat back down, rubbing her back, and continued on about her father's care, or lack thereof.

'Did you take your heart spray?' she went on, distracted.

'Yes, yes, I did, I never forget, I've promised you,' Hegs softened.

'Pull up those socks,' Jane shouted at Claire, nodding at the fluffy bed socks. Margaret Rose laughed.

'And your Prothiaden?'

Nod. Bobble-Head-Hegarty. Nod.

'Look, Claire, I took whatever they gave me ... they're too busy to be asking all your questions.'

'Always a little thundering bitch,' Jane whispered into the large hairbrush clutched in the palm of her red leather hand, before suddenly passing out on the pillow with her bottom jaw opened downwards so her chin dropped onto her chest.

Hegs had lung cancer. This was the only definitive diagnosis on the Ward. It pleased me to know something definite, an actual real piece of specific information. His cancer had travelled upwards, awkwardly, and was now to be found meandering into his throat crevices. There were spots of cancer on his liver also, mapping here and there like stars over the night sky.

Claire was the woman to give all the words to, he explained, for he had very sore eyes and wouldn't mind going to sleep and if they would just leave him be, he'd be most happy. Not to be rude. Or a nuisance. But best if they let him be. And he'd take anything they could give him for the pain that would help him back to sleep after he'd cleaned up the jelly and ice cream.

The medical staff reassured Hegs at great length that his cancer was slow and he had plenty of time, though he should be more stable and they'd be closely monitoring his odd, but rapid, demise. They didn't like the look of him. And more specifically, his colour was off. If there was anything at all that he could think of, he was to let them know, especially Ms Jo Moran, who seemed to be the most in charge, and constantly arriving, carrying a wedding edition of *Cosmopolitan*, if only to open the curtains and complain that they were shut, stylish in civilian clothes and a stethoscope accessory around her neck that cut off at her bony collarbone.

The stethoscope seemed to be her most powerful fashion accessory, hanging like a necklace or other useless adornment, and she carried a large solitaire diamond on her ring finger, that was two point five carats, bought in one city and set in another, as you do, indeed as you do, Margaret Rose said, smirking at me.

No. Hegs couldn't think of another thing that would be causing him such a rapid demise, and they should/could/would have better things to do with their time and leave him be. For now, he was just grand, he wouldn't mind if they stopped asking questions altogether, and maybe get him the pills. To take the edge off.

But the more he said he was fine, the more the Hospital staff seemed to doubt him.

Claire glanced out at them from underneath a long side-split fringe, soft chocolate brown, and while she had experimented well with honey tones, on close inspection they were brassy. She seemed tired, rather drained around the sides of the mouth that bent downwards, and the creases between her eyebrows were deep like an unformed W. When she flicked her hair back, there were significant greys above her temples. Her face had an odd serum-like texture, a duck's moist eggshell, wide almond eyes held a long nose stuck between them, slightly lower down on the face than where a nose should sit, like a Picasso line drawing. But her skin, for all its pretty texture, had an unnerving whack of corpse about it, dark downy fluff growing impatient on her jawline. Her figure was clean, nipped at the waist with incompetently skinny calves. And every so often she would blink her eyes furiously, as though congratulating herself or suddenly remembering a personal triumph.

Jane screamed, 'Shutupshutupshutupshutupyoufucken bitchshutyourmouth.'

'Why is Daddy mixed in with ... well, with female patients?' Claire asked loudly of Molly upon her return, holding out a kidney dish in front of her. Claire was getting flustered now at the screaming Jane, and darted her eyes around the Ward as though looking for an escape route, or another person to dump blame on. 'Look here, it's obvious we need a private room, in fact we deserve one, we've got private insurance, premium plan, and, really, if the Minister for Health could see this, you know, he's very good friends with Daddy, despite, you know ... being rivals.'

'Opposition,' Hegs said.

'Yes, opposites. And we have ...' she said, 'contacts.' She waved a folded *Sunday Independent* at Moran as if this were the contact, or as though it would pay heed to

Hegs and his shared doom/dorm. Claire Hegarty had an interesting, if naive, faith that highlighting the lack of facilities in the shoddy unhealthy service was going to do Hegs favours.

'And my God,' she said, 'but surely there's some sort of protocol?'

'Protocol?' Moran said, eyeing the paper.

'Oh, anything could happen to him on this *mixed* ward. That's why we don't mix boys and girls at school. It's very dangerous ... and really,' she lowered her voice, 'he's a government official, he's doing his duty to – and for – the public sector. Bode you all well to remember that.'

Hegs was a county councillor in a political party that was failing badly since it had destroyed itself and the country's finances during a hedonistic (for some) Celtic Tiger. Defending himself, he wanted it known that starting out as a young politician there were not many alternatives in Ireland after the foundation of the state. It was really a frustratingly bi-partisan-imperial-theocratic-male-option, and he followed in his father's footsteps. Centre or right of centre. But Hegs wasn't awfully keen on us interjecting in his political monologues and countered it with a, where would you move to, love?

(Love, ugh.) It's not the done thing, he explained, just to party hop because the country was up shit creek, sure he hadn't even been to the Galway Races, don't mind ever indulged in a bottle of champagne or even a helicopter ride, and he had most definitely never received a brown envelope of any kind, but he had an allegiance to the party, because it was tradition amongst his people, and he was a popular choice in the local council elections, out west, past Galway city towards Connemara, further than Beyond Barna and just shy of Ellis Island. And what was I looking for? Surely not gender quotas. He was wary giving exact geographic coordinates. The Ireland apparently saved from colonisation. He cheered softly. Giving us all a fat thumbs-up, as though the colonisation were last week. And saved from Cromwell. Both thumbs up again. That part of west that was full of rocks and full up with sadness in the little sacks grown men develop under their eyes, the accumulation of tears they don't cry as they walk along, shut down, like an out-of-season seaside café.

But he was mistaken in his defence for I wasn't judging his party allegiance.

'You know, I could just take him to Lithuania,' Claire said, labouring the *could*. 'I will actually just take him ...' she said, as though freeing herself and suddenly excited, 'just you all watch me. In fact I just heard on the radio, that's where the best medical help is, and you get respite because really, this place is a joke. Daddy needs a private room. Now. Today ...' And she clicked her fingers.

But nothing happened.

'We're doing our best,' Molly said. 'Your father gits a lot of minding, we're keeping a close eye on him. Really no need to drag him out of the country, darl.'

Darl. Eek. This would be official complaint Number 1.

'But of course feel free to go to Lithuania, naw one will stop you.'

Ms Jo Moran shot Molly a look. Claire curled the *Irish Independent* into her narrow hand again, and shoved it under Moran's chin. 'You really should put some manners on your nurses.'

'Excuse me?' Moran said, stepping back fast and putting her hand to her ear as though she had misheard.

'I'm not looking for round-the-clock help,' Claire said, backing off a little. 'I'm a reasonable woman, nor am I looking for a one-to-one nurse staring in at him sucking on his ice-cream spoon. I'm looking for a private room

–' she took one big long inhale – 'where I can shower and sleep, and a room –' she took another inhale – 'where Daddy can watch *Prime Time* with a little bit of peace ... Now is that –' and she slowed down and uncurled the paper, letting it fall from her hand – 'is that really too much to ask for?'

It appeared it was.

'Well, you're his daughter. Perhaps you know best, and in which case, take him to Lithuania if you like,' Moran said, and snapping the last words, 'off with ye both, see how far you get ...' and scanning the Ward, she turned on her heel and left curling her own *Wedding Cosmo* rapidly in her thin hands, its glossy pages filled with promises of all the mod cons weddings now enjoyed, fish 'n' chip trucks, crisp sandwiches, vintage record players, barns, dress-up, sweet stands, Chinese lanterns.

★

I took a Lithuanian bus trip from Vilnius to the seaside town of Nida as a student and for the five-hour journey, an old man sat beside me holding a small glass jar of honey on his lap. Squeezed together on the seat, I noticed how perfectly straight the crease in his grey trousers was. He didn't remove his colourful anorak for the entire trip, and he didn't speak, not one word. When the bus stopped to allow us a break, the man remained all the while sitting perfectly still, as we all got off to stretch our legs and stare up at the acres of dying trees poisoned by the cormorants that were shitting on them.

Later that evening, drinking local wine, I enquired of a man in a bar if this behaviour was part of life, as he knew it here. My new friend, who had good English, told me this man was most likely gone into his head. This was a regular occurrence and happened often he said, as he gestured at me with his hand flat outstretched just below his forehead, to show me how someone lives in their head, as though the brain had permanently dipped down into the skull a little, bobbing in the fluid, just above the eyebrows. 'We call it introvert,' he said to me. 'You know, how do you say it, trauma perhaps, you know, from all the years as a partisan, and all the years the boys were in the woods. Forest Brothers, hiding out or escaping and maybe, in the end, truly lost. Some, well, some never came back, you know? Sometimes people had nothing to come back to, no one, or no place. And even when they did return, most had stayed away, you know, on the inside.'

The next day, at sunrise, I visited Thomas Mann's summer house on the Curonian Spit. I couldn't remain long inside the house – it was claustrophobic. I went on and wandered along the pine groves, over the sand dunes and eventually came face to face with a wild pig. We looked at each other and I stayed absolutely still until he eventually tired of snorting at me.

I would have liked to escape there, live near the Mann house, hide out, and live out my life with a wind chime and pottery, drink mead, make mead, drink mead, repeat, but I couldn't enter the sea there, there was no proper swimming, and I couldn't live in a place where I couldn't suddenly enter the water, to cool off, or at least know I could if I needed to, so that the water would hold me for a little while, allow me to float, alone.

★

On that rare occasion Margaret Rose had no visitors, Hegs engaged her in a little political discussion, while avoiding it entirely with me. Perhaps he was afraid I might ask him for something he couldn't deliver, or afraid perhaps I'd bring up Anglo-Irish Bank, or worse, NAMA. Hegs took the politics for granted, and he told Margaret Rose that all his nods at consultants, who knew to offer praise for his soft-foam surface just laid in the local playground, were part of the game, and also thanked them for the praise of the footpaths, as he had them widened in his town and built a cute feeding bridge for the ducks over a miniature lake in the park. It was a town where many of the Hospital's consultants and young careerists lived, a popular area amongst 'blow-ins' with its water and grey stone and farmers' market and Atlantic spray. Hegs knew how to keep the younger professional voters sweet, he explained to Margaret Rose, winking at her, and of course it involved the obligatory funeral attendances, and he said he liked to visit schools, open a new library and complain about the blow-ins/strangers behind their backs, fill up some pot-holes, promise a path from here to there, push through the odd grant to an up and coming artist who maybe went to one of the local schools and was not too risqué. He wasn't into art much himself, he confessed, but asked after my musical tastes, nodding at my headphones as though they were contraband, and after Alex's profession, his people, where he came from. We spoke a little pidgin architecture. I said I liked fast buildings and fast songs. He said he loved song lyrics, especially country. Margaret Rose agreed about country music, she loved it too. Country music is popular in East Galway, more than West, they both agreed and I didn't disagree, as we all wondered why that might be, but I liked lyrics too, I said. And I read a little poetry, the odd time, once or twice, you know, loved it in school. They knew. Nodding at my books. Hegs liked the poem about the daffodils and I said I liked the Heaney poem about the child dying but Hegs said they only read the British poets at school. And no, none of us could figure out the why of that.

Hegs explained to Margaret Rose that he popped into the local funeral home just as the remains were about to be brought to the church – sure, otherwise he'd spend his whole life in a queue, and she agreed – and grab the hands of the mourners, but this had taken its toll, all the dead corpses and all the new births and the whining locals who wanted the path to circle the entire village and not just the private estates, or wanted braces for their children, or a free eye test, or a stairlift and some were mad enough to be looking for a cycle greenway, and not even a proper road in or out of the city. I tried to engage him more in politics, pushed him a little on planning laws and where the government could improve on housing, but he was suspicious of me, though both of us recognised it was a mess, especially the horrendous traffic in Galway, and the docks was in real need of some planning. A mess indeed, and I explained that all of my developments were abroad, and he nodded, relieved that I would make no requests of him.

★

Father used to drive like a lunatic around the docks. He'd chase off mercilessly at high speed, in tight situations, around the water's edge, now with their new

sprays of graffiti colours, bright bold colours, silver sig-
nage, fancy dentists, purples and royal blues with yellow
egg-yolk splashes. Old contemptuous oil tankers used to
dock there when I was younger with wispy blonde hair
that I would suck in my mouth, attempting to nibble
away the split ends. The tankers terrified me with their
honks and bellows, big metal sea monsters, old robot
giants in a sea war. Our gold car would semicircle the
docks, and I'd panic, squeezed in the back seat, taking in
fast breaths. I was afraid they could blow up, these oil
tanks, if anyone decided to light up a ciggie; or that
Father would just crash into the sea, finally having
enough of the lot of us. I calmed myself thinking that if
Father did veer off course, we'd be swallowed whole
like the toy submarine that I played with in the large
enamel bath, watching the air escape from its soft plastic
belly as it dropped to the bath floor with an easy thud,
eventually settling itself beside the melting Imperial
Leather soap. The submarines came free in the bottom
of a bag of cereal. I knew the air could suck our bodies
to the water surface if someone managed to wind down
a window.

This never happened, our car never veered off course.
Although the first time we went electric windows, I
fainted.

★

That afternoon, Margaret Rose couldn't concentrate the good or bad eye on her *HELLO!* She answered the phone twice and both times her caller hung up on her.

'What are ya in far?' she asked of me, gently.

Aggressive. Months. Treatment. Time. Tell. Talk.

'Chest,' I said.

'Thought so,' she said, 'terrible thing a bad chest. And yar so young ... very unfair. Have ya always had the chest bad?'

'You're right, unfair, it's more than unfair, isn't it all so unfair,' said Jane, scanning the room and then focusing her attention on something outside the window. 'Just watching for the postman,' she said.

'Yeah. Always,' I lied.

I thumbed a pamphlet Molly had gingerly left by me. A smiling woman in many lavender hues, jumper slacks shirt, grandchildren at awkward angles to her chair, one on her lap, like on stage, not real life and she was holding a yellow flower, but nice graphics. 'Dying is one of the few certainties of life.' I shoved it to the middle of my *Mindfulness* book, one that I'd bought out of duty from those travelling salespeople who drop books and knick-knacks into the office staffroom.

Observe your thoughts. Slow down. Watch what is happening inside your head. Fuck sake.

'The chair ... OK if I ...? You know ...' Molly said at me, as she began moving furniture.

'Oh yeah, yeah, sure, take it away ... have it,' I managed, motioning the departure of the chair with my right hand. I was defensive of the chair, considered it Alex's and yesterday's curve of his arse was still in the leatherette. He'd have to share my bed and strain at Frank Underwood on the clammy screen of my iPhone, compliments of Shane's Wi-Fi. Watching Shane's catheter bag was so public. I focused on it for hours. Sack full in. Sack full out. Clear to yellow.

in/out/in/out/in/out/in/out/in/out/in/out/in/out/in/

Claire snatched a baby wipe from her bag and lifting Hegs's large hand she began to scrape out the underneath of his fingers and scrub the back of his palm.

'It's high time you met a man,' said Hegs, quietly.

Jane announced to the ward that she was about to teach a Latin class and began. 'Morior, Moreris, Moritur, Morimur, Morimini, Moriuntur,' she sang out and waved her hands, conducting.

After the hand cleaning, Hegs leaned over his nightstand, picked up his plastic mask and attached it around his head, snapping it onto his red face by its blue elastic. A sort of a getaway as a puff of mist escaped through the side holes and he settled the machine pug-like on his lap, snorting.

I plugged in Ray LaMontagne, attempting a sleep. His raspy voice was so fuckable. It was a Cup of Teatime, which is very different to Actual Teatime.

'I come to you last, see ... last,' Michal shouted over to me, over the rasping LaMontagne, winking as he pushed his trolley of goodies out in front of him with great importance. He was a poor replacement for the singer and his beautiful vocal chords, his denims, one leg thrust outwards sitting near a fountain or on a swing hanging off a large tree, looking sexily depressed, a mountain with snow, a cabin with a red door, crocuses making their way through and he'd pick one and put it in a vase on the centre of the table. Oh, and a log fire, and he'd pick up his guitar and sing 'Shelter'.

Michal rattled biscuits out of packets.

I would never wank in here.

It was full of interruptions.

Besides, all self-pleasure had gone entirely astray since Magpie landed. Everything filled up with her plumage, the terrifying whiteness of her breast. I couldn't bear to touch myself. Even brushing my teeth was nauseating.

'I keep you best Sunday biskits ... maybe even little cake.'

Chapter 5|

Hey

... Hey there! How're u? (Hug emoji)

Horny and tired ... You?

... Fuck. Soz. I'm OK

I want some sweets

... Ah poor you - chocolate? How you feelin?

No - apple drops. Come in with some, please, might die if you don't xoxoxo

... I'm not coming in - can't xoxoxoxoxo

Y? (Crying emoji – full tears – gushing one – almost could be laughter)

… Kids asleep ya twat (Three small bed emojis)

Leave them

… No x

Fuck you. Ah no only joking, **don't** leave them (Sideways laughing emoji – def too much)

… I won't … stop worrying … so no better?

Nope (tearless sad face)

… Soz xxx

I know, such a balls (Basketball emoji. Total accident)

… You missing the kids? They all send love hearts, Nathan has made a dino card this time … Brachio-saurus x

Sweet. Yeah, yeah, send them some back xoxox-oxoxo (Three hug emojis and a turd)

… They're fast asleep … Joshua made dinner; well put pizza in oven without box

Sinéad typing. Undo typing …

Ah nice. Fair fucks Joshua. Yup soz indeedy. U drinking?

Long Pause … .

… A typing … not typing … typing again …

… No (Monkey covering eyes emoji times two)

Bullshit

… Just a small one, beer

Fuck. Ouch.

… Soz

Stop fucking saying soz. I'm watching Suits (Heart emoji – red)

… That shite?

It's not shite. What you watching?

… Grand Designs (Small house emoji)

Liar

… I am, swear, repeats … the one where they build the house out of hay

Ahhhhh … without me (Sad face – one tear – most distressed emoji imo)

… SO Soz

I'm still horny (Aubergine)

… Wank to Hegs

GROSS (Green vomit face). Feel like I'm gonna die (Automatic coffin suggestion. Deleted coffin – fuck – fuck suggestions)

A typing … not typing. Long pause. A typing again …

… You serious? Wanna talk?

Alex would be sat at home with a large bag of cheese puffs, doors and windows all open, radio blaring, TV blaring, pale ale of some description with a wolf on the front, in a small can like on Australian soap dramas, but classier, and perhaps it would be a grapefruit beer (or blood orange of late).

I didn't want a call.

Shane began to groan, his laptop charger had disconnected. I got out and plugged it back in; his eyes were not in focus, one was wet like a tiny pool of water on a beach far from the tide. He seemed way more distressed than before. I asked if he'd like me to put on some music or something, but he didn't answer. His bag of piss was full, bright yellow, and I said I'm so sorry as I stared at it. And then I went back to bed.

Talking to Alex via text was much nicer than dealing with his breathing and humming and hawing and real-life him. He was more eloquent or direct in texts, and they allowed little room for me to get edgy. Emojis offered due emotion, quickly and without complication or effort. I was ever so grateful for them. Especially my mother's, even if she sent them mostly by accident, they made her look utterly emotional, which was brilliant, especially the mad weather ones and the completely out-of-character, big bursting-red hearts.

No, too noisy

… Don't die, but fuck off with the horny text. It's your meds driving you cray cray

Most men would be thrilled to hear their wife was horny. Honestly, apple drops. Begging. Pleaseeeeeee.

… Not if they're an In Hospital Wife. Horny in Hospital wives – not a turn on. They still make apple drops? Shit, I can't rem last time I had them (Hospital emoji)

Lolz (full stop? Ouch. Bit much.) Yeah. They do (still make them).

… Nightnightnightnight. I love all your punctuation.

Night. A few bags, please, surely someone can sit with them?

… NO. Who? Now seriously fuck off. I love you. I'll bring some tomorrow xXx

A typing … not typing

… PS don't die. Rem to floss. Bye (monkey covering little eyes) PPS I'm in bed now. Beer gone. Wrecked. Love you xxx

Hegs began to snore and Jane was nibbling Bourbons like Minnie Mouse.

Floss. The sum of our love.

★

Hospital Sundays were strange. I felt strange and although time was moving, it was stuck on strange same. It was just another Hospital day, without the good doctors who were off in their holiday homes or running marathons or whatever else it is that doctors do when they're not doctoring.

Outside of here, Sundays smelled free, if being free has a smell, like rusty wood incense, leather or cold air. Sundays smelled like Alex. Male. I didn't check emails on Sundays. (At least not in front of him and definitely not until after sex and a shower.) It was coming to the end of the Premier League season. That was the hot topic. And their hot Sunday topics sometimes got in on me.

Everything so cyclical.

After the season ended the transfer markets would open and then the boys would divert onto some European thing. Except Nathan. He excelled at the role of middle child with a terrifying love of dinosaurs, Thomas the Tank Engine, socks with sandals and rational-thinking-that-bordered-on-catastrophic-thinking. But among the other three, there was talk about the World Cup qualifiers around the corner, the corruption of the Russians, and sadness in the FIFA world, which was hurting them. Not a lot of food in the house. Which was hurting them too. They were now living on pizza, which wasn't hurting. There'd be much talk about men wearing earrings and hairstyles and left kickers, and the most pressing question of all, whether or not the English team would be allowed to bring the wives to next year's World Cup, if they qualified, considering the media frenzy following around Victoria Beckham many years ago in Baden-Baden, the chariot with the horses and the sixty pairs of sunglasses like glitzy Tommy fucken Shelby's.

I missed having my daughter to talk to, though the thought of it also frightened the life out of me. I would be too strict, just in case she turned into that woman following her husband's success on a chariot in Baden-fucken-Baden. Nothing would be appropriate, not her hair or her smell or her clothes or her swagger. I'd be too tough on her. In the way mothers are with daughters, because they know, mothers. They know how different it is. Boys were fine. Besides, they had coped well without me for years. Ten.

I was ten years working madly and thinking about manoeuvres and strategy, so that at the end I'd have photos to hang all over our concrete lives (aka The House) and everyone would be comfortable and none of them would want for things, the way I had wanted, that crippling awfulness of not having The Things; clothes and runners and schoolbags and music lessons and gym gear and labelled denims and fancy stuff and days out and Irish summer college and keyboards and hamsters and roller blades and computers and the best games and if they had all of that, then no one would notice them in the wrong way, and therefore if I did a little groundwork, you know, when they were small, when they'd hardly notice my absence at all, then we'd all be safe from judgement. I wouldn't have to rely on a man leaving money on the counter in a small dim kitchen for our survival. When the mood took him. Or not leaving it. When the mood took him.

But this was bullshit and in the end, my business was really an addiction. For once I knew the other personalities up against me, it became personal, and though I could logically analyse my addiction, every small battle was a cortisol flood, a problem I could solve, and I couldn't leave go. Even a rotted shed in the Hebrides would get me going, wherever they are.

I never planned to have my children so quickly. They came along. My grandmother often said, once they get in they have to get out. There's only one way out. And after they came along, the act of parenting was so brutal.

It was the happy/sad/worried.

Sad with the manic stress, sad with the rejection, sad with the crippling brutality that having mortal children brings with it. Happy with the small everyday OK. Happy when we laughed. Poo. Dick. Fart. Willy. Stupid words that made them tear up laughing. The routine. Happy with the smell of their necks in bed at night, asleep. Superhero movies. Soccer. Happy when the day went OK when nothing was too good or too bad. Happy for a non-event day, but then the long twisting before sleep, that comes when their mortality punches you again. Or the nights they make you promise that you won't die until they are old, and it's a terrible promise that you can't possibly keep. Stressed with the other parents that parenting brings into your world, especially the judgy ones. Ones you never asked for. Ones you'd ordinarily run a fucking mile from. Social situations you would never go near. I left most of that to Alex. I ignored them. School parents. Hanging around the gates in tracksuits, sippy coffee cups and large sunglasses. I am good at ignoring people, like a mime artist. I've even done this to Alex. The ignoring. I was outside Boots' pharmacy once and spotted him out of the corner of my eye, and then in the sharp turn of an instant, I completely avoided him. Freeze. Then the moment passed, so that to suddenly shout his name would have been so terribly awkward, the delayed wave, grimace. So I ignored him. My own husband. I just kept walking. Later that evening we had roast chicken. He had stuffed it with plums, I remember because he apologised for burning the plums and I said it didn't (really) matter, that the plums gave flavour and made it moist.

His parents had accumulated all their life, cars, children, potted plants, life-insurance policies, golf clubs, secrets, savings plans, short/mid/long term, enemies, safeguards (boarding schools, first-aid books, home insulation), lamps, crystal, deep pile carpets, Rolex watches, diamonds with big claw settings, holidays, frosted-glass doors, perfect gardeners, jumpers to throw over your shoulders when a breeze came, best lawn feed, fridge cleaners, everything matching, no books, no clutter and because of their drive to accumulate things, he wanted nothing. Nothing. And in this way we were opposites.

But we had things in common, and we promised when we were old, we'd search each other for them.

Chapter 6|

'Ye speak ta yar father yet?' Margaret Rose asked. Her boys were back after Sunday evening tea at a chip spot and nodded their baseball-capped heads downwards like obedient stable horses. They fussed over Margaret Rose's eyes for what would they do if Mammy didn't see properly again? Margaret Rose dismissed such fears with a gentle swat of her hand, as if sight were an irrelevant condition of the modern age. As she spoke about their father's absence, the mammy matador fixed her pink hoody high up on one shoulder.

Everyone has blips.

Margaret Rose was not oblivious to the knocks of the world and to the wants of a man. Just as she was finishing the last of the chips, complaining about a heavy hand with the vinegar, a man in an oversized checked sports jacket and hefty ginger moustache arrived on the Ward.

He seemed uncertain as to whether he was in the right place, bowing down deferentially at myself, then Shane, across to Hegs, until he tracked back and arrived heave-ho to the end of Margaret Rose's bed. Jane shot straight to him and greeted him in a flimsy night top with spaghetti straps like a dancer in a burlesque club.

'Well now, who have we here, and a very good evening,' she said, front-of-house. 'Is Tom with you, I really do hope you brought him along for a pint?'

'Indeed he's not, I'm afraid, ma'am ... very sorry,' he replied, gentlemanly.

'Ah that's OK so, you see, what can you do?'

'What can you do indeed, ma'am?' he said, nodding.

'But now, you see, that cow is a desperate long time calving, the poor thing. She'll be exhausted if ye don't pull the calf soon.'

The younger boys greeted the man quietly, by shaking his hand and nodding. One boy moved the bouquet of carnations that had lain on Margaret Rose's nightstand down to her feet, showing them off, and in a swift changing of the guard, the boys gave up their space around her bed.

'More power to ya, Mags ... well, aren't ya looking fresh?' he said.

'Jim, fetch a vase,' she demanded of the visitor, and Jim mithered for a little while, awkward in the ill-fitting jacket, and a vase being unfamiliar territory. He eventually fell upon a flimsy plastic cup beside the sink, that would, they both agreed, do for now. And wasn't it lovely of her sons to bring her flowers, how well she had reared them, she agreed.

Shane, like a blocked sink suddenly freed, let out a terrific guttural noise.

Jim pulled across the curtain and in a familiarity that only comes with growing up together, they had a long and earnest chat. Ah, Mags. Someone had a heavy hand. Yarself? Ah, now ya overdid it today. Face looks like a rock. Yarself? Oh, how can ya inject yarself? Yar mighty. Dentists are most peculiar. Ya knows they say they kill themselves a lot? High rates of suicide. Rally? Dentists. No way. Easy ta get their hands on drugs maybe. Should I ask him if he's all right? Stop, yar terrible. Hardly a word out of him. 'Tis a strange wan though. I'm terrible sorry it's come ta this. Are ya sure ya knows what yar at? Hope you know what yar doing? Paddy is no fool. A prick ... yeah ... but no fool. He might never come back. Donna set yar face like that for ever now whatever else ya do or ya'll be in some pickle. Ah, he'll come home. He has ta. 'Tis a bit far now. No. Of course. Shocking. Indeed. Fuck it anyway. To Hell. So. Tired. Exhausted. No. One. Yet. They're in the old house. Bernie's mam's place. Bermingham. Up behind the Old Quarry Cottages. Have the number. Here. I'll just lave it here. OK? How're ya fixed? If ya had ta travel? Ya sure? Of course I wouldn'a send ya alone. Ah no, the Hospital is lovely. Long as they leave me alone. Haha. No. No no. Not at all. 'Twas a very dark night. Ah, that'll be spring. Ah, right. I do think it's the right plan. Not looking likely that the shame will smoke him out. Soon. 'K. Too young really. Ah, but now. We. Will tame. Her. We'll try. Paddy better come back soon or I'll tell ya. Niquita. Worried. So easily led. Very like Krystal. Jonathan – ah right little cunt. Don'na warn him. Not yet. I'll see how it's going. Oh, sweet Jaysus but Paddy better come back ta not disgrace us. I said I'd bring him back. Settle yarself. Just hope that's where he is. But a course it is, he has no imagination. Homing.

Like a dirty pigeon.

Angelus bells faintly called out from the cathedral.

One. Two. Three. Four. Five. Six.

Jim promised Margaret Rose that he understood a sickness was the best way to tug at the heartstrings of Paddy, and specifically to shame him among family and friends, publicly. But Jim also wasn't convinced that Paddy had strings attached to his heart, and he was, in his opinion, beyond shame. And while Margaret Rose agreed a little, she said that he was a proud man, wouldn't like the talk if she did up and die for herself, and he'd never live down the shame of leaving her alone to die. Jim washed his hands in our little sink and left the Ward.

The last segment in Sunday evening's triptych of entertainment was the arrival of two young girls, dancing and stretching, bending upwards and forwards in short neon tops, bright greens and pinks and pristine white frayed short-shorts that showed their bum cheeks.

'Well, Mammy,' they both said, kissing Margaret Rose in turn, then they opened back her curtain, and sat either side of her bed, flanking her, but it was short lived. They'd pop up, suddenly, sometimes to braid each other's hair, or play that game where you clap at each other, mirror like, leaning against each other, dabbing their split ends back into place between their fresh lips, fingers popping each other's large gum bubbles, in colours that matched the neon tops.

Michaela and Niquita Sherlock were the youngest daughters of Margaret Rose. They spoke quickly, were high-pitched, swirling around topics, at times hysterically, as though any minute someone would drop dead, at other moments, quietly, as they began edging their way past boundaries. But mostly, they were deferential to their mother. Lightheartedly, everything was open for their criticism, from her pyjamas to her facial paralysis, but never her decisions.

'Did ya watch Jacinta's wedding on the laptop far ideas, Mammy?'

'I did, Nick, I watched it again and again ... ma God, she was beautiful, wasn't she?' said Margaret Rose.

Both girls nodded.

'I want me own ta be just like it,' Niquita, the taller of the two, said.

It was time to get a move on with the dresses. Margaret Rose told them to slow down. Paddy had to return before they could move on with it, and though Niquita woefully protested, Margaret Rose ended it, but she'd need more time and besides the stroke had made her very weak. Both girls blessed themselves at the mention of 'stroke'.

It was what it was.

And they weren't to bother Mammy again, for a little while at least, until she had recovered, and talk about weddings could commence upon Paddy's return.

Seeming content with this plan, and just as they took leave, the smaller one said, rather like an announcement, or that she'd been plucking up the courage to spill it out, 'Jonathan's calling Niquita names again.'

'Ah, fuck ... Loveen, I don'na believe it,' Margaret Rose said, looking in earnest at the taller girl who shot her a sharp look. 'Are ya joking me? Fuck this. I thought this had all stopped. Again?'

'Yeah, he is, like, I really wanted to tell him to fuck off for himself, but neither yarself or Daddy are at home now and I just didn't think 'twould be the best thing ta do. Ya know. Bringing bother.' Michaela lifted her tiny shoulders forwards in a hunch, and one of the spaghetti straps fell down along her narrow arm.

'Lave it, Mic ...' Niquita said, pulling her sister by the arm, and when Michaela resisted she punched her where the strap now lay, giving her sister a dead arm.

'Ouch, fuck sake, take it handy ... I'm only trying ta help ya,' Michaela said, rubbing her arm, then shaking it vigorously in an attempt to try and wake it up.

'Ya OK, love?' Margaret said to Niquita, nodding slowly.

'Help? Yeah, right,' Niquita said to Michaela. 'Ah yeah, I s'pose. Yeah, I'm OK, Mam,' she said, dropping her head and shaping her fingers into childish knots.

'Look, yar not OK, tell her ... I saw them,' Michaela said, '... on the wall outside Neary's.'

Niquita lunged at her sister, twisting her arm up behind her back, and tried to gag her mouth with her other hand. Michaela shoved her tongue through her fingers and continued to blab.

'Back at Neary's? What were ya doing there? Fuck me, haven't I bloody well told ye all to stay ways from it?' Margaret Rose said quickly, her face red with temper. 'I've asked ya both not to be hanging there ... I must have said it a million times. Jesus, if ye'd only listen ta me ...' She raised one eye to the ceiling. The other stayed fixed ahead.

Both girls looked crestfallen.

'Look, I am trying my best ta protect ya both, but I canny do it if ye won't listen ta me, tisn't trying ta make life difficult far ye ...' Margaret Rose took a deep inhalation, red circles appearing on her chest and the side of her face, then she lay back on her pillows. 'I have ta try ta keep ye both safe. Safe as I can. Well, that little prick … I knew damn well he'd go down this road …' Both of her eyes narrowed.

'I'm so sorry, Mammy,' the taller one said.

'I'm sorry too … ya know, far going there, but like that's literally where everywan's hanging out,' Michaela said, whispering cautiously. 'It's just dat all our friends go there.'

'Everywan? Who's everywan?' Margaret Rose shouted, sitting up again. 'I warned ye before about everywan, bad news hanging out there, the place is not fit far … far rats, and look what's happened? No wan of us there ta protect ye is all is all … that's all. I'll just be worrying now … worried sick.'

Margaret Rose took another deep breath and composed herself, recognising perhaps that there'd be no more blather from the girls if she chastised them over spilt milk. Or that she was passing the spot of parent warning that entered into unnecessary fear and would make her daughters overly cautious to live out their lives with some semblance of independence.

But Michaela was not stopping. 'An' them girls of the Lally's was walking past … and Johnny starts at Nick, calling her bad words.'

'What kind of words?' Margaret Rose asked.

'No, please, don'na ask me ta say them again … just names, like … bad names.'

'Did ya do anything? Or say anything?'

'Yeah … well, Nick like, she like told him ta stop, but he walks right up ta her and like made this kind of face …' Michaela moved her head up and down and leaned over her mother, with her hands behind her back. 'And then,' she whispered, quickly, unlocking the hands that were behind her back as she shoved Margaret Rose gently to imitate young Jonathan, 'he pushed her clean off the high wall … harder like than that … then pretends it was all an accident.'

'He didn't mean it, he really didn't …' Niquita said, quickly and breathless.

'Shit.' Margaret Rose, then composing herself. 'He push ya hard?'

She listened to the details of the shoving-off-the-wall and the name-calling while giving the girls some biscuits. She listened to their sobs that turned into a flushed nervous laughter, they made shapes to leave and said they would be back tomorrow and every evening, laying on Mammy's bed until Margaret Rose was home in her kitchen sitting on the same couch she fell off and with the stove lit and minding little Evan again. And just as it was Falling Asleep Finally Time, Niquita seemed unsure about making a break out the door, and suddenly began to sob miserably.

'I'm late.'

The vestal virgin. Shit.

It was awful and she was late and there was no sign of her friend atalltalltall, sobbing still, shoulders heaving, and Johnny had told her before doing it that it couldn't happen the first time, he had made her so sure, convinced her, because if it did happen the first time, it would be because she wasn't a virgin at all, and that it would be because she was a slut, and so she believed him, because she is a virgin ... was one, but she was sure Jonathan O'Keefe would still definitely maybe marry her, though he couldn't wait any longer, because there was a long queue of good-looking wans of the Lally's ready for him, and she knew deep down in the place where women find answers, for she was soon a woman, and all the bother and blather that was coming down on her, but for now it was maybe all over, she didn't know, still, a part of her was convinced he'd still marry her and they could tell a white lie to make it all much better. Pretend the baby came early. Or something. But a part of her wasn't convinced at all, and she was so very sorry. She heaved. Then retched. And she was also starting to get fat already, well, more sort of thickened around the waist, bloated, but her Michaela felt it was nothing good Spanx wouldn't solve. Margaret Rose rolled her eyes to heaven, and of course Niquita wasn't happy about this at all, because now he was laughing at her most of the time for being fat and seemed to be trying to make a pure fool out of her, and she remembered what happened to Auntie Krystal when her waist started to thicken like this and the wedding dress was a fiasco and no one ever let her live it down, as if everything that happened in her life and the lives of those close to her, good or bad afterwards, was all her own fault for bringing sin in the door. And Mammy should really get up out of bed, now this minute, because the wedding would need to be tomorrow or at the very latest next week to stop everyone knowing that she had a thickened waist. And Niquita began hyperventilating and shaking and shaking. Margaret Rose pressed her daughter about who knew. No one knew. Except Michaela. She sobbed. She knew right away. And now Mammy. And she flicked her eyes downwards. Promise. Swear to God and hope to die.

And there it was all over the Sherlocks, shame. It lay heavy in the middle of my marriage bed every night, shame, and Hegs had a face of it, shame danced slowly all over his sad hands as they lay below his belly button, shame, and Shane couldn't tell us one way or another, but I felt it by looking at him. Jane was too astray in the head maybe to feel it. But it dropped in and out of her like KerPlunk marbles. You needed to be fully astray in the head not to have it. It was the most contagious thing inside and outside Hospital.

Margaret Rose knew exactly what was ahead of her young daughter as she cradled Niquita's head into her breasts to muffle her crying.

We were all absolutely silent for some time.

Later as both girls eventually slipped into the night, Michaela leading Niquita out the doors of the Ward, rubbing her hand up and down along her sister's spine, Margaret Rose called her daughter back for one last question.

'Niquita, love, come here … just a sec … how late?' she whispered.

At two a.m., a time reserved for bringing news of the dead, Margaret Rose Sherlock made three phone calls.

★

I played football as a kid in the large field beside the cowshed, repeatedly kicking the heavy leather sack up and back against the pebbledash. My grandmother would sometimes cycle past on her bicycle, and tell me that football isn't a game for a girl and neither is the way I ride the ponies astride not sidesaddle. I took no notice of her, but her comments about manners and womanhood lingered. When we go to Dooley's restaurant on a summer's evening, I order the Farmhouse salad, to remind me of her. I take the cutlery in my hands, like she showed me, elbows inwards, though this isn't easy as I have a very broad back, and I usually give up halfway through and lump my elbows up on the table, but I try, for a little while, to be ladylike, like she asked. I notice they don't pickle the beetroot like she used to, so that they look like jellied fruit delights on my plate. I drink gin, because this is the way of me. Alex drinks tea, because this is the way of him.

After Magpie, I was so tempted to lean into Alex in bed with his tea, and tell him all about it, about being terrified, terminal, but I thought it was a dreadfully selfish thing to do to another person, fill him up with worry and uncertainty, to try and make him figure out death, because that's a dead end, a spiral, even though it's always there, inside us all, death, creepy and skulking around. I thought if I waited, that I might have some words of consolation to follow Magpie. So I waited, and waited, as big yellow and white daisies returned their withered heads into the tarmac, ditches that overflowed with beginning again started to hush and by September's end the green blackberries ripened to a deep purple as wild heathers bloomed.

In the fields among cow shit and wet yellow moss, we'd swing a hurl and knock a sliotar back and over to each other, my brothers and me. The ball came back harder and faster than it went from me, and often struck me hard, between my floating ribs, vulnerable, the pelvis reaching up to defend. The smash of the ball to the hollow made me cry and fall over, like children are allowed to do, panting uncontrollably.

This empty sack is now riddled and eating me. Great peach. Brown stone. The body remembers.

Ah, what in the hell would girls know about sport, go in, go inside to your mother and ready us some food, and then come back out and you could whitewash the gable end of the cowshed, I'll mix it for you, because that's a terrible job entirely, the mixing, and one you'd probably get wrong, you wouldn't know the right measures. You're always drawing attention to yourself. It's embarrassing to be straight about it. And why haven't you any friends? But sure who'd be your friend? You can be very difficult. Give up those books. You have a lovely face. Use it. You should try to be less difficult. It's an awful way to be in the world. Now g'wan, inside, ready the food. And come back out. And do a proper job, not the cunt of a job you did the last time.

I'd get the measure perfect.

Well now and I declare to Christ the light is closing in on us, so if you bring the sandwiches to the field and then I'll have the lime mixed and you can get on with your job as quick as you like. I can't trust you with the mix. Quick.

Quickening.

Good girl.

I could tell the size of the field by looking at it. The square foot of the cowshed to the litres of the mix. Meters. Grammes. Kilo. Milli. Centi. Magnitude. Feet. Inches. Pounds. Hands. Length. Mass. Time. Electromagnetism. Thermodynamic temperature. Luminous intensity. Quantity of substance. Sfumato. Fast-dying fresco. Warm water. Oil and Venecolori. Lapis Lazuli. Colorito vs Disegno. Caravaggio's painting was found. Hanging over the fireplace in a dining room. Society of Jesus. Hydrated lime. Near Dublin. It was the hands they recognised. Salt. *The Taking of Christ.* Telltales. Light. Closes. In. Around. Us. Mixture will be thinner than paint. Stings my eyes.

Judas. Two graduate students found a mention of Caravaggio's painting in a notebook in Italy. Be meticulous. Notice things. Cut in the corners with precision.

Ah, sure what would a girl know about mixing and painting. Amn't I right, lads?

Father added the hydrated lime hurriedly to the salt water – instead of first dissolving it in warm water, he hadn't the patience – clumsily, as every job. I rolled the whitewash all over the gable of the cowshed. Mother arrived in a pixie with her overcoat and cut in the narrow spots for me, we stayed silent the whole time. When I was finished, I dumped the leftover contents of the whitewash into the neighbour's field, where Father never looked and the neighbour never told. He had, of course, got the mixture wildly wrong. We could all keep our secrets around him, safe inside our heads, until they'd leak into all our cells and their memory, their future prints, would seep out, like all noxious poison does eventually.

Chapter 7|

First Call.

'Bernie ... Hello ... Bernie ... now look here, I know that Paddy is with you ... don'na mind asking where I got yar number and ya gone all public with it on Facebook ... I have people ... watching. I have it, finally ... that's all that matters ... I know where you are and I have no problem sending the Maughans over ta sort the pair of ye ...'

Pause.

'What? Are ya mad ... they'll kill Paddy ... we both know it, yar not doing too good hiding ... game's up now ... ah, will ya stop yar shitehawking ... no, I won'na ... not if ya send him back ... tomorrow ...'

Short pause.

'Otherwise they'll cause big trouble ... listen here ... yar only getting wan warning ... ah, here now, you and I's been around the block ...' She spat. 'And we knows that man needs something with a bit more in her pocket than you ... ya won'na hold on to him ... so go and buy yourself a strong packet of cigarettes ... tell him to be on that ferry tomorrow ...'

Pause.

'I'll make big trouble, Bernie ... ya, I'm in Hospital ... how ja think I am? Now you'll be filled with bad bother if he's not back ... ya don'na want that on your head ... or in yar heart ... ya fucken trollop ... Hello? Hello? Bernie? Ja hear me? I'm only giving ya wan warning ...'

Long pause.

'Ah, here now ... aren't ya some fool ... they'll do any-thing far a dying sister ... do you think it, do ya, ya do, yeah? ... Well, I'll make ya think it now, I really will, you'll be thinking then for a long time ...'

Pause.

'... Well ... I felt sarry far ya ...'

Margaret Rose sneezed.

Pause.

'And. Him. I will … and ya knows I will … ya might be his hoor but ya'll never be his wife.'

Second Call.

'Wedding's off now, O'Keefe … ja hear me? Hello? Ya, it's me … Margaret Rose … Let that be an end ta it.'

Pause.

'Look … I warned you before about name-calling and the passing yarself round yar doing.'

Pause.

'Ah sthap, ma brothers said they're watching ya … ya little prick … Niquita's our girl and she's easily led … 'twould do ya a lot of good ta shut yar thick mouth … I feel sorry far ya without a mother … but now look at ya … well, yar some cunt.'

She sneezed again. 'She'd be turning in her grave now, lad …'

Long pause.

'Listen here … shut yar mouth 'cause there's no necktie now, nothing … and ya should feel very lucky ya can just disappear. Ja hear me? Hello? Jonathan? Hello?'

Pause.

'If you ever so much as look at her across the street from ya … I'll break both your legs … what ja mean "show"? Show me?' She mock-laughed, then inhaled loudly with a snort. 'Oh sthap, ya poor lad … don'na come at me with yar daddy this and that, I'll sort him too if I have ta … yar a lucky boy ta be getting a clean break … So take it …'

Short pause.

'Now listen here, ya motherless runt O' Keefe … I didn't bring Niquita Sherlock into this world ta have her and yar guttery voice and yar bad habits knocking her off walls …'

There was no mention of anything or anyone being late.

Last Call.

'Jim, hi, hello? Jim … 'tis Mags … were ya asleep? Sorry … look, I need ya to come in far a chat, quick like.'

Pause.

'I knows 'tis the middle of the night. Morning like. Tomorrow will do ...'

Sneeze.

'No, I'm grand ... just a draught in on me, I think ... look, I've a huge favour ta ask ... no, not me ... Nick. She's in bother ... what ja mean what kind of bother? Women's bother ... yeah ... yep ... I know, I know ... look 'tisn't time for I told ya so's ... I know ... but these things happens ... will ya help? We need it sorted.'

Sneeze.

'What ja mean *how*?'

Pause.

'... Yeah, that's exactly what I mean ... Christ, it's been a long night ... Jim, I don'na need ya judging me too, so enough. Please. Can ya help or not?'

Babble.

'What would ya knows about it? ... Ye can just up and fuck off ... Yar not left holding on to it ... wondering where a roof will come from ... or if ya'll ever get yar life back. 'Cause ya don'na get yar life back. Ever ...'

Silence.

'Ah here ... I'm sorry ... I knows yar not that sort. But I'm afraid Jonathan O'Keefe ... well ... and God rest his lovely mam, but he's a real bad egg.'

Pause.

'Thanks ... I won'na forget this. Thanks ... but shir if I get up out of bed, I canny just up and lave ... ya knows that ... he'll never come back ... Lazarus ...' Margaret Rose laughed loudly and sneezed again. 'I won'na get another chance ... I've gone this far ... OK, but 'tis hard ta get me on me own ... Great ... Thanks so much ... I'm sorry ... Great ... They won'na let ya in till nine. Try then.'

Pause. Babble.

'Just don't bother me if you see visitors, 'K Jim?'

Pause.

'Thanks ... Look, I knows ya don't ... She's yar niece ... 'K ... 'K ... See ya ... Night ... But Jesus, not a word. Promise? Night. Byeebyebye ...'

Click. Beep.

The familiar whirr of the laptop sounded at three a.m., put to its photographic-merry-go-round and soon after, Margaret Rose snored out as she held her phone tight in her right hand and close into her chest like the dead in coffins for ever left clutching rosary beads and photos of loved ones.

Chapter 8|

Early Monday morning, Jim was back, sitting on Margaret Rose's bed licking a large pink ice-cream cone that matched his shirt and cheeks.

'I've it sorted, Jim,' she said, as she emerged from the shower and waved the Nokia in one hand and swung her washbag in the other like scales of justice.

'Jays, it's a bit early for ice cream, no? Oh fuck, shit,' she wailed out.

'Oh ... ya OK, Mags?'

'Yeah, grand, just bit me cheek. Shit. Am I bleeding?'

She patted her face and attempted to open her mouth wide, while Jim took a look inside and scrunched up his nose.

'Jaysus, you'd want to go aisy with that stuff, Mags,' Jim said, lowering his voice. 'Yar man said it's not good the amount yar at it. Ya could hit a nerve,' he hissed, looking around anxiously.

'Isn't that what I'm hoping far?' she said, laughing with one side of her face paralysed. 'Ah, don'na start now you, not you as well. I'm delirious with tiredness ... and have I any other choice?' It was a rhetorical question. 'No. So 'nuff outta ya.'

I liked when she showered first, leaving the bathroom warm and homely. The windowless square box, coated in its rectangular white tiles with a shower that had no border or boundary, only a dark brown drain that ran close to the toilet bowl, so that if you showered for any length of time the entire place flooded, and sometimes the water gushed out under the gap in the door, so much that the bottom of the door was mildewed and warped. There was the obligatory white plastic chair plonked there like a sun-bleached Van Gogh painting and an SOS cord hanging from the ceiling. That people sat to shower in the chair unnerved me. The door also unnerved me for it opened straight out onto the Ward, and there was far too much white ceramic space to comfortably shove your leg up and out to double-lock it, maintain dignity. Though here, thinking about dignity was naive at best.

Jim listened to her hushed instructions as the two of them sat out on the edge of the bed, clearing his throat once or twice after he had finished the cone's wafer. He plucked a tissue from her elaborate gold tissue box with red flowers dotted all over it, and wiped his large hands. Bits of dry tissue clung on between his fingers, sticking to the ice cream. I pretended sleep. He took instructions on tickets, collecting his brothers, the Maughans, and they would carry Paddy home he said, if they had to, even in a zipped-up bag, and yes, he reassured her that all of her brothers, according to Jim, were most concerned she'd have another stroke, and yes, even the ones not talking to her seemed the most irate about the situation Paddy had left her in, everyone was talking about it, especially after the Facebook post, which they both agreed was utterly humiliating to everyone in the family. And they were all up for righting a terrific wrong, even though there was a car auction in Ennis tomorrow night, but they were more than willing to forgo this and head over and drag Paddy home. For the wedding, and to console his sick wife, like a husband should.

'Manchester has her booked in at midday. I'll drop a pin in the place and link ya on this.' She nodded at the machine to locate the city that was to take on the weight of Niquita Sherlock.

'Sound.'

'Couldn't sort it in Birmingham. So sorry, they're fully booked.'

'Short notice.'

'Yar right, 'tis woeful short notice, sorry that you'll have to travel onwards ...' Margaret Rose said, carefully, to avoid taking a chunk out of the inflated cheek.

'Ya sure this is right, Mags?'

'What? Which part?' She raised one eyebrow.

'All of it.'

'Ah ... now ... don'na start again, Jim. Of course it's right, we canny end up embroiled for ever with the O'Keefes. And as for Paddy ...' she said, stopping, and rubbed the cheek. The wounded. 'Just, no words.'

''K,' he said. 'Sorry.'

A lispy spittal ran down her chin. I guessed Novocaine. Manchester would deal with the bother in the uterus. Like it had helped so many times before, with Irish women, rollie cases, taxis, coffees, airport toilets, sobbing, solitude, trauma, travel, Solpadeines, secrets. Jim was accompanying his niece, and he'd see her right, well, as right as he could manage.

'It needs sorting. Jim. Simple as ...'

He nodded again. He promised to look after her very well. He was then to go on to Birmingham, meet up with the brothers.

'And Jim, when you go on to Paddy's place ... best leave Nick a night in the Travelodge, in the honour of God, last thing she needs is travelling onwards, after ... it.'

It.

'She has a real soft spot far Paddy. So say nothing too bad about him.'

Keep Niquita happy. White chocolate. Topshop, though she mightn't be up to it, and Solpadeine. Blister pack. Twenty-four. Passport bottom drawer, key here around ma neck. Here. Take it. Marie Stopes. Manchester. Birmingham.

'Lots of Solpadeine. She's like myself. And remember ta keep it all ta yarsells. Not a word.'

''K.'

She handed him a tower of magazines and a phone charger.

'OK, OK, Mags, jeez, calm yarself or ya'll have a proper stroke.' Jim had the face of a man who remembered none of the exhaustive information he had unwittingly procured for himself.

Michal wheeled in his steel trolley of Monday's breakfast and brushed hard against Jim as he was leaving in a hurry to get himself organised. The glossy magazines fell asunder. Margaret Rose raised her eyes to heaven as Michal and Jim fumbled on the ground. Her phone rang as Dolly Parton's 'Nine to Five' blared from her laptop. She quieted it. Answering the phone, 'Ah, shush yarself, pet ...' she said, pawing her rosary beads and waving Jim onwards. 'I knows yar upset, Niquita. Nick ... ya needs to slow down ... yar breaking up, love. Hello, hello. Nick ... What is it, what's happened? Nick?'

Pause.

'Ah, love. What's all the tears about? I canny make out your words, love ... yar in very bad coverage, move around ... No, no, it's not ... it's not me ... ah, better.'

natter natter natter natter natter natter natter natter

'Ya'll have ta slow down ... Who rang ya?' She placed her hand flat on the top of her head.

Margaret Rose knew exactly who and what it was had upset Niquita Sherlock.

'Calm down ... I'm sure he wasn't drunk ... Look it, if that's what he wants, Nick ...'

She lowered her tone.

'Yar far better off without him ... What ja think I mean? You knows well what I mean ... Oh, now, hush please, love. I hate hearing ya like this ...'

Jane screamed out from her bed. 'Is it morning? Agggh. It's raining. Damn it.' Jumping up and out of bed she plucked handcream bottles and cups and pillows and began thrusting them into the middle of her bed. 'Everyone just needs to lie down quietly and later we should set a nice tea out on the big lawn, and hope that the rain stays off. We'll do our best to avoid the thistles, cursed things those flat thistles and if it looks grey or nasty sure we can bring out the umbrellas.'

'Yes, Niquita,' Margaret Rose said. 'No, 'tis just poor Mrs Lohan. Woman beside the window … uh-huh, yeah …' Then covering her mouth with her hand, 'Ya'll be all right, I'd say, love, and ya don'na want ta hear this, but my gut feeling is he did mean ta break it off … Why? Well, for wan thing, he probably knows yar too good far him … What ja mean what do I mean? I mean he knows yar too good for him … It is not a daft thing ta say … Look, fuck'im, Nick. Respect yarself. Plenty more fish in the sea … Ah don'na hang up … Love? Hello? Hello? Nick?'

Jane stared long and hard at a box of tissues, then plucked out five and folded them into perfect triangles, placing them down beside the heap of items on her bed. At first she seemed pleased but then she began crying into them. 'Rain, no one said it would rain. Rain. No rain was promised. This is really dreadful.' Jane howled at the window.

'Ah, great, yar still there … Look, there's bigger shames in life than Jonathan breaking yar line … I knows yar upset, peteen, but that's the way. Now tell people 'twas you broke it off. Ja hear me? Don'na give him wan more inch … No, I agree, yeah. Yeah … True, ya aren't exactly comfortable with time on this. Sorry.'

Long silence.

'I know ya don't want ta lie, loveen, but ja really think telling him the truth now will help you? He won'na marry you now far sure. It'd be a lot easier if ya made a quick decision. Less invasive.'

Niquita was as strong-willed as her mother. Some minutes passed and Margaret Rose blew upwards, her bottom lip protruding.

'He's no good ta ya ... and he won't be a good father ... Ya have to listen to me, please, love. Jesus, Nick ... it's far the best.' Margaret Rose was beginning to sound exasperated. 'I know well it's yar choice. Think about it ... OK, well, that's good then ... Maybe come in and we can chat face ta face. And chat with Mic ... Really? Well, maybe ya need ta take her advice ... She loves ya so much ... Yeah, I know, it is pressure, yar running outta time, love, last thing ya need is yar father or wan of the Lally family finding out and going blabbing it.'

It was quiet now. Jane sat down on the floor, disgusted with the rain that was unsettling her picnic planning, and thrust herself forward into Child's Pose, head between her outstretched hands.

'Don'na mind him ... Do not tell him ... Are ya gone mad? Remember what Mamó said, the lie told with good intent's better than a bad truth ... That's right, love ... That's right ... Shush now ... Shush ... Ya'll need ta bring a bag ... Oh, I don'na know ... A coupl'a loose tracksuits ... Pads.' Pause. 'In the bathroom press, love ... Jim will bring everything else ... stop now ... That's life ... 'Twill be OK, love ... Loves ya too, see ya very soon.'

★

Niquita Sherlock arrived back on the Ward very soon after the hurried phone call, her eyes bloodshot and puffy, draped in a black Juicy Couture holdall across her body. She was inconsolable, but certain. And then she was in no need of consoling and totally unsure of it. This flip-flopping went on.

Jane lay humming in Child's Pose as Niquita stared at her while lifting the bag off over her head and placing it down on the ground.

'I'm sure, certain, I'm so sure ... What the fuck's up with her, like?' she said, distracted, nodding at Jane. Margaret Rose smiled. Niquita then lay on the bed and her mother stroked her face.

'I think it's yoga,' she said. 'You know, love, you've more time, you can think about this ... You don't have ta, I mean ... 'Tis very quick ... Maybe I'm rushing ya?'

Niquita hissed that Jonathan O'Keefe was a cunt. And she wanted rid of him. Margaret Rose corrected her language. But agreed he was a bad sort. Then popped her daughter's gum bubble with her finger, clearly happy with the sudden change of heart, and they laughed. But soon after the laugh, Niquita began to wail out again, and her mother ran her hand warmly along her daughter's bare flat midriff.

Niquita jumped when Jim arrived back, pulling a bright wheelie suitcase after him, at the same time Michal Piwaski was giving out elevenses, close to midday. Cup-of-tea. Custard cream. Michaela walked alongside him, she was there for goodbyes, as she picked a custard cream off Michal's trolley and began nibbling one side of it. They all laughed at Jim's suitcase. Then the girls set to taking turns plaiting each other's hair. Tight.

I imagined Margaret Rose at home, holding court in her kitchen, back in charge. I thought of my own kitchen, too large, impersonal. Joshua, Nathan and Jacob's Daily Activity lists were plastered on one wall, and we were rarely if ever there, off fulfilling the list after a breakfast full of omega and vitamin C shots and probiotics and everything else I could make them ingest to send them out into the world with minimal guilt. Jackets, hats, scarves, waterproof shoes, hand sanitiser, tissues, smoothies, water bottles, music lessons, karate, swimming, CoderDojo, violin, creative writing, drama, indoor soccer, outdoor football, orchestra, art classes and play therapy. Even when we were all home together, they'd leave for their bedrooms, often watching the same Netflix shows from different rooms.

'Look, love,' Margaret Rose said to her young daughter, squeezing her tight, 'it'll be OK, I promise, and please text. Love ya.' She then patted Jim's lower back. 'Take good care of her, Jim, ja hear me?'

'Promise, Mags.'

'Bye, Mammy, love ya too.'

'Text me when ya get there. Text from da clinic too. Text me when it's over. OK?'

'Yeah, yeah, OK, OK, quit fussing,' Niquita said, impatiently, looking away from her mother.

'And don'na forget, ta text, ya know, when … ya know. After. Ring me or Mic, if ya, ya know … ya need anything.' She muttered, 'Or ya change yar mind. 'Cause ya can, if ya like. Change yar mind.' She said it ever so slowly.

Niquita nodded and twisted her Juicy bag across her thin body.

Michaela hugged her sister tight and then kissed her uncle on both cheeks.

'Text me.' Michaela looked at her mother. ''Tis awful quick, ya sure 'tis the right thing?'

'Hush, you,' Margaret Rose scolded Michaela.

'I knows, but I jus wan'na get it done. Now.'

And the two left with the wheels of the rollie case trucking out along the corridor and Michaela swapped her sister's place on the bed and hugged Margaret Rose.

Margaret Rose looked deeply unhappy. Agitated.

'Far the best,' she said to herself over and over, until she fell asleep for an afternoon nap while Michaela drank down her mother's tea.

Chapter 9|

After lunch, two young student nurses arrived attempting to open a bottle of bright orange energy drink between them; the taller of the two women held the bottom while the smaller twisted the top with her hand, curving her hips away in the opposite direction. They began taking turns supping from the bottle, and the smaller woman opened out a window for air. Legend night. But OMG that taxi driver. Creepy. The smaller one had an arc of mascara underneath one eye and some silver glitter on the back of her hand.

Monday-morning rounds were underway in the late afternoon, and the trainees had been drafted in to keep an eye on Shane. There was some concern. It wouldn't be long. They had no idea how long and no, neither of these young nurses-in-training had ever watched anyone die. Oh God, they might die themselves. OmG like. oMg like. WTF. What if they faint? Poor man, it would be awful watching him die, they didn't feel they had adequate training for this, and instead of making them worried this made them giggle. The energy drink came down the both nostrils of the smaller one with the black arc under her eye. They took to fits of discussing last night, checking Snapchat and then standing ever so straight at times as though on sentry-like duty. Is he dead yet? Ease. To. Him. Yes, family called. But no sign of them. That's sooooo sad. Lit. Lol. Soz. I'm just giddy. Lit. But fuck me. How will we even know? His eyes are closed already. He's kinda cute, right? Right. He's lovely. Isn't he? They decided he was lovely.

I agreed, lovely Shane.

They gave him a bed bath to pass the time, make him more comfortable and maybe even blow-dry his hair, and yes, they could use Margaret Rose's hairdryer. Don't wake her. She won't mind. Whisper Thank You.

Hearing is the last to go.

Vigil at the bedside.

Hankies, phones, Club Orange, energy drinks, crisps, rosary beads and apologies.

One ran out for Juicy Fruit. And then for Hula Hoops. And salted popcorn. Sweet.

His input was nil.

His output was nil.

His peg feeds had stopped.

Jane woke Margaret Rose and they searched deep in their nightstands, tugging out extra religious paraphernalia for The Cure to Save Shane. Margaret Rose was busy. This was the best way to be after Niquita's exit. Jane was busy, as this was her only way. The search for this cure went in a hierarchy of inanimate but precious objects, with head nods, and everything was displayed on the stripped shiny mattress of Jane's bed like an eccentric May altar. The two women hummed and hawed as they pawed over beads and cards and plastic statues of saints full up with water. If they could only get in the mitten of Padre Pio or a drop of blessed oil of St Thérèse of Lisieux or even a lock of St Francis of Assisi's hair, even a hair from one of his pets, but they were unsure that Assisi had left behind any cure at all. But he was a lovely man. Yes. Lovely man. Loved animals.

Margaret Rose put Michaela on the Nokia to someone in Navan who had the mitten of Padre Pio. She'd been given it for her son who had developed itchy and incurable warts, and it would be sent down on the next bus with a trusted bus driver and hopefully make it in time for Shane, if not this evening, with any luck it would arrive by the morning. Jane blessed herself backwards which, according to Margaret Rose, was motioning in the Devil, and Jane stared at her blankly then began blessing Margaret Rose instead, misunderstanding the instructions, so we all blessed ourselves ten times at Margaret Rose's request, for fear we'd bring the work of the Devil onto the Ward, and she encouraged a proper blessing. Michaela instructed that we all do it like soccer players, and she demonstrated to her mother and Jane. They copied her and blessed themselves, kissed their thumbs, then lifted their kissed hands to the ceiling, thumbs clutched, and finally patting their hearts. With the help of good God and all of his many archangels, especially the favourite one, Michael, or so they thought, although they were unsure as to which archangel was the favourite, the glove would get here, safely, off the Navan bus.

The taller nurse leaned in, opened Shane's dry mouth and rubbed a giant cotton bud across his cracking lips, dipping it into his mouth a little, while holding his head in the crook of her arm. His face reminded me of a dying cow, down after birthing a difficult calf.

In the corner of the Ward, under the bright German bulbs, Margaret Rose began washing her hands like the plastic noticeboards told her. She scrubbed up to her elbows and linked her hands and scrubbed under her fingernails, using her elbow to turn off the silver tap lever, and dried off with paper towels. Jane stood behind her, crying now, and so Margaret Rose removed Jane's fingerless gloves and followed the same procedure on her with determined vigilance. Then she combed Jane's hair and Jane went out on the corridor to see if the bus driver had arrived, immediately forgetting why she was out there, returning promptly to ask.

Margaret Rose began the prayers. Our Father Who Art. As many decades as she could. All the mysteries.

Our Father Who Art in Heaven (once).

Hail Mary Full of Grace (times ten).

Glory Be to the Father (once).

Repeat.

I would not die in here. Not a chance. I would decide my death date. I'd put a hefty bet with a Chinese bookie.

And to the Son and to the Holy Spirit. As it was in the beginning. Is now. And ever shall be.

That evening, I went mad with Google. I'd tire myself out in the great vantablack hole of it. Letting Go. The Acceptance Gap. Seek Safety. Death is always a surprise. The amount of sugar in a custard cream. If someone dies right beside you, do you feel it? The average IQ of a nurse. The average IQ of a student nurse. Why do nurses wear watches on their tops? The amount of sugar in soda bread. Ordering apple drops online. What lighting a match would do to an oxygen machine. Hiding tattoos for your wake. Best make-up. How did Yorick die? Gravediggers. Do they really jump down on graves? Saved by the bell? How many? When? Is it a good idea to place a bell in a coffin? The weight of the soul.

Amen.

★

Shane lasted through Monday night. In silence. The vigil holders had left, but had promised to return early on Tuesday morning.

Hegs had a restless night tossing and turning until the early hours. So by morning, they goosed him up out of his bed coaxing him all the while, then they sponged him down with a big yellow sponge you'd use to wash a minivan and dried him with Shane's large Liverpool FC soccer towel. You'll Never Walk Alone. Walk On. Walk

On. With Hope. They took his blood pressure five times until they swapped machines and took it one last time, dismayed at the numbers.

Jane, with a face of etched concern, began searching for a minor charm for Hegs also, not of the magnificent mitten power, but something, a miraculous medal maybe, and after some success she perched a plastic glow-in-the-dark cheruby thing at the end of his bed. It had pretty yellow buttocks, polished and bare, and its wings were outstretched and out of proportion like Batman on the top of a Gotham building.

The morning nurses had a swift and quiet handover, which was unusual, and they told Hegs he was due to go for an emergency CT scan. Ms Jo Moran arrived swiftly beside a young doctor with gimpy swagger, neon lime crocs, all business, and skidded at the edge of Hegs's bed. Hegs was asked all sorts of questions, and looked perplexed as Ms Jo Moran was getting him to tip his nose with his left hand and right hand and left foot up, right foot up.

Michal came in all prepared with a black leather wheelchair, lifting it up on its back wheels like a BMX bike.

'Patreeeeck, I bring you now for CT brain. Get your bed coat, come now, good man.'

Molly Zane handed Hegs's file to Michal in a thick brown envelope, sealed, to be brought to the scan and brought straight back – the entire life and medical history of Patrick Hegarty in one flimsy and rather damp-looking cardboard file.

Hegs lifted his two legs with his hands and brought them to one side of the bed, but they didn't move as far as he'd hoped and just when Molly and Michal thought he was about to mobilise, he threw his pale head into his two overgrown toddler palms and sobbed. Eventually, they placed a maroon Tudor bed coat over Hegs's robust shoulders and gave him some tissues. The footrest on the wheelchair had broken off, leaving Hegs to heap one foot upon the other and Michal set off singing a U2 song in Polish.

After they left, Molly began emptying Jane's swollen purple bag, again, and then busied herself with neatly fixing away the contents, but Jane screamed.

'No, no, leave it so ... Would you leave it be,' Jane said, swatting at Molly, and grabbed the stuffed bag to her chest. 'I have my secrets wrapped up in here.'

'You do not, Jane,' one of the young student nurses said. 'Not all of your secrets, surely,' and she winked at the old woman and laughed in that sad way the young play the old.

'I certainly do, young madam, I saved it from downstairs in that awful horrid filthy place, you should really go down now and clean it up. And don't mind your winking. Or you should perhaps read a book, and learn some manners,' Jane said.

I stopped reading. Years ago. When I was a kid and my mind was filled with Father, I needed books. Growing into an adult, I longed for them. There was nothing safer than fiction. But then as I started out on my own, I was so busy. Books reminded me of all the shaking and screaming and suffocating and hitting. I couldn't concentrate on other people's stories. Fuck the Cave. And the shadows. Fuck the peach with the friends I needed, they were never coming; talking insects didn't take me to New York, and a man didn't show a keen interest in me taking over his chocolate factory, a teacher didn't come and pluck me into her world of hair ribbons and shiny Mary Janes. Dickens made me feel like I was exaggerating, because there was no workhouse. Or undertakers. Dylan Thomas made a hash of it all. And when Kate Brady ended up walking all alone and destitute in London and never reconciling with the big thick fuck of a father in the third of that trilogy, this finished me.

Jane began to fuss about Hegs in his absence.

'Try not to be worrying about it all, Jane, he'll be grand,' I said, turning over to face her.

I tried to distract her like I would do with my own children, half-heartedly waving my phone in her face, as though she could play Tetris or go on YouTube and watch some twats play video games.

She looked puzzled.

'Ah. Now. Should I use your phone, my dear?' Jane asked me. 'But who would I call?'

It hadn't been my intention to mither her or encourage a call.

'You have the most lovely skin, is it real? Is it really your skin? It's lovely,' she said, inquisitively perching at the side of my bed.

'Thanks, yes, it's my skin . . .' I said as she shimmied along on the bed. I moved my legs to one side. She rubbed down the bed sheet over and over, and then, patted my thigh.

It was all the permission she needed.

'You know, I think I'll ring my daughter. Why not? What d'you think?' she went on, still patting me. 'I need her to bring in my Sunday clothes and to pluck these buggers off my chin.' She pulled at some wisps of hair. 'Would you mind?' she said.

'No, Jane, it's not the weekend, you don't need your Sunday clothes, not today. Today is Tuesday.'

She was eyeing the phone on the bed and then picked it up with her two tiny hands, and held it like you might do to wring out a facecloth.

'One always needs one's Sunday clothes, especially, you see, in a nice place like *this*. Now, if you wouldn't mind, can I have it?'

I stared at her kitten whiskers. 'Oh yes, sure, of course. Yes, here, have it, of course. Here. Ring away.'

'No cord?' she said. 'Ah.' Her eyes were a bright turquoise like the glass jars and baubles you find in wicker baskets outside knick-knack shops on a Spanish promenade. And they had a most peculiar line of mustard yellow running vertical through both irises. Jane had strong oily black eyelashes. The skin on her face was etched with spidery lines especially on her cheeks and round her nose. 'Well now, isn't this just lovely?' she smiled, still holding the phone. 'And while I have you here, madam, I don't suppose you'd have a brassiere?'

'What?' I said, holding her stare for too long, 'A bra? Really?'

'Yes, you see I just can't bear it in here without a bra on my back, and for the life of me, I can't seem to place my hand on mine,' said Jane, shouting loudly now to aid my comprehension. 'I think I left it somewhere along the long way here, while they were bringing me here, and what with all the scans and taxis and needles and bars, and, leave it there to all the restaurants they took us to, it's marvellous really, all the different foods, but it's been a very busy trip altogether now, and for the life of me, I can't, well, I can't seem to ...' She looked downwards, grabbing her breasts between her hands. 'I just haven't a bit of comfort, with these two sitting down on me all day.' She squeezed them. 'And I mean if I needed to take a swim in the sea later, well, I know it's all the rage to go in without a top on –' she threw her head back laughing, then stopped most abruptly – 'well, to be honest, I wouldn't really be keen to swim without one. But I will if I have to – skinny dip.'

'What? Are you serious?' I said, laughing nervously.

'Oh yeah, she's serious,' said Margaret Rose, and looked down at her own pair.

I had a spare large black-and-cream Wonderbra shoved in a bag under my bed, that the ambulance staff had snapped off me. It was encrusted with pink star diaman-tés across the cups. 'Babe' times two. It was a hideous thing, really, with empty hooks for the missing straps. I lifted it from under my bed, and pulled the cups together in a rather vain attempt to make it look a little more innocent, or perfunctory. I tried to pluck off the dia-mantés, but they were stubborn. It was monstrous, but I hated nipples uncovered underneath my clothes, so I could empathise with Jane. Any bra is better than no bra at all, except at airport scanners with the metal wire and all the confounded beeping.

'Jane, here, this is all I have and really I'm awfully sorry about it, and ...' I said, 'I'm sorry, but there's no straps.' I paused. 'Well, see, it's ... strapless.'

'Oh, my,' she said, grabbing it, 'you see, look at this now, isn't it marvellous? Thank you, thank you ever so much, dear.'

Jane ran her hand over the diamanté stars and walked across to her cell, pulling around her curtains, as though it were a changing room in an old drapery store. She stirred behind the curtain. 'Oh my,' she said as she emerged and strutted forwards to me, her shoulder blades folded back like a mangled book. She had entirely abandoned the idea of the cream blouse. The skin on her belly fell downwards like a deflated wasp nest.

'Success,' she applauded, as her small belly wiggled. 'Oh, my, that's better, ever so much better. Ah. Great success. This is a very lovely shop you have here, dear. Will you parcel it up for me now?'

'Would you not prefer to continue wearing it?' I asked.

'Ah, yes, great idea, now, thank you, dear. Ah yes, sure I'm wearing it, no need for the fuss or the parcel. My apologies.'

'Thank you,' I said. 'Enjoy it.'

'Oh, I sure will.'

In terms of a successful transaction, it was daylight robbery but it was the best this boutique could offer to Mrs Jane Lohan. She was delighted, but only so briefly a satisfied customer for next she put her head down, as though I had been caught laughing at her, or told her a dreadful lie, or done some other atrocious thing to embarrass her.

'You OK, Jane?' I said.

'Ah,' she said, applauding her memory, 'I almost forgot. The call, we need to make it. I knew I was forgetting something. You see, I'm ever so hot and bothered now. I don't like shopping so very much and I got ever so distracted. Now we need to make it before our swim. Could you dial it up there for me?' she asked, expeditiously.

I hesitated.

'I'll pay you up for the units,' she said, noting my apprehension. 'Perhaps it would be best if you timed me, set your watch there, dear, I have money, I'm good for it, then we'll know how much I owe you.'

'Oh, no, no, it's not the money at all, stop, I don't need money, Jane.'

She had her daughter's number scrawled on a beermat, with its edge slightly torn.

'Can you dial this, dear, I've no glasses?'

I dialled. I returned the phone to her ear, but she fast waved an angry hand in the air and continued her swinging legs at the side of my bed.

'No, no, no, you must talk to her for me? She's never happy when I'm away on my holidays. You see, she's a jealous sort. I don't like to speak much on your phones, case I do anything to them, break them, press a wrong number, dial a stranger,' she said, motioning it this way and that, 'feck it up on you.'

She was getting frustrated that I wasn't playing the game, her game.

The phone rang out and out. Margaret Rose eventually, sensing my apprehension, made a hang-up sign by lifting her thumb and little finger upside down and dropping it slowly downwards.

'Maybe she screens anonymous calls?' I said, but Jane didn't take the bait.

'Call her again,' she insisted. 'Go on, dial her again ...'

Daughter in a kitchen. Large red presses. Slate floor tiles. Surrounded by lilies. Attractive. Golfer. A guess. All appliances hidden. Integrated. Little signs of life.

'Are you sure you don't want to?' I asked. 'Maybe try her?' offering her my phone.

'Ah, now, my dear, I wouldn't know what I was saying,' Jane fussed.

'I don't even know her name, Jane.'

'Oh, I know, but don't worry. I don't know her name myself, half the time.' Jane extended, laughing and swinging the legs at hip height and with sprinter velocity, she was fit as a fiddle, mind astray, heart pumping. It was a cruel combination.

'Pretend you're a doctor,' she laughed. 'G'wan, you can, put on a voice, a doctor voice,' and she began pulling stiff-upper-lip faces and miming a stethoscope around her neck and lifted it to her ears.

'And you see, ask this precious daughter of mine,' she said, growing excited, 'doesn't she care at all for her mother? Ask her that.' She paused, then lifted a hand to her face. 'Oh, and be sure to tell her we're having our tea outside today on the lawn, all of us. Me and all my friends. That'll drive her mad.'

'It's not picking up,' I said.

'Oh, she will, just wait a minute, have you withheld the number?'

'But it's not your phone, Jane, does that matter?' I said.

'Pardon?'

'I'm ringing off my own number.'

'Oh, yes, you're right, she'd love the excitement of a secret number, see, she's a little bitch like that. Make sure and tell her about the big tea we are planning. About the front lawn and our plan to bring ... bring ...'

Margaret Rose took a sharp intake of breath. 'Umbrellas.'

'Brilliant, yes, umbrellas. Thank you ... make sure and tell her.'

Jane's picnic tea set was wrapped up still in the bed sheet. We would each dine on a tissue and a set of rosary beads.

'Ask her,' she said, holding a tight grip of my chin now, her face deadly serious, 'what's her problem with me? Does she not care, and she having a fine big car in the driveway, ask her what did I have her for at all?'

Her eyes were fast and intent on mine.

My jaw wobbled, unused to being held to ransom like this.

Dinnertimes. Father's hands. Mother. Throat. Neck. Choking. Dancing off the ground.

'I can't say that,' I said, resentful of my inability to be assertive without being angry, without provoking.

I deadened the call.

'I'm not telling your daughter what you said,' and I handed her my phone, 'and keep your hand off my chin, it's a trigger.'

She threw her head back, laughed and pointed forward with her index and middle fingers firmly together like a gun. Shooting. Pow. Pow. Pow. And she blew the top off her fingers.

'Lave her be,' Margaret Rose said. 'I've a phone here ya can use, and I'll ring your daughter and pretend to be the doctor far ya, love.'

'Thanks,' I mimed at Margaret Rose, embarrassed and guilty that I'd dragged her into this.

'Maybe she's busy?' I said, attempting to console. 'She'll visit later. Try and sleep, lie down, they'll be in with some tea soon, or try and rest maybe?'

'You're only a coward.'

'OK, I'll ring her for you this time, just this once, mind you.'

I redialled the last number.

Hello, Lohan, Lohan, Mary, answered the phone, rhyming off the number, and calling out her surname twice. Mary. Hello. Hello. Irascible. There was a brief and adequate conversation about medicines kept in the top drawer and Meals on Wheels for Tom, locking the top bolts of the gates and door, something about the large Yucca plant in the bathroom – its roots rotting from over-watering seemed to anger her, and trying to mind Tom's hands when he opened the tins of dog food. I didn't recommend a bra or knickers drop-off. I hung up. She wouldn't be visiting. Everything was fine. Goodbye.

'I've my husband at home, you see – Tom,' Jane said, and giggled. 'I'm his carer. Me, I care for him, I shouldn't be in here at all, you know, with all I have going on, we're two right old codgers.'

'Oh, that's a tough gig, Jane,' I said.

She trailed off.

'He's terribly forgetful …'

Margaret Rose sensibly asked if she was getting the Carer's Allowance but Jane screamed at her to mind her own business. Margaret Rose said she just thought it might help. Jane told me she was getting the allowance, but not to tell anyone, they'd take the eye out of your head that sort, as she dismissed Margaret Rose's concern with hand swats and smirks. She got new curtains with last year's Carer's Allowance, she said. They were lovely. She couldn't remember what room they were in, but they were yellow, same colour as her tenth birthday dress, when she had her first kiss. No. No. She can't quite remember her name, but yes, she distinctly remembered her face. Her husband's name was Tom. But she never wanted to marry Tom.

'I've nine fine children. Mind you, they're all away now. America, Australia, England and I've even one in Mexico. Mary didn't go away though. She was always a good girl, Mary, but I often wished she went too because everyone needs to go. Everyone needs to get away. It would give me great peace if she went away ...' She didn't finish.

I wondered how a woman could grow nine children and end up here, without a bra or even a clean pair of knickers.

'D'you know, you're a lovely girl? That second girl I kissed went away, you know ... Did I tell you I could smell St Thérèse of Lisieux. It's her roses? They're drifting in off the corridors. I just know he will, he'll spare you with her help. I know it when I can smell this. It's the roses, you see. It's all in the roses.'

She held my fingers in a newborn-baby grip. I closed my eyelids tight, unsure of where to look. I sat, deferential, as though in prayer. But I had no faith. My parents were devout Catholics. Father with Old Spice on his face, at mass on Sundays, not daring to ever sit far up the church or receive the host, a sinning man, but he was proud that he somehow knew this, like all good honest men; this was a good thing, he convinced me. An honest hardworking man that held his wife up by the throat like a raggy doll in our sun-filled kitchen to watch her dance. But that was just temper, everyone needed it. Temper. And sure, couldn't one repent it? In the end. On the very last day. Judgement.

I had sprayed some of my rose perfume behind my earlobes.

Jane let go of me abruptly, dead-staring at me.

'Who went away?' Margaret Rose said.

'Patrick. Hegarty.'

'He's only gone for a scan,' I said.

'Ah, good. I know Patrick Hegarty very well,' she said, 'and . . . I know his mother.' She raised her eyes to heaven and held her hand to her mouth.

Margaret Rose opened her eyes wide. 'What, ya sure?'

The sheets on Hegs's bed were tossed. Unmade beds unnerve me. Molly had left without fixing it.

'Yes, I'm sure, certain that I'd have killed his dirty rotten father.'

Chapter 10|

'I settled on decapitation. Chopping his head off,' Jane said, her face sweaty.

'Jane!' Margaret Rose screamed, and then laughed tentatively.

'This is no laughing matter, Margaret Rose,' Jane said, remembering her double-barrel name. 'First, I'd wash my hands in lavender soap like I do when a cow is calving, cleans them from infection and it's great for it gets the smell of afterbirth off your hands.'

'Oh, now, Jane, that's a dreadful thing ta be saying,' Margaret Rose said. She lifted herself from the top of the bed to the bottom, and sat there.

'But you see, you're not a farming woman. Besides, I have often thought about how,' Jane went on, ignoring

Margaret Rose, 'but I couldn't lay my hand on anything that would have done it cleanly, quickly, and to be honest, really, I don't think I have it in me, to kill a person. Do you think that's something you're born with?'

She looked at us both.

'No,' I said.

'Agree,' Margaret Rose added.

'Well, maybe then it was a, what do you call it, a dream, a ...'

'Fantasy,' I said.

'Yes. Fantastic ... so to save me the stress of hacking at him, maybe I could have bought an axe.'

'Jesus, fuck,' I said. My stomach began to throb, and the sides of my face to flush. There was pressure between my thighs.

'I have a good swing. But I'd never find him. I didn't even know what he looked like. If I'd even one lousy Polaroid to go on, but New York City is a big place, plenty murdered there, isn't it a shame we don't have a telly here?' she said, throwing her arms towards the window, where a TV would naturally plonk itself. 'Great shows on the box from there, we'd have a great time, us girls,' she smiled, and weight settled on the back of Jane's shoulders as she dropped them slowly.

'Ah, don't worry, I wouldn't have dared do it,' she said. 'It'd be impossible to get a good swing on an axe in New York, it's so full up with people. People everywhere. Maybe I'd use a gun.'

Her eyes stared at the ceiling's mould and up at the sickly tiles that sneezed on us each time the wind would lift one up and down. She clattered her false teeth into a pink froth in her mouth like one of those reduction things they whisk up and place over poached eggs and asparagus with a silver spoon on a fancy cooking programme.

'I know exactly what's up with Patrick. Poor boy. I could fix him, but it's too late, it was too late the day he was born. He's pretending not to recognise me,' Jane said. 'You see, I pretend I don't recognise him too ... you know the way ...'

'I think you should lie back into your own bed, Jane, get some rest, and leave it so – you're very tired and we're all drained and maybe if you slept?' I said. 'Then Mary will be in.' I closed my eyes. I had pain everywhere. Throbbing. 10. Ten. Pressure. Stinging. Flushing. Pulsating.

'She might come in today, and relax you, they could give you something to help you sleep? Do you take a sleeper?' I said, arching my back forward to take the pressure off.

But there was no talking to Jane.

'I'd never find him. You understand this, don't you?' She was flustered now with an anxious energy. We both nodded silently. She quieted down a little then, and began buttering and marmalading a wheatened cracker from her nightstand, and crunched down on the thick chunks of pale yellow butter and blobs of orange-rind marmalade heaped on it. Her thoughts were uncontrollable like daft pups. 'Would you care for one, dear?' she said, as she coughed, the crumbs going against her breath, coughing again. She offered me nibbles on the palm of her hand.

'I'm grand, thanks,' I said.

'I think you should tell us out that story, Jane,' Margaret Rose said. Eager.

I shot Margaret Rose a look.

'I'll put a sliver of marmalade on it, first for you.' Jane wasn't giving up. 'If we can't picnic outside on the lovely lawn, this will have to do.' I'd eat her concoction, and Margaret Rose would eat it too, poorly, out of one side of her mouth and perhaps bite her numbed cheek a couple more times. 'Come now, have one, maybe they'd wet some tea for us, isn't this nice?' Then, as though she'd been struck hard, or wound up, she began. 'I taught Claire Hegarty.' Bingo. 'Ever since she was a little girl, y'know?'

I licked the sticky mess off my fingers.

'Oh, really, Jane? No, I didn't know, I don't know her very well at all, his daughter,' I said.

Margaret Rose grimaced. It was nice being alone, the three of us, without Claire, easier to chat, though we were conscious of Shane, nodding at him sometimes, and fussing when the students came in and out, telling them that they should wet his lips, or close the window near him, for it was not nice for him to be in a draught.

'Ah, no, you don't, sure why would you? Well, Miss Claire was a pupil of mine ...'

'No way?' I said.

'And tough as nails. I'd give her velvety stamps in her copybook, you know, to tell her she did well ... she loved to be told she did very well. Preferred being told she did the best, and even then she'd ask, "Am I the best?" It was difficult to disagree with her. She liked stars in her spellings notebook, her maths, Irish verbs, music. Everything was always in order, except that awful walk.'

'Ah, ya,' Margaret Rose agreed, 'noticed that ... very flat-footed.'

'Yes, yes, very much so,' Jane replied. 'Well, she'd wear cerise-pink ribbons tied high up on her head and when she knew an answer, which was all of the time, you see, she'd put her arm up straight over her head in the air and keep it there, like one of those swimmers, paused.' Jane mimed the action, holding her own hand high above her head, then thrusting her arm backwards, she continued, 'She could hold it there all day long, sometimes I'd just leave her be. I'd let her sit and hold her hand up all day long.'

Alex texted.

I ignored it.

Jane took a long breath, snapping one of the crackers in half, but didn't bring it to her mouth. 'Really she must be just like her grandfather, the one I want to kill, you see, because I don't know where she got the brains from,' Jane sighed, 'and the rudeness. And you know, another thing, she always knew the correct answer. Miss Claire Hegarty. Miss. Miss. MISS. Hand up, shaking it now, so impatient to tell me everything she knew, I knew it all already, she didn't need to try so hard. So I'd strike her.'

Margaret Rose took a sharp in-breath and shut her eyes tight.

'Don't be so critical, you —' she whipped around and pointed at Margaret Rose — 'I couldn't allow her just to plough on forward and pass everyone out, you know what they say about too much praise? Besides, it'd have done her no good. All that praise.' Jane spoke quietly now, not wanting anyone to hear. 'We'd better be quiet and not pretend a thing, or we'll never get out, they'll never let us home, and we'll have no tea outside later.'

The Hegartys never acknowledged Jane. And in turn she had kept an iron fist of silence on her story. The wind was blowing up outside, but the rain was lifting and the late-afternoon sun was showing itself. Leaves billowed and big seagulls cawed out, landing on the crumbled balcony edge and flying off, startled by the banging windows.

'Her hair was braided so very tightly, you see,' Jane said, making a tiny O out of her thumb and forefinger. 'And let me tell you, ladies, it was not Claire's mother who did that to her hair. You see ... she did it to herself. The child. That tightly to herself ... that it almost stopped the blood ... but she had to be just perfect.'

'I always liked putting my girls in plaits. Kept it neat,' Margaret Rose said.

My sons. Barbers. Six weeks. Short back and sides. No razor. I'd go get a coffee and leave them in the place with music videos, scantily clad women, men with tight chinos swaggering, narrow combs in blue liquid with pretty teeth, lift-up seat for the smallest as he eyed himself furtively in the mirror.

'Ah, I have you now, I have you,' Jane shrieked at Margaret Rose, scanning her up and down. 'Well, aren't you the right one, and you named after the princess, the bitch, the whore one, went off with the photographer, Margaret Rose Windsor, that's you, right? Wonder what ma'am would think of that?'

Margaret Rose laughed, 'Ouch. But ya, yar correct.'

'In fact, there is no way in this wide earthly world that Claire's mother would give a damn as to what her hair was like,' Jane said, going back to her tale and raising her tone now. 'Claire Hegarty's mother didn't plait her hair. She put plaits in model dolls, mind you. But she was never going to touch a hair on the head of her own child. It seemed there was just something about her.'

Margaret Rose shot me one high eyebrow. I reciprocated.

'She's a lovely woman though, you know?' Jane said, invitingly.

'Who?' I asked.

'Patrick's wife, gentle, could never understand why she didn't take to Claire, and in the end Claire did everything for herself and her father. At first, little Claire began asking my year's plan, and said she loved maths, but all I could think of was Ann . . .' Jane said and sighed. 'I was years teaching at this stage and let me tell you, there were few put it up to me as Claire did, not at all like the older brother and older sister.'

'Really? He has more children?' Margaret Rose said, surprised.

'Oh, yes. Two. Joan's in Saudi for years, teaching, and John married a lovely woman from Colorado and they set up a music shop. John loved music but he was tone deaf, I used to have to ask him to mime in the choir, only move your mouth, good boy, John.'

Lucid.

'Would you like a chocolate?' Margaret Rose said, and shoved a box shaped like a blue coffin towards us both in turn, rattling around a few red-wrapped ones. A lone orange one held Jane's attention. She jumped up, reached in and fished it out.

'No, no, ah sure, I'll take this orange one, is it a hard one? Oh, wait, Jesus no, no, it is not, it's soft,' she said, grimacing and bruising it with her fingers first, then opening it, and placing the cracked chocolate volcano on her tongue to melt like Jesus, the syrup dripping into her throat. Cu. GU. Cu. GU.

'But who's Ann? Did they have another daughter?' Margaret Rose asked.

'No, no. Ann Hegarty was the most beautiful woman,' Jane replied.

'Hegs's wife?'

'No, no, no, not his wife at all, his mother!'

'What?' I said. 'You knew his mother?'

'Of course I do,' she said and blessed herself. 'She was born on July fourth, six days before myself and that was trouble. Independence Day, see, wild as a March hare, and the first chance she got she left for New York.' As Jane spoke her eyes darted towards the ceiling, as though she were bringing up files. The past wasn't difficult. The present impossible.

'Ah, so many left,' Margaret Rose said, sadly.

'Ah, they did sure, nothing for many really, but to get away. We'd all grown up together. They were the next house over from us. Ah, they were lovely times really, we were mostly left to ourselves ... head to the beach. I loved school, but Ann, well, you see, Ann hated it, always trying to take me away from learning. She was wild. We loved going out off on the bikes, especially to go as far as Roundstone. Do ye know the lovely beach, Dog's Bay? Ann loved to swim.'

'Yeah,' I said.

'Ah, ya, so beautiful out there, isolated,' Margaret Rose said, twisting open a red foil paper by pulling it with both her hands like a Christmas cracker, 'but I never gets in the water, freezing.'

We all agreed.

'There's never enough sun to heat the water,' Jane said. 'We did what was asked of us at home. I loved the books, and Ann loved the music. She played guitar. She'd sit in on her bed for hours just strumming it, while I'd lie there, listening.' Jane made an odd noise and began to lift her shoulders up and down and again.

'You OK, Jane?' I said. 'Jane?'

She paused, sat still, eyes frozen fixed straight ahead of her, her right foot going around and around in a fast circular motion. Margaret Rose glanced fast at me, unnerved, 'Jane, ya were saying, the guitar and Ann, lying on the bed ... remember ...'

'Ah, yes. I can see the guitar, and I can hear her, laughing, but I can't rightly remember her face. Oh, damn this, she keeps floating off ...' She put her head in her hands. 'It's no use, I can't see her, damn it, damn it ...' she said, getting agitated.

'It's OK, Jane,' I said, 'take your time, maybe have a sleep? She'll come back.'

'Promise?'

'Promise.'

I was just about to close my eyes, breathe through my own pain, when Jane lurched forward again, energised. 'Oh, now, the guitar, yes, well, you see, she learned of an old Martin guitar brought back from the States by an uncle who used to live in Chicago,' she said, 'and I cannot, for the life of me, cannot, remember the uncle's name.' She was unnervingly specific at times, her bright eyes ablaze with another time; recalling people seemed to give her memory a welcome distinction. 'Ah, yes, the uncle said he was friends with Dick McPartland,' she said.

There was something about the odd specifics that was upsetting.

'And that it was Dick's guitar, after he'd had the heart attack, he'd given it away. But this is a lie, you see, Ann told me that she believed McPartland never played a Martin guitar, these kind of things held great importance to her, and I never forgot a word she said to me. I remember it all, verb ... verbal ...'

'Verbatim?' Margaret Rose said.

'Yes, that,' Jane said. 'Ah, Ann had notions, she was off to America to find jazz. Jazz! Did you ever hear the like?' she said, smiling. 'But that was Ann.'

'Where'd she learn ta play?' Margaret Rose asked.

'Ah, well, the guitar playing had come from the Hegartys' side, really, her father was a great musician, in the trad sense ... they were session musicians.'

Yeah. I knew, hard, strumming tight, feet tapping, keeping the hands close into the body, like Irish dancers, a restrained madness, attempting to express the unsayable.

Then Jane started at Margaret Rose. 'Did Tom come up the fields yet? Would you like a cup of tea? Here, I'll make it for you. This isn't my bedroom, dear, is it? No matter how much searching I do, I cannot, cannot for the life of me, find the kitchen here.'

'No ... it's not, it's not your bedroom. You're in Hospital, Jane. On the Ward ...' I said.

Margaret Rose shook her head, looked at me, and put a finger to her mouth. Perhaps it was better if we were quiet.

'Ah, yes, I'm on the Ward, amn't I? That's correct. Thank you.'

'Ya are, love, ya were talking about Ann,' Margaret Rose said back, quietly, her voice tired.

'Ah, yes, Ann. I was so sick the night Ann Hegarty was leaving. I'd a bad fever and it hadn't broken. I'd cried myself into it. Then I'd screamed and stuck my head into a pillow. They didn't know what was wrong with me and of course I couldn't tell them.'

'No, ya certainly cud'na,' Margaret Rose said, sucking a chocolate and nodding.

'She had an American wake and just ... left ...' Jane said, pulling furiously at the star diamantés on the bra. 'Ann was delighted, mind you, she was so giddy, spinning this way and that, telling me, planning it all.' She threw a diamanté bead and hit the window, startling a gull. 'She was jumping up and down as she was leaving me to go over to the wake house, where they'd a party for all the young locals off to America. I couldn't go with her. I didn't want to anyway. I would have made a show of myself. She wouldn't stand still to even say goodbye to me. But she was such a foolish dreamer and I knew, truthfully, she wouldn't last a minute. That's what everyone said. And I hate to admit, I agreed with them and, sadly, they were right.'

Margaret Rose sighed.

'Maybe I should have stayed with her, minded her, but she wanted to go alone. She never asked me. Never spoke about it. I would have gone. God, but it hurt me ...' Jane stopped abruptly, perhaps weighing up if it were appropriate to finally betray herself in front of us. Strangers. She looked at us both inquisitively, ascertaining threat levels.

'I knows ya would, Jane,' Margaret Rose offered, softly.

'You see, I told her I knew all about boats. I'd have swum the Atlantic Ocean just to be with her. We could have hidden over there and pretended to be sisters,' she said. 'And besides, the daft bitch said she was going to put her feet out at the end of the boat and tickle her toes off the Atlantic, stupid girl, she didn't seem to care about me, or that I wanted her to stay. I even had to tell her that large boats that take you to America didn't work like this. Imagine. Imagine that she was going off to America and she didn't know how a boat worked?' She laughed, fearfully. 'And that was it. We didn't laugh again ... well, not together at the very least.'

'Did you ever see her again?'

'Oh, yes, of course,' Jane said, exasperated with her audience. 'She arrived back a year to the month, on a different day. She arrived back on a Sunday. A Sunday is never a good day to arrive anywhere. I was finishing up my schooling and moving to Dublin for teacher training.

Are you OK, love?' she said, eyeing me. 'Would you like a sandwich, you're so awfully pale now?'

I shook my head.

She offered to make one for Margaret Rose.

'No, no, I'm OK, but when is a good day ta arrive, Jane?' Margaret Rose urged.

'Arrive where?'

'Ann, arrive off the boat?'

'Who?'

'Ann!' I said.

'Ann, Ann's here? Oh, my, what a lovely surprise. Well, let her in then. Christ, are we going to leave her abroad in the cold all day? I haven't seen her in the longest time,' Jane cried out, opening her eyes wide and fixed on the window, as though her friend would walk through.

Margaret Rose groaned.

'No, tell me about the Sunday, Ann Sunday. When Ann came back Sunday. She's not here, Jane, remember?'

'Ah, ah, yes, poor Ann. Oh, yes, a Friday, a Friday is a great day for a new beginning, because if it doesn't work out, you can start again on Monday. Clean sheet.'

'Slate,' I said.

We laughed.

'That awful man was the Bishop of Galway with his cigars and champagne.'

Lucid.

'Browne?'

'Yes, him ...' Jane said, cowering.

'He was a bastard,' Margaret Rose said.

'Oh, yes, most correct, a terrible man. He liked to be called My Lord, you see? Yes, a bastard. And we were not doing so well,' Jane said, sharply. 'None of us ... Women.' She took a long breath. 'Ann was in trouble ... and ... just like that she handed herself over.'

It was the early fifties and the world was all a secret affair, after the wars, turn of the decade after the terrible war. Bishop Browne was at the helm here for Virtue and

Money and General of Misogyny, for with a complicit family and a complicit society, and God plonked at the centre of everything, schools, kitchens, doctors' clinics, garages, shops, marts, sacred heart on every kitchen wall, red light, mea-all-culpa, we could once and for all solve the problem of fallen women, hoorish women, pretty women, pregnant women, poor women, women, girls, we could put an end to the shame they were bringing, for the bother with the fucking outside of marriage; no property rights; no rights to their children; rarely rape sanctions (or mentions); no drinking in bars; no drinking out of pint glasses; no pill; no property; no money; no married job in the civil service; no sitting on a jury; no free health care; no church after birthing a baby without a churching; breaking of pelvises; sterilisations without consent – list is not exhaustive.

Who made the world? God made the world. Oh my God, I thank you for loving me, I am sorry for all my sins. It has been one week since my last confession. Oh my God, I am sorry if I have offended thee. Oh my God, I am bleeding. Oh dear Jesus, I have not bled. Oh dear and gentle Jesus. Save me. I am your sinner. I am sorry for greatly offending thee. Save me. Glory be. Blessed be the fruit of thy womb, Jesus.

But these women would be dealt with, and the sins of their flesh would be discussed in his drawing room with champagne bubbles and Cuban leaf smoke, and in many other drawing rooms, and good or bad sex, no matter, there was a hefty life sentence, incarceration of the body of the woman, of her mind, and of the baby, the Holy Trinity, things good in threes/things bad in threes, and they'd soften our women coughs for us, forever in penal servitude. There was an appropriate way of solving pregnant women in Ireland. Apparently. As they decided on the fate of young women and their children, with their robes and their God and their cocks and their cigars and champagne, and sure, wasn't it only good for us? And weren't we only lucky? For their own good, and the good of the child. A bastard. For the good of everyone, for it was contagious, hoorish behaviour, like galloping consumption, and men were poisoned with a spell of passion by these young women, girls, by their hair and their eyes and the way they might wash a cup or iron your shirt and all the fleshy bits of the body women have, poisoning them all, and the awful way they might look at you, to damn you, or talk to you, or walk along beside you. Everyone must help solve it for the good of us all. And if it wasn't a good solution, locking them up in hellholes, which turns out it wasn't, it was a fucking criminal travesty, then, now, hush, God would be good to the incarcerated women and their sold or dead children. And if God wasn't good, which he didn't seem to be, not turning up for work in these places, then we all must be good and virtuous, and nice, and act appropriately, and maybe best not to talk about it at all, for what is talk but weak, and cheap. Now, now. And not bring shame, no more shame, for until, praise be, God might come back for us. And see how secretive and virtuous we all are, and oh, how many cannot recollect. And oh. Wasn't it only the way, only the way of us? And wasn't it what we all deserved?

They say Ann Hegarty didn't stay long in Clifden after returning from America. A motor car was called for and she was brought back into Galway, past the stone bridge at Oughterard, thatched cottages, and red doors. Half doors. They stopped at the Angler's Rest Hotel, where her stubbly chauffeur, who had been quiet the entire journey from Clifden with the pregnant girl in the back seat, took her in to the bar of the hotel for some Guinness, and after he settled her into the snug, the lady of the house brought a large glass jug of Guinness with two tulip glasses, and he poured. She was given a half-pint, for he insisted iron was good for the baby as he stroked her thigh and sure he could do no more damage, he whispered. And he bought another large jug for himself, before they left, in broad daylight. Ann was sickened from the Guinness pooling and churning in her belly, so she sat, faint, on the white garden seat outside the front of the hotel, and two young boys came over, offering her a basket of fish they had just caught; five silver bodies lay on some straw in the wicker, fat and blue around the centre, dead and resting in the afternoon sun. Five fresh jelly eyes, bulging and shiny, staring back at the young woman.

They went on to Tuam and her chauffeur drove on through the town and stopped his motor car out on the Athenry road, a little way past the railway bridge, where the trains brought sugar beet up and down the line, and told her she was on her own. If she wasn't up for anything then why should he shame his car and drive her to the gate of the Home, and abandoning her on the side of the road, he gave her scant directions to find her way back the route he'd just driven out, and up and into the right.

It was dusk when Ann made her way to the Bon Secours Mother and Baby Home.

Good Help.

Good Help to Those in Need.

Bon Secours.

And it is said that sometime after the birth of a little boy, with beautiful skin, Patrick James Hegarty, Ann was eventually flung in through the doors of the Magdalene Laundry at Forster Street in the city, driven by the same chauffeur, and although rumour has it that she protested, she'd serve out her time for the sin of sex, for no one would pay or could pay the one hundred pounds bounty or release fee, demanded by the Church for her keep while in confinement, one hundred pounds to release her back to a life of hanging her head down, or leaving for England if she could raise the fare and never return. But how could an incarcerated woman raise such a fare?

A life of incarceration for Ann as Bishop Browne and his army of virtuous brought down any good man or woman who sought better health care for women. And wasn't it only what was best? For what were women only donkeys? And what was a donkey only a working ass? And what was an ass but a fool? And what to do with a fool but stick her in the corner and point fun at her, make her your slave and what was the child of an ass but an ass fool, and a chattel to sell or starve? And what of it? We should all forget it now. Bastards. Malthus indeed. And isn't incarceration only your own fault? And how we are all so convinced by each machine that replaces the last that all lost ambition is to do with the self. The self. Regulation. Impulse. Self. Live. Your. Best. Life. Everything. Is. Possible. Fight your illness. Come now. H'up off your knees. Christ.

'It was a Martin, the guitar . . .' Jane said, eventually. 'She'd gotten in harm's way beyond in America. And the nuns weren't really used to the backwards way of this now.'

I agreed.

Usually girls stayed out in America. Ann should have stayed. For better or worse, girls stayed out abroad, for if it maimed them, it could mind them. And they were never heard from after. But Ann Hegarty gave herself back to the Irish prison.

Patrick was eventually given out to a family member. Which was the strangest thing of all. It was also said, the Hegartys were *lucky* the laundry took in Ann, for the girl wasn't raped by her brother or interfered with by a priest. The father was an American. And for all intents and purposes the sex could have been decent. American sex, where you could fuck and come without a criminal investigation.

'She came back with her beautiful head down. In repentance. You should never hang your head in shame,' Jane said. 'I just can't, for my whole life, understand why she came back. Never ... NeverNever. I'll never ever understand why ... wasn't like her at all, at all ...' Jane began lifting her shoulders up and down again as she swatted at something in front of her face and grimaced. 'I was so troubled to hear everyone saying how ashamed she looked, I didn't get to talk to her properly, for once she gave herself back to Clifden, she was chaperoned, always

chaperoned, until they got her into the Home and then
... chauffeured on.'

'Did ya try?' Margaret Rose asked. 'Did ya try ta tell her
how ya felt? Did ya still love her?'

Jane looked hurt, stung. 'Of course I did,' she spat. 'I still
love her, and you can't just stop loving like that, like it's
a tap.'

'Sorry,' Margaret Rose said, 'I didn'a mean ta upset ya.
It's just so ... sad.'

'It is sad. And what else is sad is that neighbours went
around as if this was a good thing, as though this made
them feel better. What did it matter to them, to any of
them? Their tea would still be in the same place, their
boots laced, their boats with nets, nothing Ann did
would bother them, upset the running order of their
life, and yet we were so much of everyone's else's business. It was all they spoke of for some time. But it
wasn't like Ann –' Jane was crying now and I was crying too – 'to give in. Ah, here now, keep your chin
up,' she said to me, watching me dry my eye corners
with a tissue, 'especially with your lovely skin. Did
you get any tea? I'll ready some for you now if you so
wish?'

I was thumbing the cracker. I waved it weakly at her. 'I'm OK,' I said. Jane blew her nose in her bed sheets.

'I wrote to her, but never heard a thing. I went to Dublin, tried very hard to forget her.'

'Really?' Margaret Rose asked as she pulled at some tissues from their elaborate box.

'Don't "really" me. Don't you think I feel guilty? D'you think I just got on with my life? What do you take me for? She was my ...' She stopped and Margaret Rose reached forward, dropping sweet papers on the ground, got out of bed and climbed in beside the old woman. Margaret Rose held her and began passing her tissues. 'I forgot about her on purpose,' Jane said, sobbing into Margaret Rose's chest. 'Imagine forgetting about someone you love on purpose? But that's who I am. And look at you, with the royal name, what do we make of that?' She laughed weakly and looked at me. 'And mymy, aren't you beautiful too?'

The bra was gone fully astray now and hung around her waist like a make-up belt.

'Ann's aunt, Maura, well, I suppose she raised him as a bitch would a pup, and he has no idea. I don't think I should ever mention it?'

'No,' we both said, loudly.

There wasn't a peep out of Shane and his student nurses had come in, surprised and unsure what to do with us all, attempted to cover Jane, who resisted, and then left again in a hurry.

'Two weeks after Patrick arrived in Clifden —' Jane clasped her hands and her eyes shut down tight as Margaret Rose rubbed her shoulders — 'Ann hung herself —' she paused — 'inside the laundry.'

Margaret blessed herself three times.

'Oh, Jane, I'm so terribly sorry.'

'And right where all the other girls could see her,' Jane continued, 'with a thin yellow apron string, and it started cutting her wiry neck. I have this terrible dream that her head falls off completely and rolls to my feet.' And she spun around to Margaret Rose and started screaming, 'Fuck them, you know, FUCK THEM FUCK THEM FUCK THEM.'

Ann Hegarty never took the trip again home to Clifden, to see her son creeping down low in a woollen duffel coat with big peg buttons, searching for a shell at Dog's Bay, and Hegs would remain a man boy, because that's the way sometimes, when you are constantly searching the past.

'They think she's buried out Headford way near some castle ruins, but who knows? I don't trust a word they say, in the next breath they'll say that she's not dead at all ...' Jane said.

'Or that the records burned down in a fire. That's always what they'll say. Or the nuns are too old now ta be upset. But what 'bout all the families too? They were in on it,' Margaret Rose said.

'Fire starters. Every convent in the country seemed to have one,' I said. 'Sure, there's hundreds buried every-where, thrown into bogs and over walls, some say they're in that awful tank in Tuam, sure, what do you even say?'

'Jesus. That gives me nightmares. Ta think that was going on when I was young. Is that really a septic tank?' Margaret Rose asked me, blessing herself again.

'It would appear to be,' I said, quietly and unsure.

'Indeed,' Jane continued, 'others say other things. You see, mostly people won't speak about it at all. Maybe that's easier? For the best?'

'But ma'god,' Margaret Rose said, ever so slowly, 'a sep-tic tank, far poor children, babies, and those poor boys that found that tank.'

'Some say they were only in that tank because it was a safe burial place,' Jane said, 'but I know what they thought of women, we should make no mistake of that.' Her hands were shaking.

'So do I,' said Margaret Rose, oddly clutching her sheets. 'Never trust them, I amn't the best with the words, so never rang in ta the radio, but I'd have liked ta, but so many wans come on, telling us their story. Awful. But still, ma'God's ma'God. And he won'na see us wrong. None of this is God's work. 'Tis the work of the Devil. And we let the Devil control us. I knows it.'

She blessed herself. I didn't agree with any talk of God or the Devil. I thought about Ann's guitar. Where had it ended up? Hegs should have it. The body remembers, human, instrument. Somatic pain. All the pain-filled belongings we're encouraged to just dump.

'I remember her beautiful hands. Such beautiful hands and the longest eyelashes you ever saw. People were so scared,' Jane said, after a long pause. She eyed us both again, running another trust test. 'The people were scared, I don't blame ordinary people.'

'Well, I don'na know how ya'd put yar daughter into wan of those places,' Margaret Rose said, defensively.

'But they put the fear of God into you,' Jane responded, 'and you didn't even know why. What were we so afraid of? Hell maybe. Or shame? Or your parents, siblings ... everyone was terrified.' She knelt on her bed now, back poker straight, and began to join her hands as though to pray. 'But Tom is a good man now, though we got off to a very bad start, and I don't love him, but he stays to his side of the bed.' She said, 'Though he's so very quiet, hardly a word out of him, and I'm not mad keen on silence.' Jane lifted up her holdall with her narrow fists tightly closed and lay back with it on her naked stomach. Margaret Rose crept back to her own bed.

I needed a plan. I would have to find something, Switzerland. Something. And I needed to make it clear to Alex. He needed to understand. Stories last a long time after you go.

Chapter 11|

I slept badly. Ranting. Dreaming. Sweating. Raving. I was relieved when Wednesday morning arrived.

Hey, morning! Please pop in x

… Morning. Shit. What's up?

Just come in please, I'm lonely and sick/don't feel gud –

… You can't be worse? You're in the right place. Why the hurry? I'll be as quick as I can, still horny?

(Aubergine emoji. And syringe. FFS.)

Fuck you. I'm bad. Seriously. This place is too much. Pls. xx

... REALLY? OK. Soz. Gimme half an hour.

If you've prepped lunch, then come, NOW Pls?

... (Another aubergine. Christ.)

... Fuck. Soz didn't mean to send that.

K. You idiot. Don't come until you're organised. Have you prepped?

Bitch move. I always chose it. It quieted him fast. Guilt. Not being a provider. I'm so utterly afraid of marriage and its potential to become entirely catastrophic all of a sudden, that I self-sabotage regularly. I try to break the habit. But it's utterly compelling, and lately I do it sub-consciously. Yet as I watched **A typing** flicking this way and that with the dots illuminating/dying for minutes without a word appearing, I wanted to punch myself. I could never unsay them, these words I unleashed on him, I could try frantically to gobble them back in ... *this text has been deleted* ... but it never worked. Those words are utterly damaging too. Paranoia inducing.

It was time to start saying some nice things.

Tick Tick Tick Tick Tock Hynes ...

I'm sorry. Don't worry about prepping anything.
Mum will feed them. Love you.

… I really do fucken love you too, even when
you're ratty, soz too, but you've been so … ratty
… unpredictable

Just bringing the element of surprise I'll be grand
– prob just the meds xoxo

… I think you're hungry. Hangry? Remind me to tell
u bout a doc I watched on Hunger Strikers

Can.Not.Fucken.Wait.More.Pain.

Crazy shit

… I'll pop in, just need to check with your mother
and I'll get there asap

K?

K.

Heart. Red.

Heart. Red.

I picked apart a split end, amazed at how many pieces a narrow hair ending can divide into, and splayed the hair out like the top of a skinny lotus. I couldn't see my kids. They couldn't see me. Not yet. Not like this.

SPOTIFY: I Shot the Sheriff.

I muted it, I needed one of those you-go-to-too-much-power-songs for when you can't regulate your own emotions, when you know you should be sad, but you giggle, or you know you should be sad but you scream, or you know you should be sad, and you go out and fuck. No strings. Sad. Mad. Bad. Same. Emotion. I braved Sinéad O'Connor singing 'Nothing Compares 2 U'. She guts me, her voice like a pike or a bayonet. Her big eyes, that face, and the long sadness of the line where she goes to the restaurant, and just then my mouth filled with my tears.

SINÉAD: MEANING: Irish form of Jane – God is gracious. (God my hole) **GENDER**: Girl | Female **IRISH NAME**: Sinéad **PRONUNCIATION**: shin + aid **ENGLISH**: Jane, Janet, Janette.

But gawd, did Sinéad O' Connor gut me open like a fish-o-filleted.

★

I first met Alex on a Friday, start of weekend. We had both gone to the canal near the Claddagh after work to watch the swans. I noticed him and watched him standing at the edge of the bank, legs spread and his hands in the back pockets of light blue jeans, a chocolate-brown Fred Perry hoody zipped up tight to his chin, grey runners with white stripes. When he turned to face me, I saw he had deep mistrustful eye sockets, as though he were constantly exhausted, but he had a warm and generous smile, with two deep dimples. He was laughing away to himself as two Whooper swans fought over a milk carton.

He was just the type of guy I never went near. The jeans, the runners, the zip top. As the swans came closer, he attempted to pass pleasantries in my direction, about the wind, the milk carton, the orange beaks. I interrupted the swans with a flocking motion of my hands, cautiously, and tried to grab the milk carton, to break up the fight, but ended up being head-butted hard in the stomach by the most giddy of the swans, to which end he stopped laughing and ran to my attention. I knew he was an OK sort, for it was the first time anyone moved so fast towards me.

'Alex,' he said, putting out his hand after first rubbing it off his jeans. Steady handshake.

'Sinéad.' I smiled.

'I wouldn't like to see you at three a.m. outside a chipper,' he said, and we both laughed. 'Glad you've the milk carton though, that'll come in useful, I imagine.' I laughed again. I suggested we get a drink. We got many drinks. And we got very drunk, stayed up all night chatting and laughing until it turned to crying and I passed out on his futon bed in a flat with guitars and crystal ashtrays sunk into tall copper stands.

After our day of breaking up swan fights we continued seeing each other, getting drunk, getting lentil curries from a small stand near the river, getting to know each other. He'd walk me over the Salmon Weir Bridge and back to my flat with all its cliché rubbish, white bread, a toaster, an empty bottle of peach schnapps with an ivory candle stump, colourful wax hardened on the glass, skins, dream catchers, Che Guevara posters, Harley Davidson Zippo lighters, mix-tapes, CDs, Portishead, Pixies, an unframed Proclamation of Irish Independence, large grandfather clock, guitars with three strings, strings of fairy lights, a menatwork sign or a yieldrightofway sign, damp patches, mildew, pizza boxes, loo roll, broken chairs.

I felt intense pain. I always start out thinking they're amazing, the men I meet, and then getting let down, or letting them down.

But he was reliable.

And love slid up on me. I didn't look for it. I tried, if I'm honest, to utterly avoid it. I liked Alex and so I quickly showed him all my worst traits, to warn him. Still, he stayed. I had simply wanted to watch the swans, to escape, but we drifted along as a sort of a couple for some time, made no plans, visited the swans every weekend at one of the canal spots, until he proposed there, with a ring tied onto a milk carton.

The Fred Perry hoodies were the first to go, next the posters, and on and on I went, fixing him. By year two, married him, everything in a strict order, and so it began. Or perhaps something ended and something else began. Planning. House. Meals. Wedding. Baby. Work. (Daughter.) Baby. Work. Baby. Children. Money. Cut your hair, grow a beard, clip your toenails, drink spirulina, eat less red meat, drink less beer, run, walk, run again, until my suggestion of hair plugs became the final straw and he threw a dumb-bell through the patio door of the New House (which is now just The House) and the glass smashed into a million little pieces, and he screamed at me that if he were to start on a **Snag List** of me, then it'd never end. It would be the first list of an eternity of things.

And. There. Was. Nothing. Down. That. Road. He. Roared.

We patched up the door with duct tape and a cornflake cereal box that offered free trips to the zoo, which Alex immediately began cutting out, meticulously. I consoled him by saying that I didn't really notice his thinning hair, it was just a little bit John Travolta, and that he was still a ride, and not to worry and we eventually laughed.

In an effort to also not age, I tried every shade of girlie pink blusher and he said I looked like a spy from the Soviet Bloc, with the stern jaw on me and square shoulders, and duck-egg walls in the house replaced all the yellow magnolia everywhere, except where we had carefully frescoed antique white, and a bed so big, you were guaranteed to never find each other. We had two en-suites at opposite ends of the bedroom.

The fact that he was a real man and a real good man came as a surprise, like that Christmas present hidden far in behind the tree that you find on January sixth when you're lifting out the Christmas tree. And despite driving each other insane, he was so solid, like a clove drop or bull's eye or a bullet.

What I lacked in maternal instinct, he had in abundance and what I lacked (or hid) in verbal expressive ability, he made up for, and what he lacked in his pockets, I sorted, and it was topsy-turvy and often neither of us felt particularly good about it. I wanted to express more and he wanted to earn more and perhaps because we went against the status quo, or perhaps because as time went on, I couldn't cry unless I was drugged or drunk, or because I couldn't show I loved him, because of my guilt or my constant self-sabotaging that I had become masterful at. And this was the most painful of all.

Some weeks before landing on the Ward, I went back to the Whoopers. I hadn't been since Magpie. I was feeling weak and restless, and needed to get out of the house. Alex was there, standing with his hands in his back pockets. Wax jacket. A lone black swan glided along the canal water, a wine beak like a velvet cupcake. He appeared to be stooping more now and I hadn't noticed, and he'd thickened a little around the waist, his laces were undone. He had a chicken roll and a takeaway cup of tea from a petrol station, he smiled and rushed to me when he spotted me, and then very worriedly, remarked how thin I'd become, and not good thin, thinthin, as opposed to *thin*. He tore the roll in half and shared it with me.

'Do you know you break bread?' he said. 'You shouldn't ever cut it. I only heard that today. Weird.'

'Yeah, I think that's something medieval,' I said, 'something to do with knifes and hunting – blood and stuff.'

As a child I had clumsy hands and I found it hard to hold those really fat waxy crayons that the black flecks stuck onto, and I'd colour in a picture, I'd colour it with bright cyan, magenta, yellow, mauve, whatever else I had, and I'd seal the scene shut with inky ebony crayon, then take the back of a steel spoon to it, and release some colour. But the art was never quite right, for when I dug hard at the ebony wax layer, I took the layer of colour underneath also, and the wax rolled up onto the spoon, so that the house I carved or car or dad or dinosaur looked good, but faded, completely faded.

★

'Happy Wednesday ta us,' said Margaret Rose, yawning. 'How're you this morning?' Her eye was drooping towards her stiff chin, but she looked better. Facially. Fresh. Not entirely daisy-like, but she was definitely in better fettle.

Hegs was back in his place, snoring.

I waved my hand in the air, unable to speak, and lay back. My chest was a vice-grip. My stomach was on fire, and my pelvis was only safe if I lay down absolutely still; for rising up or attempting to move put tremendous pressure on it, like I was going to give birth or have some prolapse thing about to happen that I'd read about online. I desperately wanted a walk or a swim, to take the pressure off, and because each time I closed my eyes to try and rest, I saw Ann goggly-eyed hanging from the banister. Hospital rest means lying there with your fleeting thoughts on acid.

Alex arrived, his temples were taut or hollow, his skin looked dry and he was agitated, greeted me in the way he does, not by smiling, but by lifting up his eyebrows and opening his eyes wider. This irritated me, but after a few moments, he revealed he had brought some nail polish, Punchy Soup Can Red.

'I thought maybe I could paint ...' he drifted off mid-sentence, lifting my hand, and settling it on a pillow. 'You know, maybe paint your nails, cheer you up ... I'm no expert, but I'll give it a try ...'

I smiled.

'Don't stir,' he said, as he rummaged in his pockets.

I tried to sit upright, but couldn't.

'Don't,' he said, 'I can do it while you lie down. I've brought some sweets too,' and he lifted a crisp small brown paper bag from the left pocket of the wax jacket. He unscrewed the top of the bottle and dipped the brush in and out of the pot. 'Are you actually trying to lose even more weight?' he whispered coarsely, eyeing around the Ward nervously, as though they were in on it.

'Yeah, I am, yeah,' I snarled, hardly able to speak.

'Why?'

'Just drop it ... Jesus, paint if you're going to paint ...' I said.

''K.' Alex paused. 'It's just ... well ... I'm sorry but fuck me, Sinéad ... you look like ... death.'

'Fuck. 'K.'

'I'm sorry, but you do.'

He placed the brushstroke a millimetre from the cuticle and began to stroke the nail, rounding it nicely at the tip, over the nail edge. After awkwardly manoeuvring the thumb, he blew them quickly, and gently lifted out the pillow and laid my hand on the bed sheet. He circled the bed and came around to the right hand, miming his actions.

To break the silence, I attempted to tell him about Ann, but he looked concerned and furrowed down his brow. I was wheezing madly, and he told me that I was talking too much to the other patients. Wasting my energy. That ended the conversation, because it took the wind out of my sails and the moment was gone; upon noticing, he apologised, and with the tiny brush between his finger and thumb, he blew gently down again on my fingernails.

'You're in Hospital to rest and get better ... that's all ... I'm not cross, but you're wasting energy, and I'm so worried, but you'll be right as rain in no time ... you're in the right place.'

I grimaced.

'Ah, here, there's no need to sulk about it.'

I didn't respond. Couldn't.

'I've been Googling respiratory illnesses,' he said.

Shit.

'Do you know it's a major killer ... even more than cancer?'

I'd been Googling too. Animals that freeze or play dead:

LEMON SHARKS PLAY DEAD WHEN FLIPPED ON THEIR BACKS. When faced with imminent death, certain species of duck will play dead. It's called tonic immobility. Pigs and other farm animals can fall into a trancelike state. Snakes are good actors. The baby brown snake, or *Storeria dekayi*, will freeze if approached by a menacing predator — or scientist intent on a closer look. And the snakes stay in character, remaining stiff and lifeless even after prodding. (*National Geographic*)

He apologised for the nails, as the more he painted, the more his hand shook. I reassured him quietly that they had cheered me up – and they had. They were summery, and I accidentally, for the briefest moment, looked forward to the summer for the first time in ages. Then I looked down at my body; black coarse hair sprouted out of my ankles and I remembered again. This was the way it happened, forgetting, remembering.

'I want to be cremated, OK?'

'Ah, now, I didn't really mean that you look that much like death ... I just don't want you to lose any more weight. I was joking. Sorry.'

'It's OK.'

'Shit, you don't have one of those eating disorder things, do you? Where you … you know … puke? Fuck. I never thought, maybe …'

'No,' I said, interrupting him sharply.

'Oh, no … sorry, just Paul's daughter has one, and well, you're similar, you know … you fit the …'

'Fit the?'

'Nothing.'

'Fit the what? Go on, you started.'

I gripped my two thumbs with my index fingers, smudging the polish.

'Fuck, now look what you made me do.'

'You know, type A, determined like …'

'Right,' I said, calming down. This was a compliment.

Wheeze.

'I want to be cremated.'

'Fuck, Sinéad. Where did that come from? Jeez, what drugs you on?'

I ignored him, breathing through a huge pressure. 'Well, no one knows anything, when things can go ... wrong ... I mean, it's a conversation we all should have. So I just thought. Like if I were to die suddenly you need to make a hair appointment immediately. I'm a state,' I said, as I grabbed a fistful of my brassy yellow hair in my hand, 'especially the roots, and to be honest, if Chloe has time, she should think about toning it too, you know, before laying out my body, they'll all be gawping in. I'm orange, tone them down, now I'm not fucking joking, if I die, make sure you get them to dye it. It'll take time, but it's worth it. Give her three hours to do it, someone should stay with her though, no one likes a client who can't talk back, otherwise they'll stay orange, don't rush it. The medicine has played havoc with my hair, and my nails, Sarah will need to do them, not you ... no offence.' I knew being laid out would mean Gawpers. 'Oh, and don't forget a tip, I usually give a fiver, but you know, this is different circumstances, so, well, I'll leave it up to your discretion.' Round our way, they love if you're laid out at home and they get a cup of tea. They clatter the cup off things to show their presence, and walk upstairs and have a good look around your house, check if you're wearing a wig, or if the corpse has glasses on. My granny was laid out with ridiculous frozen-ice-blue eyeshadow, and she looked like Ivana Trump and not at all like herself.

'Ah, fuck off, crazy woman,' he said, laughing nervously. 'Who's going to highlight your hair when you're dead? That's really sick, you know, you shouldn't be talking like that, it's dangerous ... What's with all these insane requests?'

'Look, just make sure it's a cremation and make sure not to allow any of those knob-ends I know and hate, near the place.' I had to say it, I was afraid now, and it was all coming out arse-ways, but if I threw it into the air, he'd have to remember some of it. 'It's just, I don't want everyone looking at me.'

'Sure, y'know ... I'll send invites, will I?' he laughed. 'Are you sure you're eating? Promise.'

'Yes ... invites, invites are a great idea. Yeah, of course I'm eating, it's just the drugs for my chest, and they knock stones off you.'

'Christ,' he said, and thrust his head forward into his hands. He began pressing his index fingers into both dry temples, two dots of red nail varnish on his thumb. 'Ah, here, Sinéad, no one sends fucken invites to a funeral, they'll think you're a diva. This hospital is playing with your head.'

'I'll be dead, I don't give a toss what they think.'

'I do ... I do care about you. About it. Jesus, can we stop this morbid conversation. Is it him?' He nodded over at Shane.

'Maybe. Yes. It's so intense, you know, just watching him. And no fucken prayers, I've had enough prayers in here, none, nothing ... I'll come back and haunt you, I mean it.'

'I've no doubt you'll do that anyway.'

He began laughing hard now.

'I love you,' I said, desperate. 'I do, you know ... love you so much.'

God, it was awkward.

He tapped his fingers off the nightstand and looked upwards and then he bit his lip. I tried to appreciate this was coming out of nowhere. I rubbed his hand, to settle him, and connect. We were never heavy on public displays of affection.

'This isn't like you. You sure you're OK? There's nothing you're not telling me?' he said, and he thrust the arm away, blowing hard out through his nostrils.

'Yeah. Yeah, I'm fine, just so run down.' I paused, 'I do really love you, look, fuck it, I need you to hear this …' You can't even block out hearing things. And if you do, some part of you will remember, like a twitchy leg or an itchy nose.

They say drowning is awful.

I tried to tell him.

I think I'm drowning.

I am. I'm drowning.

Save me.

First my eyes watered, then a most ferocious throbbing at the back of my head, under my arms stung, my wind-pipe closed in like a lump of toffee had jammed in it, and my nose worked but it was a pinhole and trying to take in the air as I desired, well, the nostrils couldn't do it. The pressure was tremendous.

Alex rang the bell quickly and roared out. I hadn't seen urgency like this since he split me up from the swans. The pressure was getting worse. Ten. Pain. 10. All over. Pressure.

★

The seas remember to come in and out. The waves are solar-powered. They stay going even in the dark of night. They'll take deck chairs and towels and rubber shoes, tennis rackets, buckets and spades, beach balls and picnic tables, tins and rollies, plastic coffee cups and nappies. They'll gobble seaweed and leave it back. They'll lunge at jellyfish. They'll take your coastline. Your breath. The sea comes in hungry and can take your son and daughter under, caressing them, swallow them whole.

★

Buzzers went off and everything froze.

As I like it.

'We've given her magnesium, no more steroids, give her a break for a minute, she's crashing, some adrenaline and epinephrine, please, and perhaps some atropine. Code Blue. Move. Move. Quick as you can. Thank you.'

'Could you get out of my light? Trying to find a line. Fuck.'

Potatoes falling from the sack. Thump. Heartbeats. Thump. Onetwothreefourfive.

'Someone needs to give this more time, OK, start the count ...'

'Is that what she wants, does anyone know what she wants?'

'Of course it's what she wants ... she can't be more than what? What age is she? Anyone? Age? Quick as you can ... Age?'

'Jesus, more fluids maybe? Someone. Now. Nurse. Now.'

'What's happened?'

'No idea. OK. Line in. And move. Next. Twenty milligrammes. Thank you.'

'Who's looking after her? Any chance of that file? Quick as you like.'

'What in the name of God are on her feet?'

'OK. File ... here.'

'Read. Loud.'

'Thirty-nine. Female. Oh, shit. Perhaps Mr ... You should take a look here.'

'Are they slippers?'

'Jesus, they can't be!'

'Paddles. Ready. OK. Clear. Now.'

'Yes, they're blobfish slippers, sir.'

Charge –

Charge again.

chargechargechargechargecharge –

'FUCK SAKE NOW. Hurry up. Quick – OK, sorry, sorry, next. Another line and good. Thank you.'

Jesus.

'Why did she let herself get into this state?'

'Please stop screaming but I know, it's the twenty-first century – right?'

'Right!'

'I think she was … it seems, I don't think she attended, yeah, nothing, look …'

'Noooo.'

'Yeah, take a look, here, and look.'

'OK and clear again …'

'OK now, Ms Hynes, we know this is frightening, but just stay with us … OK … we will do all we can, just try to breathe … all we can to …'

Save you.

Code.

Charge again.

A freckly nurse pulled off my rings and frantically began removing my red nail varnish off my index finger, the paint transferred to her cotton ball in the shape of my fingernail, and she held on to it like a child grasping the ear of a stuffed rabbit.

I really don't want them to think I'm lazy. Still can't move my fingers. Move your fingers, I scream at myself.

G'wan, dare you, show them you're not lazy! That's it. Good girl.

Father again – Christ, let me not die to the sound of him. I think of waves. I lie back and do the dead man's float.

'I think she's gone. Is she gone?'

I can't see you. I can't see.

You're not sick at all, you're a fucking chancer, you really are, it's all those colourful mad vitamins your mother's giving you, and that fish oil, eat the fucken fish and don't mind taking it in a tablet, what sort of shite is that, don't be such a cunt, there's too much work for doing and you acting like a cunt, your brothers are out there already, hands frozen off them, and they don't have this sucky moody face on them, what in the honour of Christ is wrong with you? Animals don't feed themselves, you know?

My mother intervenes, whispers something.

OK, OK, well, drink up a bit of tea and put on a coat and come out, I've a horse for you to ride.

He whispers something back at my mother, he's angry now and she has her head hung low. She has lovely hands and she smiles at me with her thin lips. I think she mouths that she loves me, or maybe she's saying to unload the washing and hang it out.

And maybe two, but we'll have to saddle up the young Clover-field colt and see if he takes to you, and sure then we can have another mug of tea. Your mother will ready us something. And maybe you'll lie across the new yearling then? Lovely crossbreed, jays, he's a lovely keen little motor on him.

I can't see.

I leaned my body halfway across the neck of the young yearling, my pelvis on his withers, to eventually prepare his back for weight; he began to dance and push himself forward on his two outstretched front legs, eventually arching downwards and lifting his back up fast like a cat, he bounded forward and hurled me off, blowing out hard, terrified, as he propelled me into the sky. I fell down on the flat of my back, after coming down on his neck first, breaking my fall, the mane hot, blood spurted from my nose. Something prodded through my T-shirt. The horse escaped over the high wall, in desperation, and flipped over it, just toppled, head first, injuring himself. He cut his hock and a big knee came up, soon a second big knee. They never go down, two big knees. Unsellable. Ruined. Father caught me by the hair at the nape of my neck, to show me what I had done, how I am ruining him, Father. I will be the ultimate ruination of him, and I cried out, sorry, and shook, tried to tell him to leave me alone. He lifted my head from the hair at the nape of my neck, twisting it around his fist, and banged my head forwards off a rusty barrel, over and over. The clangs seemed to come from the next field over, like a church bell in an Italian city. And lifted and banged it again, spraying blood, until my head whooshed and I didn't feel any pain at all. I see his teeth and shaking lips, quivering, the sun was going down behind his shoulder. Red. Red sky at night. Delight. The colt blew over the wall at me, apologetic, his big wide brown eyes, head down. He had given in and I could mount him. But I passed out. The wet sand heated up all around me and was warm. I was so grateful for passing out.

If I love any horse, it is a seahorse.

And then you could wash up yourself, or do whatever you want, maybe even a bit of homework or study. But shir, what is it they have ye all doing? Learning lines, learning off reams and reams of stupid lines. Forget them. Today, today indeed today you can ride the stallion. The stallion. And forget learning lines for anyone. Make up your own. Gods make their own . . .

Indeed.

I can't move my legs. I am overheating. I dive under the waves again and I fan my hands in front of my face. The young yearling with the two big knees gently nuzzles me. We are so sorry to each other. Well, horse, we could have managed this better.

You're not sick at all, loveen, I've told you this a million fucken times. You need to toughen up.

'Did you hear me, love? Go with it, go into it, go into it, and stop fighting.'

'Can someone ask her to try and relax? Anyone?'

'Is that her husband?'

'Are you her husband? What's your name, love? Love? Name?'

'Shit, sir, quick, quick as you like …'

'Jesus Christ, GET HIM OUT!'

'OK, OK, sir, sir, you really must, this way, please.'

'Get him to leave, somebody take him out – '

'He wants to stay, he's insisting –'

'And could someone take off the blowfish slippers? I can't work on her looking at them – Christ.'

'Blobfish, they're blobfish,' Alex says. He stays.

I dive under the water again, but I've gone out of my depth and there's a net.

'OK. Everyone, as you were. Again. Count.'

'What's your name, love?'

I grab a yellow paisley necktie tight with my fist and wrap it round my wrist.

Never wrap the lead rope around your fucken arm like this. I've. Told. You. A. Thousand. Times. Now that'll show you. Don't mind rubbing your face. It's only a slap. If you do this with a big horse, and he's stronger, remember he's always stronger, he'll pull your arm clean out of the ball and socket at the shoulder and clean off you, like a Christmas cracker snap, and I try to tell you, but I can't. Do. You. Ever. Listen. CHRIST.

I try to scream, but the doctor's holding my face in his hands and they are soaked wet.

He's Alex.

Alex, his name is Alex. My Husband. And he's so far away right now that he could be standing on top of Mount Blanc. That time. We ate apricots. Drank wine. Chewed tobacco.

They shove something down my throat. I gag. I gag up my tongue. I gag up my tits, my tummy, my vagina. My legs pulled upwards and inside of me and I gag them up too. I leave it there, the gagging. There is nothing left inside of me. The fear on Alex's face is like a dirty winter's hangover from March. But we're in April now. And I love him. Guilt. And this fucking elbow on my sternum.

Now the heel of a hand bangs me and I've pissed myself. Again. I want to pull a face.

I consider diving one last time.

'Oh, sir, shit. Look, sir, I have her notes, she didn't return, she said she was moving, would get treatment elsewhere, or something?'

'OK, charge again, it's the least we can do.'

I can do the dead man's float for ever.

I'm gathering up some Connemara ponies in the Railway field, they usually run with a couple of older horses, or a donkey, to calm them down, the ponies dart among the heavier horses, no good for anyone now, their stumbling legs slowing them down, heavy swollen hocks from wallops off the stone walls, old hunters, but still the sun shines on their dappled rumps and over the strawberry-roan arches of their backs. Sheep run with them, pick and graze, shiny greased maggots wriggling at their back openings as the soil is heating up with fine weather. The dark grey ponies will turn a snow white as years go on, and sometimes, after they've left us, I'll no longer recognise them, that's if I'm fortunate enough to ever come across them, but I rarely am, fortunate. I'm not there to watch them turn into old reliable ponies for kids with ribbons in their hair who do ballet or play piano in Devon or Shropshire. Father always sold the stock without telling me, no goodbye, we didn't get one to keep, we broke them, bridle, bit, saddle, rider, ground poles, cross poles, stone walls, and then moved them on. He sold them off to a Rose Cottage or Amble Lane Farm, far from the rough west coast of Ireland with gates rusty and unhinged, squeaky and cumbersome like people, necessary, swinging this way then that then staying stuck, held together with yellow lutein baling twine, needing a good lift from the lower rung to open and shut. In the end I stopped loving the ponies when they'd arrive as young foals, plucked giddy and frightened from the mother. We simply worked them and eventually we stopped calling them by their names, referring to them by sex and colour. And when a fancy horse truck would arrive in the yard with a yellow reg to collect them, I'd hide under the bed.

I never said goodbye.

This, Father said, makes us tougher. But later it made loving harder. I was always ready to

let

go.

Chapter 12|

Margaret Rose held Alex's upper arm tight between her two hands. I didn't remember introducing them, and hoped he'd be polite. I was mad I hadn't told him about the fish with regional accents I'd read about on *Wired*. Some scientist in Exeter had been studying it for years, how cod have chats. I had meant to tell him. He'd love it.

'You're going to have to try and count, OK, Sinéad, right, you need to try, count with me, count to a hundred, count to a hundred.'

'One, two ...' I was making no sound.

'Come on!'

Count, I thought, like you're counting small diamonds in sieves, or crumbs of precious metal, or the tiny pieces of stones that were crushed under the tyre of your car, that emerald, remember when you ran over it? Count like tributaries going to sea, like the hairs Alex left on the bed on the last morning before you ended up here. Seven hairs incidentally. Five lines now attached to you. Spells trouble. Count the days you whined for yourself. Count the number of times you watched *The Simpsons* and fell asleep. Count the number of lazy days you've wasted. Count the number of days you've wasted, hungover. Count the number of days you were late home for dinner. The number of days you stayed out until the next day.

Count the number of times some fuck told you to smile. 'A smile is the prettiest thing you can wear, girls.' Smile, love. G'wan. Prettiest thing you can wear. FFS. (Unless you're a soldier or an undertaker or a surgeon or disciplining your children or a million other things you could be doing where a smile is wholly inappropriate.)

I laughed to myself, then suddenly as a bonesetter's triumph, air came in, air. Just air, simple but lovely lapping popping air.

Alex was screaming wildly at me. I had a bag on my face and couldn't reply, he was making an awful fuss and now he seemed to be holding on to Margaret Rose, really tight. He was always so gentle, but here he was now, going mad, screaming my name over and over and over again and he had an odd way of emphasising the end of my name. Aid. AID ... I needed to see my children. I imagined them. I could retrace each face. Phew. Limbs long and awkward, the crease of their necks. Little fingers in paint. Worms in spring wriggling in their fists. Tears. Lost teeth. Santa.

And all through the house. Not a creature was stirring. Not even a mouse.

I lay naked and shaking. Young doctors fussed about with syringes and bags of fluids. No one considered a sheet, not even a T-shirt. Across the way, Claire, unfussed, picked up her glossy and sat back down as she flicked through it, keeping an eye on Alex and me in turn.

The balloon inflated and deflated.

Alex was a tragi-cross between withdrawal and a terrific solitude. Ms Jo Moran stood upright and all serious beside us, and Necktie stared out from behind her as he set about explaining things. ICU was jammed, RTA, I would have to stay put on the Ward, and no, they know it's not ideal, no, everyone should calm down, everything would be OK, everyone just needed a little time out, calm down, calm, a hand–held telemetry and wires would play Big Brother. He was mostly counselling himself.

I was freezing.

The cancer was causing serious respiratory failure.

It was a shame that I hadn't wanted treatment.

It really was a shame.

For such a young woman.

But choices and individuals and well, policy.

Alex stared at them like a clownfish.

'Today is manic in Hospital,' said Ms Jo Moran. 'Sorry, but we will try to keep your wife stable and comfortable here, and now, don't . . . try to talk, Sinéad . . . just rest . . . OK?'

I tried to speak.

'It'll be a while before you can talk again,' Moran smiled, looking down over me as she was tucking some hair behind her ear and settling the stethoscope on her neck.

'The tube may have damaged the vocal cords ... I know there's plenty you will need to discuss with me ... but try and rest ... later we can talk.'

'What?' Alex shouted, moving out from Margaret Rose's grip and approaching her, his eyes dancing. 'Will it, is it ... you know, will she be able to speak?' He had a dry mouth, staring at Moran's scope. And Moran went on. Thankfully they didn't need to leave it in. Or fully intubate me. Bate me. Yet. But it was time we both had a chat. For that's end/end. End/end/end tube. Poor fucken choice of words, doc. In the meantime she would leave a writing pad for me. And they would all accept my wishes, whatever they might be. She pressed treatment. Urgently, if at all. But urgent. Again. Choices. Respect.

'Is she a Mormon or a Jehovah's Witness?' Necktie again. Christ.

'What the fuck?' Alex said, his jaw dropping open. 'Who the fuck are you?'

'I'm Mr ...'

'And what the fuck is it to you ... She's a ... She's a, you know, like you, I mean, me. Like me.' Then he screamed into his hands and began shaking his head. 'She's a fucking atheist. I mean an atheist. Sorry. I have no problem with her being ... I mean, I'm an atheist myself ... Christ.'

'You sure she's not religious? This seems conscientious.'

'Conscien ... What is wrong with you?' Alex squared up to him and shouted again, 'What? What are you saying to me?' Alex was eyeballing Necktie now and Moran put her arm up, nodded at Necktie to leave, swirling her head to the door to give him directions on the fastest way out. Necktie muttered things as he obeyed, walking away. Well, in any case. An awful pity. But this is hers. Choice. She made it. We are all here for you and the children. Here's the bell. Lingering. The bell. Oh, yeah, sure. And he took a grasp of it as though he were now also a patient.

'You OK?' Moran said to Alex. 'Maybe someone could make you a cup of tea?'

'Tea? What? No, no. No tea. I'm, I mean ...'

'Watching someone crash like that is an awful shock, but she's ... she's OK now. She seems out of danger. For now.' Moran focused on the machines, lifted a line coming from me, rolled her thumb along the little white roller to speed up the liquid, then squeezed the bag.

'Choice,' he screamed. He stood over me as he stared down, white with rage. 'What the fuck does she mean you chose not to know?' He looked at Moran in desperation. 'What the actual fuck, Sinéad? You CHOSE not to know? What the fuck?? Is this some sort of a fucking wind-up?'

Moran shook her head.

I was so glad they had shoved a tube in my throat and damaged my voice. I put my hand out to catch him, my finger, to grab some of his anger or something, like a mother puts out a tissue, but he hurled it back on the bed. So he could piss off with his anger and his shock.

Whose business was it anyway? Rhetorical question.

'I don't want to ... I mean ... I can't actually even ... touch you, sorry,' he said. 'I mean. Christ. Oh, Sinéad, love, oh, my God, look at the state you've got yourself in. Jesus Christ.' It was the lines and tubes. They said Sick as Fuck. He pulled a sheet up around me, and then covered me with a quilt. Finally.

'She doesn't have cancer,' he muttered finally. 'She's ... a cold ...'

'I'm so sorry,' Moran said to him, 'but she choose to keep it to herself.'

His eyes widened and he frothed at the edges of his mouth. 'Are you mad?' he screamed. 'You choose fucken kitchen blinds, and car hybrid engines. You CHOOSE a fucken takeaway. You even CHOOSE a bottle of wine. And my God, you're good at that.'

Ouch.

'Ah, no, they can't be … It can't be serious. This has to be some sort of wind-up?'

He was pacing to the toilet door and back. Jane was following him, turning just seconds after him at the doorway and re-entering the Ward like two demented soldiers.

'It's a joke … it is a joke, isn't it? I mean … they just said *Terminal.*'

'They did, correct,' Jane said, fanning him, 'terminal. Yes, that is indeed what they said.'

'Maybe you need to calm down a little, this isn't helping anyone,' Moran offered, as Margaret Rose unscrewed a bottle of lemonade and offered it to Alex. He stared at her, then at the drink, bewildered.

'They're wrong, aren't they? Aren't they?' Alex said to Jane, who continued to fan him.

'Well, she's very thin, I don't think they're wrong, but they're good in here, though I have yet to locate the kitchen ...' she said, scanning the Ward. 'I mean, they dressed me and I'm very happy now, you see ... I've made new friends.'

He looked at her, puzzled, and put his hands up to his head and then down, and up and down – he repeated the same action over. 'I mean, I've taken, I've been, I ... I've booked our holidays ... and see, we have a new fridge coming, and the kids have, the kids, you know, they've concerts, and Nathan has a thing in the aquarium with the seahorses. Nathan loves seahorses. And the fridge is great, it opens the other way, so it won't be constantly banging at the door and I think you'll like the way the hinges ...' He trailed off.

Seahorses. Beautiful creatures.

And he paused. 'Oh, Jesus Christ, oh, my fucking God, they mean to tell me, she means to say, and the kids, the kids. Your KIDS. What the fuck is wrong with you?' he screamed down over me. 'You had three fucking children. Did you just forget that? You have them you have them. Have them,' he went on, correcting his past tense. 'You know this, right? Do you need me to name them?'

'Oh, please don't be cross with her,' Jane urged. 'She's so very lovely.'

'Lovely? You sure? You have her mixed up with her.' He waved at Margaret Rose who was screwing the lid back on the bottle slowly; he softened his tone and started blubbering. 'Oh, God.' He took the bottle off her, and cracked it, it spilled out over the dilseacht engraving on his wedding band, and dripped onto Shane's Adidas catch-all bag. Alex jumped up and fixed a Liverpool FC jersey and towel back in the bag and as he zipped he flipped the bottle into the bin and began crying hard and cursing.

Seahorses are mates for life.

And the males do all the child stuff.

Wish I were a fucken seahorse.

BTW correction.

I had four children.

But no matter.

It was possibly for the best I couldn't talk.

I closed my eyes.

They're not my boys, they're just boys. Our boys. They are themselves.

This was far worse than the time we sat up all night after he found receipts for rounds of Maker's Mark and Cokes from a hotel close by that we never frequent. I'd shoved it in my jeans, the receipt, into that little pocket where everyone knows to go to find secrets. It was the Coke that threw him. He knew I hated mixers. And plate-throwing that followed after.

Nodges, pills, wraps, receipts, condoms, the bold pocket.

It was worse than the afternoon he found blue Ray-Bans and a Harley Davidson cigarette lighter in my backpack, this was cringe, and he binned them too, after attempting to crush them in his hand, failing, which stoked his temper. Eventually he gave up finding things, or looking for them. I also got better at leaving no trace, like we do when we go camping or on a walk to the woods, or maybe he just binned them, but this was the worst look I had ever taken, because you take a look, don't you? In defence, I said I never looked for this shit on him, that I respected his privacy, and I muttered something utterly weak about trust, but it was falling flat so I let it fall, for surely he had some lip balm somewhere, or a gin-and-elderflower-tonic receipt. That night, Alex lay in bed and he said the worst part about me was that I didn't even bother looking.

Shots Fired.

Chapter 13|

Margaret Rose cried out loudly the next morning. Shane was dead. They wheeled out his bed, his face covered over with a white sheet that was crumpled in around his left leg leaving his toes uncovered. I felt enormous guilt. Worried I had taken the resources, crash team, doctors' attention. Molly watched on in silence as they removed Shane's body. Margaret Rose was blessing herself.

'So sorry,' Molly said. 'Not the best for you, ladies.' I began to shake, pluck my eyelashes, and noticing, she sat by me. 'He died, darl. But he wanted to die. You didn't. That's it. It's OK. Live a nurse-life long enough and you know those who want to go just go. We have choices, we all have fight, but we all know when we've fought enough, darl.' As she turned to leave after the porters and the body, she turned back. 'It's personal, death. Has to be. For everyone. He was comfortable, darl ... Try not to worry.'

I was cold.

Michal arrived shortly after, a pained face of something approaching mourning, lips and nose pinched, and he was kind, persuasive with his coffee and warm porridge but my throat was on fire. I had slept the night through, heavily sedated. Sedated the night through. Thank fuck. 'Poor man ... and so so tough on you all here and ...' he whispered, nodding at the bed, 'poor Shane.'

'Good morning, sailors.' Jane was up and out of bed and pirouetting, she'd rise up slowly and suddenly fall over, rising and falling, over and over.

Shane was dead.

I couldn't stop thinking it. Then suddenly forgetting it. I had heard about death rattles. I heard nothing with my sedation. My heart was palpitating. I wanted to see my mother, but all I could focus on was breath. The puckered creased sheet underneath me was stopping any relaxation, that and the sight of his toes, five. Five toes. I needed to text the boys. Joshua would send a paragraph of emojis. Heart beating. Someone had dressed me in a theatre gown. It was huge and gaped and my arse cheeks were uncovered as it pooled either side of me.

I tried to speak. I gurgled.

The windows banged perhaps to protest loss. The curtains around Shane's bed were wide open and every trace of him gone, apart from a tiny water stain air-drying on the blue mattress where it had been cleaned.

I had a direct view out to Galway's gloaming dawn. I tried to focus. I imagined the courthouse hustling, the sprawling buses full of believers arriving for mass at the cathedral, the cynical courthouse and the lofty cathedral oh so close to each other. Fitting. The green dome of the cathedral faded since I was young, from a day here and there of sunshine or from the constant dirty deluge of rain, and the clunky strength in the brick style seemed amateur. But everything seems brighter, more alive when you're young. Bigger. It was once a prison, rebuilt (Browne again, he didn't rest), and now a large cold church under the grey Galway fretful sky, ghosts of inmates could be imagined beating their chests for redemption or love inside its walls.

The Corrib River sneaks herself like long fingers through the city, labyrinthine, slyly moving around the cathedral, forking out at Nun's Island and in past the Salmon trap to enter under the Salmon Weir Bridge. Around the city's shop walls, greys and reds, and late at night down by the canals, cola-brown Buckfast bottles lie decapitated here and there. The people are an odd mixture of bog and bohemia, students and shoppers, city and country, of chatter and shopping bags and a village nature, and the city itself is often considered A Graveyard of Ambition, exciting tourists and frustrating locals.

I tried to follow the river from memory. I started tracing her routes. My heart slowed. This reassured me. But the water had an angry hurry about it, in a tremendous rush to the Atlantic. Things slowed down on a handful of ochre sunshiny days that came late spring and left before summer could take hold. July was usually wet. And rain fell often and heavy. The horse races entice some clowns who take over the place, dressed up, their own theatre for a week, swag and a story, but here's the thing about escaping, you must take yourself along. Mostly the waterways remained angry, desperately seeking some attention, often sucking in people, their dreams and sadness.

Past the cathedral, the river moves along, into 'town' and by the Spanish Arch, built to protect the city's quays, and where the old Fish Market used to stand, which stretches prettily down by the Long Walk, bright with duck-egg palates, lemons, magentas, swans, rowing boats. Tourist selfies. Bushing. The cranes have disappeared. It's all pop-up fooderies, pizza places, falafel spots, Mexican street food, craft beers, wine bars, high rents. Eventually turning back, towards the docks with its murky waters, the pastel colours and glass of the newer buildings of the Tiger decade.

'Karolina is so tired and so sick,' Michal said, abruptly. 'She 'ees so cross to me, and I am trying, y'know? I really am. But shifts are so very long. She ees not able to get up for work today. I tell her about you, about you and your children. About what happens to you? Think she care, think she care about you or me? NO. I tell her she is a selfish woman. And she laughs. She laughs at me.'

Michal was loose with information about his pregnant wife, Karolina Piwaska, who worked on the deli counter in the small grocery shop across the road from Hospital, spending long hours on her feet, stale coleslaw, hot chicken rolls, ciggies, balloons, cards. Happy New Baby, Happy New Man, Happy New House, Happy Old House, Happy Driving Test, Happy Valentines, Happy Happy Happy.

She enjoyed trying to perfect her accent at work, and he helped her also, for he had more time to learn the nuances, Hospital was full of different people he said and for that reason, he considered himself a linguist of sorts; customers come and go, patients stay longer time, good for learning. Yes. Good for learning. Galway vowels could be suddenly very sharp, high-pitched and pushed fast down your nose. Hiya, loveen. And all the nuances that took time. City. County. West. East. Mighty. Shir. Craic. How-ew-ya? Terrible. Jusht. Musha. Arra. Michaleen. Sthap. The city kids were the most difficult, he said, the speed of chat. Just the speed of talk, the speed of youth.

Byebyebyebyebyebyeslánslánslánslánslán.

Karolina had made some good friends who worked shifts beside her, splodging fried eggs into baps, toasting BLTs for teary Hospital visitors, and making one-filling sandwiches for the kids putting themselves through college. 'Karolina loves questions ...' he said. So did he. Michal could disarm you with questions, while reaching over with the coffee. 'So ... you having scan this morning?' Michal said, arching an eyebrow.

'No.' I shook my head.

'I'm sorry, I just hear them at station this morning, when they giving us the orders, always hearing, hearing always hearing. So sorry.'

Margaret Rose was under her running shower. Steam crept out beneath the door.

Jane had fallen back asleep after her morning salutations and revelries.

Suddenly like slaying spectators, numerous teams of doctors descended on our peace.

clip-clop clip-clop. winks. pinches. oh, but no, you doctor. oh, no, but you doctor. my my. oh phelbbbbbbbotomy. you know. and blood. you know. iPhones. clip clop clip clop.

Ms Jo Moran looked more delicate than usual, and was without her *Cosmo* as she made her way to the edge of my bed. Her followers swarmed behind her, glancing this way and that. One young intern whose Ted Baker glasses had fogged up, tripped over her and she shrieked out like a kitten. He wiped his lenses on his tie and then let them fall to the floor. He would never make it. Hegs coughed loudly and they all threw a fast glance at him, like a mother at her son in Tesco's to have manners, leave the sweets back.

They shut my curtain around themselves.

'So, how are you today?' Ms Jo Moran asked.

She repeated the question and Ted Baker lifted my head-phones out of my ears and clean off my head, without permission. He began rolling them in his hand. All business. Fuck. I had him wrong. 'You gave us a right fright yesterday, but great you've no tube … that's great. It was your heart more so, and not so much the lungs … but still we're concerned …' Ms Jo Moran said, with lispy emphasis on 'still'.

Speak Up. For Fuck's Sake. Speak Up. But it was no use, nothing was happening. I apologised. Again. No one heard me.

Some head consultant arrived, late to the party, partially shaven, leaving behind an odd clit-tickler under his chin. Looking for bloods and age and occupation again, over and over again this diagnosis of my socio-economic situation, my diet habits, my childhood trauma, and anything else that could make that picture society needs to see. He directed none of his questions to me. How society can help me succeed, or not succeed. He'd met me before. But forgotten. And before. Forgotten that time too.

'You're reading, I see, do you like reading?' First look at my eyes. 'I like reading. But never have time. You know,' he said, tapping his stethoscope. Pretend-pleasant, to feel himself more connected, and more at ease, but he wasn't letting me in on the secret destruction of my own body. He broke eye contact. Those were secrets they kept to themselves. If he only knew I was just beginning to trust books again, and he wouldn't fuck this up on me. I reimagined the canals, the waterways, and the salmon – their journey. He leaned his shoulder towards the canary-yellow neck of Ms Jo Moran's cashmere turtleneck and looked at my belly, then he noted a long list of instructions, his chin moving down and up. 'We're going to order another scan, how's the pressure in the abdomen, do you mind if I?' as he laid his cold hand on my gown. I could feel my knickerless bottom on the bed. Please don't roll me over. 'Hmmm. And maybe another abdo scan, if that's all right with you?' he said. 'Shouldn't be too long, though that said, we can't be sure there won't be a big RTA on the M6 and then you're not a priority, are you?'

Oh, Shane, I thought.

'We're so very sorry for disturbing your breakfast …' he added, noticing my shock. 'What is it you're having?' he went on, snorting, poking a pen around on the table, miming the stirring of the porridge pot like Father Bear. 'Porridge, oh, can't beat the porridge, can you, Ms Moran?'

guffaw guffaw guffaw guffaw guffaw guffaw guffaw

I had no doubt at all that Ms Jo Moran had made him the odd bowl of porridge. Off he winked himself away at her yellow-canary top, very pleased with his morning's monologue and upbeat spirits, completely oblivious to his M6 faux pas. But I imagine he lived his life in a certain contented oblivion.

'You doing the Connemara marathon?' he asked Moran, as he took leave. 'Maybe we could pair up?' She nodded. They would jog together.

Someone, for the love of good God, bring me a grumpy fucker tomorrow.

Oh, Christ. Waterways & Waves & Father & Alex & seahorses. Yesterday.

And Oncology came.

And Respiratory arrived.

And a nice woman from Palliative Care popped her head in. And would pop her head in again.

And then they all went off and sat around a big table.

At a Round Table Meeting. (Via email.)

And decided what was best (for me/without me).

But no one will ever tell me. What. To. Do. Ever.

I didn't even get an email or seat at the table.

Moran reminded me of Elizabeth Taylor in *Cat on a Hot Tin Roof* and oh, how she swooned at Paul Newman and how he, the most perfectly fuckable man in the world, hobbled around on one crutch guzzling a load of bourbon, and how even the most fuckable man in the world had an ailment, and that allowed him to be a dick. For some reason Newman was all I could think of. And fuck, how I wanted a shit-ton of golden bourbon just then.

'Jane, wake up for us, good lady, come on now, come now, the consultant is here, Jane. Have you any family with you?'

Jane groaned.

'NO. No, oh, really, sorry now, good lady, sit up for us now. Will they be in to see you today, the family? You do have a family, don't you? Are they coming in TODAY?'

Someone shuffled awkwardly through Jane's large pile of notes and they fell whoosh whoosh down on the floor.

'No.'

'OK, well then, now good lady, we've looked at the scans and there's a lot of water around your heart. And what will we all do about it?'

'Swim in it?' Jane said.

'Hmm. Well, Jane, we'll make you as comfortable as we can and … THEN … we'll move you out to another ward later. Maybe even later today.'

'Where?'

'Today to ANOTHER WARD, Jane,' he shouted.

'I don't want to go, no, no, I'll stay put here, I'm more than happy here at home, I'm fine and I have my little dog here, and young Patrick beside me.' Jane waved over at Hegs's bed. Two student doctors in matching head-scarves frantically took to scribbling on their Harry Potter notebooks. Both Hufflepuffs. Predictable. Pet dog – scribble. Presentation. Onset. Symptoms. Scribble. Scribble. 'Now, Tom will probably only have a sandwich. Just the one. I'll just fix him one. Of course I'll put the dinner down this evening, so maybe I don't need to ready him any food at all, oh, Lord, but I never got to the butcher, ah, sure, time enough, sure besides he never likes to eat too much in the afternoon. He has one of those things. What do you call them? Oh, you must know, you must know what you call them, those things that'd pierce through you when you eat. Especially dry food.'

The consultant looked around, agitated, and bobbing his head, he counted us, calculating the time it would take as he probably had an eighteen-hole to tackle at three or a bike to cycle somewhere in tight Lycra with his arse lubed for the saddle; he certainly didn't need to know anything about Tom's tea. He sent a woman back, the lovely woman who spoke Portuguese to the air as she dusted, to settle Jane.

Michal wheeled over a commode to my cell. 'Throw on hoody, miss, you're going for scan. It's all I have today, I am afraid,' he said, apologetically. 'Wait. I lift you. Here. Hold tight on to Michal. Hegs broke one-legged wheelchair yesterday like, I'm sorry but so what am I to do?'

A fucking toilet.

I couldn't answer. But an answer wasn't required.

I hoped he'd take me to the pub across the road. Bet he took Hegs to the pub across the road. The Blind Man's Inn. Indeed. Some of the porters did that with the old men who had cancer. For a pint. I tried to get up and put my feet under me, but my knees buckled and I fell backwards onto the bed. Michal came behind me and lifted me up by the hips. ''KKKK, good, OK, try move your bottom back, and back, good.' Michal grabbed another white theatre gown and he lifted it round me like a shirt, doubling me like the young lad in the off-licence who double-bags my wine. Margaret Rose rushed over with knickers, pulling them up along my feet and dragging them, until she settled them between my legs.

'Ah, she's vary weak,' Margaret Rose said to Michal. He nodded as he tied the top gown at the front. 'Are ya sure yar doing the right thing taking her off like this? I think she'd be better back in bed. Scans, they're all on about scans. How'd they feel if they were stuck in a scan as sick as her? Poor Sinéad. 'Tisn't right.' She pulled the tag off a new pair of bed socks, awkwardly with her front teeth, and unrolled them on my feet. 'Yar feet are vary puffy.' She pressed her fingers into them.

I got up to walk and Margaret Rose and Michal grabbed hold of me. 'Nooooooo,' Michal shouted. 'No, you not allowed, I no allowed, please you have to stop making my job so harder. I allowed to make no decisions. You're too weak, SinAID,' he said to Margaret Rose and me in turn.

239

'Get her hoody so or she'll freeze ta death ...' Margaret Rose, concerned, noticing my teeth chattering, rubbed the palm of her warm hand on my face. They both tried to lift me on to the commode, but I kicked at it, there was no way I was sitting on it in public. I was not somebody who took a taxi on a loo. 'Do that, go on, and see how far you get with yar kicking, you won'na get to the door of this ward, Sinéad, please. Stop,' Margaret Rose pleaded.

'Yes,' Michal agreed with her, 'this is not good ...'

The Ward spun. I wanted to vomit. My stomach was dizzy, gawking and rasping. *Uhuhuhuh* Margaret Rose held out a kidney dish and Michal got paper towels and cleaned up to my barrage of silent sorrys and helped me into pyjamas bottoms as Margaret Rose tied back my hair and pulled the hoody up on my arms.

'Don't worry. I leave it far outside the unit and carry you a little.' Michal said, kindly reassuring me. I made a grab for my red lipstick on my nightstand and Margaret Rose picked it up, twisted it out from its tube, and then she dotted it along my bottom lip. 'Pout, good,' she said, but my lips were so dry it soaked right in. She pouted too as she put another few layers of dots on both lips, like a Seurat painting, and then a little on her fingers and rubbed it into my cheeks, like one of my kids' paintings. Michal and Margaret Rose stood back and clasped hands like I was a daughter they had dressed up for a debutante ball.

★

Inpatients and outpatients share Hospital waiting rooms, so that arriving in an outpatient waiting room after being a Hospital inmate is a shock to the system The suddenness is disconcerting, coming up against outsiders with their handbags and raincoats and umbrellas and proper make-up, real people.

'I parks chair,' Michal said. 'You catch tight my arm, don't worry, I hold you. We leave the chair on the corridor, hiding. No one will steal, you know?' he said and he winked at me.

We both laughed. A little sound escaped. Maybe I just needed to get out. Alex hadn't texted. I understood his hurt, it was overwhelming, all of it, what was happening, what I'd gone and done with my secrecy, and I wasn't sure it would ever subside. Betrayal. But for practical reasons, I could do with a dig-out or an interpreter. Michal repeated the instructions twice and in polite parenthesis told me not to feck it up. I was not to let go of him. I was not to say I needed a chair. Otherwise we'd be all day waiting for a taxi back to the Ward.

There were strong apricot vibes on the walls in the MRI area, a crate of fruit on the roadside in France without the Monet sun. A little child with skinny hips and a large head was unsettling counters on a toy. Blue. Yellow. Red. Green. It was wooden and stark, with remnants of flecks of pizza peppers matted into the beads. His parents sat directly opposite each other, as though embarking on Battleships or Connect Four, feet shuffling, awkwardly coated in heavy anoraks. There was an angry cannula in the child's thin arm and his skin was rejecting it, reddening. He tugged at it, and his mother jumped up and moved to him like a penguin trying to make it out to sea.

Michal and I approached the desk and the receptionist asked Michal questions.

'Cannula? Piercings? Tattoos? Implants? She pregnant? Sure? How so sure?' asked the receptionist. Michal watched me as I shook my head back and over. No. Yes. No. Yes. Point to teeth. No. She kept bobbing her own head up and down to catch Michal's gesture. 'Lost your voice, love?' We both nodded. Yes. Yes.

'OK, well, we need you to do a test first.' She handed Michal a small clear bottle for urine. She pointed to the loo. We both stared at her. 'Pregnancy ...' she said, looking up, exasperated by my translator and me, and then caressed her wedding ring, twisting it in a clock-wise direction. Perhaps she still made wishes with it, fresh wedding rings, troublesome. Then she stopped pulling the ring and recoiled behind a large old printer, which banged, managing to put ink on a page.

Michal sat down, picked up a magazine and stuck his head into it. *VIP* magazine. Some rotund celebrity chef was trapped on the front with a hipster beard.

'How I Learned to Forgive my Tubby Hubby for his Flings and Make him Accept me for Who I Am.'

'Sinéad Hynes?'

The queue was large and grew unsettled and noisy. Still no sounds arrived. I tried to get up.

'It's OK,' Michal said, '... I come with you.'

I was so grateful.

'This way, please.'

Inside the scanning room, everything was blue and it made a change from the orange hues. They instructed me on length of time and consent and so on, asked the same questions as Michal answered the same answers. I wasn't pregnant. No one really knew how to react to this. I would have said, I told you so, if I had a voice. I lay back on a long tray as one of the radiographers placed my head in a cage, bright topaz Nikes on her feet, loose yellow laces. 'Here, press this if you need us,' she said, placing a cold plastic buzzer into the palm of my hand. 'Thumb into the red button if you need assistance, OK?' The plate chucked backwards, stalled, and tuttedtuttedtutted backwards again.

'You OK, Sinéad? Remember press buzzer, once for OK, twice for not OK? Test it now.'

I pressed my thumb in. It was a leap of faith to imagine the button was red.

'OK, great. It'll be noisy. Try to concentrate on your favourite thing. Quite noisy. OK?'

Fuck. My favourite thing. Shit.

The kids. Anxiety.

Wine. No. Pukey.

Husband. Guilt. Shit. Shit. Visualise something. Not water.

Michal reassured me while Norah Jones sang out.

I settled on the Whooper swan, Molly's lips, Newman's eyes and finally the whirr of Margaret Rose's hairdryer.

Michal Piwaski called out, 'You OK K K K K K K K K K K K K. SinAID, you KKKKKKKKKK. Press once.'

I pressed once.

★

'She's not supposed to be out of that chair, Michal, ya naw this, darl ... Jeez, what are you trying to do?' Molly said, sitting on Shane's empty bed mattress with her legs crossed, fixing her bandana back in place on her forehead. Michal helped me back to bed and then sat beside Molly, gently moving a few stray blonde hairs back under the bandana, flicking his finger gently on her jawline, teasing her.

Margaret Rose lay on top of her bedcovers, smiling as she read. 'Nice yar back.' One eye was on the magazine, the other flickering about me, going from my eyes to my abdomen and back up again. The kitchen staff had left a tray in my absence, white doily, glass of milk, jam patties, butter patties, plastic small containers for drugs, and my blood–thinning shot, urine test pots.

'Ya able far that?' she asked, nodding at the tray. 'How'd it go? You all right, loveen? Ya look a bit shook, if ya don'na mind me saying?'

I nodded.

'Ya sure, pet? Ya OK?'

I nodded again.

'They're very noisy those scanners. Tell ya the truth, I don'na like them, they're frightening.'

She came over and tucked me into bed, and rubbed my hair back off my face.

'Look, love, there's lots to think about. Ya have upset yar Alex, though, badly. Ya nade ta fix it. Did they let you see anything on their faces? Good or bad ... in the scanner?' Margaret Rose asked. 'Did they look bothered?'

I shook my head.

They didn't look at me at all.

Norah Jones had sung out, and the local hourly news had come on Galway Bay FM, with its talk of death and new roads and a new Ireland I had forgotten all about, as I lay there, encased and listening to the news of others and how they had died. Road accidents, war, early spring swimming.

Margaret Rose put my phone into my hand and climbed back into her bed.

'Send him a text. It'll get him outta yar head and ya can rest.'

She moved back to her own ringing Nokia, looking for my approval to take the call. I nodded. Any distraction.

The dinner arrived. It was always arriving.

No, I didn't want any ice cream or fruit or fruit yogurt or fruit ice cream as I had missed the lamb stew.

No, no, I didn't want prunes.

I shook my head.

No, I didn't want another glass of warm milk.

No, I didn't want any jelly.

Yes, I do feel awful that these are at worst my own first-world problems.

Yes, I am a cunt.

Yes, I am more than aware that we are all terminal cases.

Yes, I do feel awful and no, sometimes I don't have the correct words.

Yes, when I find the correct words, you'll all be the first to know. If I can ever speak again.

Thank you very much.

I have lost my voice and I don't think I ever want to find it again. But what I really wanted to say just then, was that being dead doesn't scare me, in fact I give it very little thought. Dying does. Those few moments. They terrify me.

The in-between.

Fuck.

Margaret Rose looked refreshed after her phone chat and tucked into a cold lamb stew, finishing it off with prunes and ice cream and then asked for some custard, for she said that anything cooked for you is better than anything you have to cook for yourself. A few bowls later and both lips were now dancing in synchronicity. She smiled over at me as she turned up her radio and began to sing along to Tammy Wynette's 'Stand By Your Man'.

She waved her *Take a Break* mag at me.

'Here, loveen. I'm going to sleep now. Wud ya like Michaela ta sit with ya this evening?' she offered, gently.

I wanted to say yes. But, really, it was Margaret Rose's life I was after. I could manage a philandering husband and a pregnant daughter, in fact, I'd welcome it, and not the handsome man who smiled at me and kept coming back for more. Not the decent man that I was about to abandon and who would soon be alone in the world with three sons. I needed someone neutral, or entirely disinterested in me, to pour myself out to, to tell them how sometimes I felt a kind of loneliness with such a force that I needed to lie down, or vomit or take myself into the sea.

I would have told Michaela that night, if she'd sat with me, about the Night of Peach Schnapps. I was about her age then, perhaps a little younger, and I'd like to tell her that once I had looked like her (a little) and how many times I, too, went off into the midnight air in only hot pants (OK, jeans) and a skinny slink of a top (OK, T-shirts and big jumpers) while boys gawped at me, and oh, how I loved it but pretended not to even notice. (OK, I would keep this bit to myself.)

I would tell her that Magpie swooped in and destroyed all my good memories, that it ruined my entire fucking life, that it inked itself all over everything. Magpie had so quickly surpassed Night of Peach Schnapps as the most bursting-out fuck of a day in my life, swooping in with its beady eye, wings all outstretched, and just landed in to destroy me, uninvited. I would say it was a fuck of a rude bird and that every thought that fleeted through my head since Magpie, felt either wrong or very wrong.

Wrong for thinking about flippant things, very wrong for not thinking at all.

On Night of Peach Schnapps, it was coming to the end of summer. Darkness arrived earlier, the stretch in the evening evaporating. It was dark by the time I headed out to a disco at the back of Dwyer's Hotel, in the next town over. East Galway. From the minute we'd left our coats in the cloakroom and stood around a tall sticky table, I spotted a guy, fair curls, long flat arse, goofy, flat mushroom freckles on his lips that the club lights illuminated. He had good teeth, even from a distance.

I had chosen him because a) he stared at me all night as I pretended not to notice, b) he was wearing a colourful woollen friendship bracelet which I considered to be a safety signal (I couldn't envisage a guy with a rainbow friendship bracelet as rapey – though I have since displaced all theories on correctly identifying rapists), and c) I was slightly taller, OK, I was about a foot taller, and this was important at this juncture.

I eventually approached him and asked him if he wanted to head out and up town to get chips, or go sit by the lake and smoke. The music was loud, 'Children' by Miles, trancey. I shouted, he shouted back. What?/ where?/you?/lake?/what?/sorry can't hear/yeah/yeah/ go ... to ... the ... lake? OK. Great.

As we walked towards the playground at the top of the town, he went into a biker bar for alcohol (on my insistence) and came out with a light grey bottle of peach schnapps. It was all they'd sell to him, possibly not knowing it had the same percentage as top-shelf liquor, but what with its soft orange peaches and the delicate feel of the glass bottle, no self-respecting barman in a hardy town would believe it was as strong as whiskey.

When we reached the playground, I lay back on the merry-go-round, and he pushed me around for some time. The lit cigarette made bright orange circles in the night sky. I smoked one cigarette off the other in that way you do when you're excited. Or nervous. In the middle of the lake was a house, and the light was on in the front window, McGahernesque – the local bishop's palace, perched on the island in the centre of the lapping water. We played at guessing what was happening at this hour of the morning to deserve a bishop's attention. Eventually we agreed that whatever was happening at two a.m., or shortly after, was bad news.

The smalt mist rolled in, near us a swing clashed in the dark, the plastic seat was broken in half. We took turns with the bottle, chatted about music, teachers, the light in the house, the sugar content in the alcohol, the Leaving Cert. Then we kissed. He put his hand down the front of my velvet tan hipster pants and kissed me harder and I kissed him back, open-mouthed. I was lovely drunk. The lake water lapped up near the playground. Sweet papers whipped up in the tennis court. Someone switched off the light in the house as we finished off the end of the thick liquid.

I never liked peaches.

I tasted his hair in my mouth, cheap body spray, my hips were tense, the skin on my stomach like bodhrán goatskin, stretched and pulled tight around its wooden frame, then nailed. My skin stung.

After, as we lay back on the merry-go-round and ran our feet off the ground, he told me about his mother, how she liked to keep everything spotlessly clean so that he'd rather stay out of the house for as long as possible, often for days on end; she rarely noticed his hiatuses, but immediately screamed at him to remove his shoes as he returned, as though he'd never been gone. She made him play piano and read poetry aloud at Christmas for a house full of guests he'd never met before. But mostly, when there wasn't an occasion, his mother just hung around the house, spaced out. His father was a judge in the courthouse that sat beside the playground. I knew his father's name from news reports about farmers round our way who kept dogs locked up or put cheap diesel in their tractors. He wasn't for me. She'd hate me, the mother, who sat at home polishing and forgetting about her son, except during Christmas when the piano-playing and poetry recitals were required. I didn't suggest we see each other again, though I wanted to. But I knew his mother would make sure he didn't waste his time with girls like me, and in that way mothers know best – I didn't stand a chance.

A cormorant landed in slo-mo on the water's surface, its black shadow flapping down on the dark water and in that lovely drunk, he said he was really into me, and I laughed and told him he was fucking daft, that I was actually quite a cunt, and he laughed, and said that kind of soft talk was mad. Sometimes it's even dangerous talk, he said then, seriously. I tried to explain how mostly I was utterly mean. Or frozen. We settled on frozen. But he said that it was the drink talking – he didn't believe it for a minute. We promised each other that this moment was the world, the best spinning drunken world we could muster. I said I'd better head on, it was so late, and he'd said grand, and that he'd have to sneak in his bedroom window for he was freezing. I reminded him to take the shoes off. Then he asked if perhaps we could think about going to the cinema or even for chips sometime. I laughed and said no, no way, I was busy. Washing my hair, hiding under my bed, going mad. I walked off quick into the dark night as he called out after me and I blew a kiss to the dark. I carried the peach schnapps bottle off into the night and the sugar hardened like a sweet glass coat as I sat in our garden and waited for the sun to come up.

Years later I met Schnapps at a business lunch in a fancy fish place. A loud woman with bouncy curls and shoulder pads was seated at our table. She handed over the large leather wine menu and told me to choose an appropriate wine, fast as you can, dear, as she flicked her hair towards him. I quickly chose a thick honey Chardonnay, for such was my limited experience and limited pronunciation of wine back then. She guffawed loudly like a pig might (and everyone there for her importance guffawed like little piglets and found her exhilarating, in the way wankers like people in power, finding them endlessly funny). Peach Schnapps rose up and said there would be no deal today or any day, then pushed his thin café chair backwards and threw some notes on the table. He kissed the side of my face and said that the wine, whatever fuck of a bottle the lady chose to choose, was perfectly fine by him, as it was accompanying crab. And crab, he said, sits at the bottom of the ocean and eats shit.

Lady.

He was the very first. Peach Snap. Large peach. Moreish.

Morello. A dark sweet cherry. Morning after. Delightful.

Morning-after pill. Necessary. Morning stars. Beautiful.

More of them hollowed out from the black sky.

iloveyouiloveyouiloveyouiloveyouiloveyouicanlovei-canijustneedtorememberourlovemylove

More time. please. IlovehimilovehimilovehimIcanlove. Morphine. More time, I beg. Mother-of-pearl.

Midnight. Morgue.

Mortuary.

I went to sleepzzzzzzzzz.

Badly needed.

Dreamed about mud falls and large peach crabs at traffic lights.

Chapter 14|

The sun was spinning, wisps of light danced across the apricot floor, refractions from the rainwater in the gutters. There was a low hum of dawn chorus and some wood pigeons hooting. Jane, perched beside the window like an arrow in a quiver, drowned them out by singing *Amazing Grace* at a ferocious pitch and then sat and pretended to knit a baby's bonnet or a small tea cosy, something tiny and delicate. She needed a different shot. Nothing had been done with her since the lovely woman who spoke Portuguese to the air was sent in to calm her.

'Stop that nonsense, Claire Hegarty, at once, stop that nonsense at once and sit yourself back down,' Jane bawled out, abandoning her singing and knitting, at Claire who was attempting to raise a coffee cup to her lips.

I circled my finger at my temple. Margaret Rose laughed.

'Oh, please,' Claire said, hesitantly, and then sipped from her morning's coffee.

'Keep singing, Jane, 'twas lovely ...' Margaret Rose prompted, devilment lurking in one eye.

'Sit down, sit DOWN. Sit back down at your desk immediately, MISS Claire, or you'll stand out on that tiled area for the rest of the day ... d'you HEAR ME? You see, Miss Hegarty, you are an awful sort of a girl, you really are not behaving like a scholarly student at all with this sort of ruffian behaviour. Now let that boy's hair go, or I am absolutely warning you. I will get my ruler and you'll know all about it.'

The word *all* went down her nose, slowly. She was so terrifyingly precise.

'Uh, oh ...' Margaret Rose said, switching on her radio.

Don't think Twice, it's All Right

Molly blew upwards at her pink bandana, as she arrived with meds in a grey kidney dish. It fell back into her eyes. 'Well, good morning, Sinéad, nice to see ya look-ing a bit brighter. Some drugs?' she said, attempting cheer. 'Hi ya feeling, hun? Blow into this, no other arm, too many in there, thanks, oh, wait; OK, we'll go with this one. Jeez, you're like a pincushion. How's this one feel? Naw. This OK?'

I winced.

She flicked her finger a few times to the back of my hand. I winced again, it was a cold pain, sharp; as she flicked the swollen hands, clear water ran from the little cannula holes dotted on my fat hand.

'Sorry, darl. OK, I'll just try maybe flush them through, OK?' Molly said, distracted.

''K.'

Her eyes were darkly dull and pale ivory make-up congealed in the pores around her nose and in the creases of her eyelids.

Michal arched his head round the door and his panda eyes were even more pronounced. He shot a glance to my hands and winced. I shut my eyes.

'OK ... now, hun, a little pinch, sharp, you feel that?' Molly said.

'Yeah, yeah ...' I said, my voice unreliable.

'Really, you sure?'

Yes. I'm sure. Pain is pain. Visceral. Sharp. Pounding. Tightening. Slicing. Throbbing. Separating. Forgetting. Losing. They tell you it's entirely in your head, and yes, precisely, it's in my head, my pain, in my fucking head, processed by me, my brain. All in my head.

Bob Dylan finished his song. Margaret Rose turned down the radio and picked up the phone and called Niquita, to ask, in her coded way, if she was all right. If it was all right? If it hurt. If she was all right again? And the words were brief. Margaret Rose let out a long sigh, staring at the phone after the call ended, then shook it, maybe wondering if there was a static that had reduced her conversation with her daughter to such stilted fragments and not at all like the chats they were capable of having.

'Molly … hey …' Michal said.

'Hi … you 'K, hun? Ya looking for me?' Molly said, twisting back to him.

'Yes, ya, no rush, yes, someone here wants to see you … visitor from …'

'She got a seat? Give her a seat and till her I'll be there in one sec,' Molly assured him.

'No, no seat, no seats. Nothing. Nothing in this place. No even wheelchair for SinAID. No pads either, or no milk, no shampoo, no razors, no coffee, where'll I put him to sit, eh?' he went on, reddening.

''K, hun,' Molly said, calmly, 'no problem.' She continued flicking my line with her thumb and middle finger; the nails tapped the soft plastic, gently coaxing more fluids through. 'Tell her I'll be there in a minute.'

'It's a man, he ... I said he ...' said Michal, throwing his arms, defeated, in the air and turning at the door, walking away. 'Few ticks, now, darl,' she said to me, ignoring Michal. 'I'll be back ... in a sec. I need to page the Reg to put a new line somewhere, this one's in a miss. So sorry.'

All better. I kiss it better. You all better now.

'Back in a jiffy.'

It was gruelling without Shane's Wi-Fi.

'That's her. No just here, left, blonde girl, red eyes, just there, there ...' Michal said, pointing at me, his watch hanging from his wrist.

A tall man walked towards me with a flamboyant Avengers bag slung over his lean shoulder. It banged off his hipbone. He was skinny and tall like a sailboat and looked down over me, large squirrelly nut-brown eyes, neat navy cardigan zipped tight and fitted onto him like a cheese wax, beige canvas Tom's, sallow feet, ambitious for April. He leaned his head towards his chest like a stallion being tucked under by a good rider, an *appoggiatura*.

'Hey,' he said, lifting the three fingers of his right hand and fussing with the strap of the bag.

'Hi.'

I was so fucking glad Michal had dressed me.

'I'm really so very sorry to hassle you. Hey, I'm Stephen,' he said as he extended his arm for a handshake, turning his eyes downwards.

'Oh, shit, shit, you're bleeding, you're, actually ... fuck ...' and he trailed off, fanning his left hand over his lips.

Jesus.

You are now entering a Hospital – there may be blood and crying and dying. Buckle up.

'Hi.'

He didn't look like another weirdo religious converter ready to take me away from the black hole of my god-lessness as I fast approached my own death.

'Hi, lovely to meet you. Bet Hospital's not much fun, huh?' he said.

Correct.

'Hi,' I said, again.

He placed a coffee on my tray-table and lifted the man-bag off over his square head.

'Look, I'm sorry to just ... drop in ... I'm Stephen,' he said, again, and placed out his hand, again.

'Sinéad ...' I whispered, but he already knew who I was.

'See, Shane,' he said.

'Stephen, no?' I said.

'No, no, I mean Shane ...'

'You're Shane?'

'Jeez, sorry,' he said, as I glanced at the coffee, Costa, and attempted to guess the contents. Americano. Double shot. No milk. Actually – coconut milk cappuccino. Double shot. 'I'm Stephen. I have. I mean. I'm here to. Hold on ... one sec ...' He tried to open the man-bag. The zip was sticky. 'I'm being very unclear,' he jittered. 'I'm Shane's brother, Stephen, the ma didn't call us both Shane.' He tried to laugh. Couldn't.

'Shit. This about Wi-Fi?' I blurted. 'I'm genuinely sorry, it's just I'm so sick, and so sick bored, and I was so bored, I didn't think it would matter, I mean, I tried to talk to him, but I was afraid I was making a nuisance of myself. Look, I'll fix up with you for it ... it's just I have no money with me ... I mean, I have money, they just don't recommend it ... keeping it here.'

'What?' he said, perplexed. 'Wi-Fi? No, no, thing is I hadn't seen him in a long time. Do you need money?' He rattled in the leg of his jeans.

'No, no, sorry ... right,' I whispered.

'None of us had, you know ...'

'Cared?'

'Visited.' He coughed and put his fist to his mouth. 'Maybe you just don't understand, you see ...'

'Right,' I said, lifting my inflection at the end, question.

'Not after Da ... you know, died ... oh, I don't know, it all became too much, the care and the minding and all.'

A text lit up my home screen.

My mother.

Good morning, Love. x.

I turned the phone upside down.

'And the carers rely on us more, you know, like the more we were there, see, when we weren't there they didn't seem to need us at all, you know, like I found this odd, if I could have chatted to him, and left everything, you know, the way it was when he was, oh, God ... this is hard,' Stephen went on, lifting the white plastic lid up and down on the paper mug.

'Mind if I?' He motioned to the edge of the bed.

'No, you're fine, sit ...'

He sat down on the end of the narrow bed, fidgeting.

'Anyway, he was always so fucking cranky too. You know?'

He started to cry.

'Ah, here,' I said, offering him a tissue. 'No need for that, it's OK, don't cry ... please ...'

'No, no, it's not OK, but nothing was right and you know ...'

I nodded.

'Ma just couldn't lift him, and it was so expensive with the feeds and the lifting and really it was too hard, too much ... much too much. You know?' he said, head bent low, and rocked his body forward, allowing its eventual collapse deep into the bed. He picked up the Costa cup and set it down again. I would have liked to see the action his lips made when he drank, but he didn't. There was certainly a resemblance to his brother, around the lug of the ear and across the nose bridge. Their knees were identical.

Assert yourself.

'Yeah, look, I understand you're sad and all, but to be honest . . .' I said, my voice almost inaudible, as he leaned in to me to hear, tugging his earlobe to help, 'I'm sorry he's dead, and all, but we didn't speak, much . . .' I offered, trying to snap this stranger out of his melancholic regret. I thought of my mother's text. She would be very ashamed if I was cruel to a dead man's brother. 'I'm so sorry he died, it's so sad, but maybe it's a relief?' His crying began to anger me. 'Oh, fuck knows,' I went on, annoyed. 'But it's no way, it's no way to live, the way your brother was living.'

He looked wounded. 'Yeah, I know, oh, here, I know I should have tried, you know, I just . . . left it. We just, we disconnected. Like I hope you don't think I'm a bad person . . . like . . . you know?'

'Ah, look, Stephen, no, course I don't, besides, roads are deadly, not your fault . . .' I said.

'Oh, yeah, yeah, suppose you're right,' Stephen muttered. 'They really are.' He looked thankful as he began to play with his hands. 'She never wanted him to have the bike, you know?' he sighed. 'But he always got his own way.' He turned and looked squarely at me. 'What happened you?'

'Nothing . . . just sick,' I said, defensively.

He eyed the picture of Santa's grotto.

'Got kids?'

'Those? No, I stole them for the Christmas card.'

'Shit, shit. Yeah, sorry, stupid question. Shit. I'm just awkward in these ...' Stephen laughed quietly, and then made an odd kind of chapel out of his hands. 'Aw, fuck, they must miss you, poor guys, and you holed up in here?' He stared at me, my heart pounded and my mouth filled with water. He was so good at holding a gaze that it made me queasy. 'Shane left you a note, a note thing for you, on his machine,' he said, changing the subject.

'What? You sure?'

'Uh-oh, hmmm ...'

'For me?'

'Yeah, I'm sure it's yours, he wanted you to have it ...' he said, lifting a MacBook Air from the bag. 'I mean he was quite clear,' Stephen said. 'He typed his requests.'

'He did?'

'Oh, yeah, of course,' Stephen said, noticing my uncertainty. 'His hands were fine – quadriplegia, but some nerves had rerouted, imagine, nerves can do that. Isn't it amazing? I think, or somewhere in that region, L something, T something, oh, I dunno, to be honest I'm not really sure of the mechanics of it, or the numbers, Ma knows all that info, but I ...' He wavered, sighing, discontinuing his own banter. 'I didn't really listen to ... details.'

Stephen was growing impatient like a dog at the front door waiting by their leash. He raised an eyebrow to move along the business.

'You really sure it was me?' I said, spelling out my name slowly, *S-I-N-E-fada-A-D-H-Y-N-E-S*.

'Yes. Sure.' Stephen pointed to the machine. Eleven Inch.

'OK,' I muttered. My voice was so shallow; none of my replies could hold weight.

The man needed to be let off the hook.

'So, here's the machine and I'd like to get this sorted, let you ...' he said. 'And push on, you know, to let you have some rest.' Then he started to cry again and on impulse, a rather cringey impulse, I rubbed his thigh. It was an odd reflex response; the static energy gave me an electric shock. I apologised and we started to giggle, hysterically, prone as I am to wholly inappropriate reactions. He shook out his leg like a worm arriving up from the soil.

'I have a charger here somewhere,' his head back down rummaging in the bag. 'I'll plug it in for you.'

'No, I get out the odd time, you're grand, I can get to the plug,' I said, wryly. 'They let me off out, you know, to piss or shower.'

'I'm sure you do,' he said, his eyes lingering longer than before over me, scanning. He pulled his abdomen as far into himself as he could and turned towards the door and checked his exits. 'I'd better head on,' he said, trotting his index fingers along my nightstand, previewing himself walking out.

My phone vibrated. Margaret Rose coughed loudly, and coughed again.

'I hear it,' I acknowledged her.

'Well, check it,' she said, shooting a nasty glance at Stephen.

It was Alex. I didn't open it.

Stephen was focused. He needed absolution, and people in need of guilt removal or absolving from sins are usually completely self-consumed in their own mission. I was familiar with this.

'Where'd he sleep?' he said, as he stood up to take his leave. I pointed to the vacant bed, blue mattress – the wet patch, last of Shane, had dried in – and Stephen moved himself, side-stepping awkwardly to Shane's cell beside me, the curtains opened back.

'Yeah, yeah, just there, there ...' I whispered, my fists tight. I didn't want to discuss a bed with him, not one with a metal hoist and a rubber mattress, or try making idle conversation about the bars they hoist up, clang-clang, which keep you from falling out.

'I'd better run ... you know, before ...' Stephen said, trailing off, excusing himself by bowing awkwardly, and took his leave. Hulk's angry face stared back at me.

I wanted to say I'm Sorry. I wanted to tell him how handsome he was. I wanted to say that it really was a tragedy for him and his brother. I wanted to say that I missed his brother's smell, as awful and noxious as it was. I knew this was a lie of sorts, but it might have made him happier. I should have said that his absence created a draught and that's the most any of us can hope for. But he was too far removed from our world on the Ward not to take that as an insult. Then I wanted to tell him that I was dying too. I wanted to ask him if he had a wife, and if she was dying, what would he do? What would she do? Would she have rushed home in the Volvo, summoned him to a meeting in the bedroom, spilled the whole fucking sad lot of it out? Would they aggressively Google every known drug and cure and procedure and American oncologist and yogi and kefir grains and spinach plants and reiki and mindfulness and everything they could to save her? I bet they would. But she'd die anyway. And all eyes would be on her. And all energy into phone calls and tests and trials and everything would revolve around her. And fuck that. And I worked up immeasurable anger with his imaginary wife. Because she'd probably do everything perfectly, just like other people do.

'Bye,' I whispered to myself.

'I'm Angela Lansbury, you know?' squealed Jane as she woke. 'Remember me, Angela?' She began mime typing with the leather gloves.

'Indeed I know, Janey,' I whispered. 'I mean, Angela.' And she smiled.

I fixed my oxygen mask back firmly on my face and tried to keep my own counsel, think things through, make a decision.

★

Friday passed in a blur of loneliness, for Alex, the boys, for my mother, and much sedated sleep. The cathedral rang out for the angelus at six. Michal arrived and tugged a plastic apron from the pull-out roll that hung outside the door. I tossed and turned in and out of wakefulness with an odd taste of sweet caramel. The plastic aprons unravelled in a heap like butcher's sausages.

Margaret Rose was perched on her bed like the last summer peach in an ivory fruit bowl.

Michal balanced a cereal bar in his pale mouth, while tying the flimsy apron at the small of his back. He was fussing with my magazines and books and began wiping the face of Heaney with a rag cloth.

I snapped.

'You always so angry?' he said. 'Why, always so so angry cococococo?'

'Don't cococococo me. What the fuck type of noise is cococococo' I spat in a whispered hiss.

'Co? Co? What is? What you going on about, lady? Why you getting so angry all of the time, is it that you're sick? And all the time angry at your nice Husband. How does he stick you? Hmm?' Fuck knows. Michal went on wiping. But his face was sympathetic, his eyes glossing over with a film of exhaustion.

'You think I'm stupid, huh?'

'No, no, that's not what I ...'

'Just another stupid Polish man, because I fill your tea every night and give you biskits, you think I don't know history and books, your history, mine, because I clean for you? I will be kind with books. No need for worry.'

I thought of him calling out to me in the scanner.

'No, no, it's just ... I'm very sorry,' I said, quietly.

'Yeah, well, I know how special books are. I know ...' he said, and placed the book down gently. 'But no need to be so cross. Is it special?'

'Not really. My father gave it to me.' I nodded at Heaney.

It was the first time Father'd shopped alone and it was the only personal gift he'd ever bought for me, probably because it was on a Best Sellers' list in one of those bookshop chains with a three-for-two offer, poetry and two cookery books, one for me. Sorry for everything, here's some poetry. Enjoy. Your mother is leaving me. Goodbye. And all I've done for her. I gave her a cookery book. Goodbye. Your mother is leaving me. I was so happy with the book, but then he said that he'd watched him on the *Late Late Show*, Heaney, or some documentary and that he was a good farming man, like himself and not a poof, like most poets.

'My father is dead,' Michal said. 'When I was five.'

'Oh, Michal, I'm sorry.'

He was stuck rummaging in behind Jane's curtain, and attempted to prise the card from her hands as she screamed out, 'The pain that you've been feeling, can't compare to the joy that's coming. Can't compare to the joy, to the joy, the pain can't compare ... lalala,' she sang out.

'I sorry too,' Michal said swiftly, coming back to me.

'Oh, no, no need. I was way out of line.'

He sat on the edge of my bed. 'So, what was he like, what he want?'

'Who?'

'Your visitor?'

'Ah, he was just upset, you know, for Shane.'

'Sad for his brother, no? Why? He never visits him, why they never visited?' But Michal didn't wait for a reply, the question didn't warrant an answer and he got up, and fixed Jane back to bed.

★

'Hey.' It was Alex. 'Evening coffee! Ta-da!' he said, warmly. He sat on the bed, and moved up closer to me.

'Oh, Alex, I'm so glad you came back. I'm, I'm, you know, very sorry,' I stuttered, beginning to cry, and I lurched forward. 'I don't even know where to start. I'm so glad, so happy, you came. I'm so ... glad.'

Glad. FFS.

Relieved.

He placed the cup of coffee on the bed table and began to look dejected. Maybe we were meant to play ostrich again? Maybe I wasn't meant to cry. Fuck knows.

'How're the kids?'

'Grand,' he said, circling his wedding ring about on his ring finger. 'You know ... considering.'

'That's something,' I offered.

'Your mother has them ... said she'd keep them for a few days. As many as ... I just can't, you know. I don't seem to be able to. I could hardly drive. I mean, I could hardly change gear. I drove straight through a red light. I'm not ...'

'Great, good that she's taken them. She won't mind ... she loves ...' I interrupted myself. 'Oh, fuck, Alex ... please say you didn't tell her?'

He paused.

'Alex? Oh, fuck, no ... Alex ... did you say anything?'

He looked bereft. 'No, Sinéad, no, no, I didn't ...'

'How'd Joshua's game go?' I asked quickly.

'Lost.'

'Fuck.'

'Yeah ... but he's grand, got man of the match.'

His gaze fixed across on Margaret Rose.

Claire was wearing new pink bed socks.

'Look, love, I'm so sorry, I just couldn't, I couldn't believe it fully myself, and then I really tried to ...'

'Nails OK?' he said, interrupting me, searching the crumpled white sheets for my hands. The varnish was destroyed but one nail was perfect, red and shiny, triumphant, and I tried to lurch it up on top of another, but one lone perfect fingernail wasn't enough to cover four others that were a congealed mess. I began crying. I tried to think of political leaders naked and of Paul Newman. Nothing worked.

'Jesus, ah, love, come now,' he said, 'not fucking tears ... you know I can't cope when you cry. Dry your eyes, mate.' He raised an eyebrow. 'Remember it? The song? Jeez, it's a long time since I heard that on the radio.' Alex loved remembering the last time he heard songs on the radio.

We were at a music festival the summer 'Dry Your Eyes' came out. It was infectious, addictive. Everyone would break into it over the weekend, especially throughout the campsite with its big fuck-off chip vans, pancake stalls, knicker-hawkers, monster beer bars, filthy dirty portaloos, spray paint and garbage, tins and cans, tents on fire. The Streets weren't even on the line-up. But nothing really mattered then. Starting out.

'Yeah, yeah, I remember.' The red nail was waving back and over like a bobbing life buoy.

'Shit ... where's my chair?' he said, looking around quickly. 'Whoa, you moved me out fast.' He smiled and winked at me. A thaw. 'Look,' he said, 'I know we need to talk,' rubbing my left hand, right down over my knuckles, catching and squeezing the middle joint of my pinkie between his index finger and thumb.

I was useless with kindness.

'The kids are good, they're great, you know, they're fine, totally grand ...' he said, unsure, finally, not letting go of my finger. He was predicting a difficult conversation he would try to avoid. He spoke faster. 'You didn't miss much, the match wasn't great, they were slow on the pitch, laboured, and actually, you missed nothing.' He laughed, nervously, grasping at anything that might disconnect us from Magpie, and from her shitty offerings. I never went to Joshua's matches. They were played late on Friday evenings when I drank espresso Martinis in some posh joint in town.

Ms Jo Moran landed in then to call it. Give our weekend a big lift. Push us in some direction, to deliver news. She looked blankly at the bed first and then lingered a while, staring at my knees.

Tall. Needy. Roomy. Nice tits. Pet scans. Thymus. Thyroid. Tonsils. Sentinel lymph node mapping. Hepatic capsule. Elizabeth Taylor. Perfect lips. Going. To. Run. A. Marathon. Thingy.

Metastasising.

'But look, in all honesty you can buy yourself time, Sinéad, maybe, if you just try to *consider* your options. But you know, it is ultimately up to you. I don't want to force the issue.'

I nodded. Half-hearing her.

'I'll leave ye for some time ... think on it. Sure, look, I'll pop back in later.' She motioned to leave, and twisted back around the curtain. 'They're really lovely in oncology. I know you all got off on a bad foot. But I've talked to them.'

Buying. My decision. Her decision. Shhhhh now. To buy. Buying. I have bought. I will buy.

Mine. I could see Alex's lips moving, as though saying it made him less culpable. Or even blameless. He remained quiet. Maybe he wasn't blameless. But it was poor timing for this, to ascertain his role in our marriage. To give that thought.

I made no decision. I only waited. Please leave me. Please. It was horrid timing.

Of course I still love you.

Of course I still love you.

I will always love you.

Come here to me.

After Moran, words sounded forced, stupid almost, our world spiralled into a frantic free fall as if these results were news to me. It was somehow very different, now there was a witness.

You know you looked for this, right? I've watched you, Sinéad, you can't settle yourself on anything, look how I can begin and end a task, you just leave it high and dry, you do, you so absolutely do, and I think that you'll never amount to anything, because first, you have to do what you need to do, shir here I am raising a girl in a household of lads, I'm responsible for you, you know that, what a big job that is, me, your father, and it's a damn tough responsibility, I mean I've watched you out there on the pitch, and when you throw in the towel, it's gone, it's over, you don't even fight it, I can't believe how much competitive streak you lack, it's a crying shame really, but you are indeed, solid fucken useless, and that's all now I have to say on the matter. Ready us some tea, and for fuck sake, do it right, last time, you didn't rinse out the teapot, the old tea leaves, still there, it was disgusting, so do it right this time, OK, and Sinéad, one last thing, will you stop biting down your nails? And let them grow long, they're disgusting, look at your mother's hands, how beautiful they are, though they're not much good for anything else, but they are very lovely to look at, let yours grow as long. Though I doubt you'd have that in you either. Self-restraint. Doubtful.

Later that Friday night, without any Martinis, Alex sat beside me and stared at me for the evening, glassy-eyed, and so I finally did it. I told Father to fuck off. Direct language was best. Or I'd swap his voice for Alex's reassuring timbre, until he took the hint. I wasn't quite so convinced my own amateur version of cognitive therapy was going to be effective, but I could try. It was over. I couldn't take it any more. Then finally, I'd think on the boys, their smiles, and their missing teeth. This was the end of it.

Sleep didn't come, and I closed my eyes twice during the night, only to feel my throat close in and my head spin. Alex had fallen asleep by midnight on the returned chair, with his head on my bed. Shock made him sleep. Late that night, or by early morning, a phlebotomist with short wiry grey hair whisked in, and pretended not to want to disturb anything, yet she disturbed everything, even turning on the big lights over everyone's bed.

'You awake, love?' she whispered with a long drawn-out sigh.

'Yeah, yeah, I am,' I said, hoarsely, accidentally imitating her, but it put us both at ease. Alex started on the bed, yawned and then darted his hand to my wedding ring, without opening his eyes. His hand fiddled with it and it fell off without coaxing.

I offered her the hinge of my elbow.

'No, no, I'm afraid I'll have to go in on the back of your hand again, love,' she said, kindly, poking my hand with her gloved fingers. Its new black bruising covering the older bruises as they wilted on my skin. I no longer recognised my own hands. My wrists were childlike.

'Where're you living?' she said, chattily. And without waiting for a reply, 'My, but God, aren't you both so very young looking?' Though Alex was heaped on the bed looking like shit.

They must all know. I didn't answer her.

Go back to sleep, love. Back to sleep, my love. Sorry for the intrusion. Try to sleep now, my love. And you both so young looking. My God.

Sleep now.

Chapter 15|

On Saturday morning, Michal Piwaski rolled up his trolley heaped with plates of soggy toast and mugs of tea like a New York hotdog vendor. He seemed unnerved or excited that Alex had stayed the night, chatting flamboyantly about how decent and caring my husband was to sleep beside me. He asked if he had fallen asleep, or had he planned it? And if yes, then we should have asked for a roll-out bed, although, of course, there was no guarantee we'd get one given the crisis the place was in, and don't get him started about the crisis the whole country was in, and on and on he went. He was persistent, Michal Piwaski. He went into abundant details before he obliged us and gave us both milky tea and soggy toast from his plate.

'How's your wife?' Alex asked, unsure about anything given our circumstances and the scan and decisions, and with the new surroundings that were now inflicted on him, for ever. Michal had to think for a moment.

'She's pregnant, isn't she?' Alex asked, flustered.

'Yes ... yes, she is,' I said, trying to save him.

'Oh, my wife, yes, Karolina, well, she is doing good, now, good,' Michal obliged.

I started to shake.

'You OK?' Alex said, his head still fallen over on the bed.

'I was dreaming all night.'

'About?'

'I was locked in the boot of a car.'

'Fuck.' He sat up, and yawned.

'Yeah, I dream this all the time ...'

'Nightmarish?'

'Yeah, especially the teeth one.'

Alex ran his finger along his top row.

'But usually locked somewhere, tight. I'm so used of it by now ...' I trailed off.

'Really? Shit. You never said.'

'You never asked.'

Alex thought a moment, seemed to take particular care with the next sentence, and he lifted his head from the bed again. 'What model's the car?'

WTF.

'Fuck knows ... I'm locked in the boot.'

'Oh, yeah, sorry. Just wondering ... some boots open from the inside.'

I laughed. 'It's a dream, Alex. It's just, when I was a kid and we'd play hide-and-seek.'

'Love it.'

'Game or dream?'

'Game, told you ... don't dream ...'

'Weird. Yeah. I'd hide out in the press in the small hall-way, you know the one?'

Call out. Ready or not. Keep your spot.

'Yeah, I know it, with the green slatted doors?'

'Yeah, yeah, that one, I'd crouch in there.'

I was shaking hard now.

'Love, you're shaking, here, take this, don't talk about it ... it's only a dream.' And he placed his jumper over me, warm.

'I want to talk ... I mean, I need to. I want to try ... I'd crouch down. Tiny.'

They're closer. My brothers. Near me now. Closer again. Little eyes peer in through the slats in the press.

Cold. Hot. Hot. Hot.

'Hearing myself breathe was terrifying. I hated it, the game. Absolutely hated it. I'd try to breathe really deeply but that wouldn't work. I always had a snotty nose like Nathan.'

We laughed again.

'I'm sure I could be heard outside.'

Ready or not. Keep your spot. Or you'll be caught.

'I'd see my brothers' eyelashes fluttering and my whole body would pound. First my heart in my ribcage, thumping, but then my head and then my whole body. Even my teeth would chatter.' I stopped, took a sip of water, crushing the plastic cup, the sides were sharp and they stuck into my palm.

Here she is.

Alex's eyes were fixed on me uncomfortably. It was rare we spoke like this.

'And eventually ... well ...' I hesitated. 'I'd stay there so long that I'd ... I'd eventually ... wet myself.'

'Fuck.' He stood up from his chair, backed off a little, and then sat near me on the bed. 'Shit, Sinéad, you never said, I'm so sorry.'

'Oh, it's not a big deal. It's fine.' I shrugged.

'Did it upset you?'

'Course.'

'I can imagine. Actually, no, sorry, I can't ... I can't imagine.'

Ready or not keep your spot or you'll be caught.

'You ever win?'

'Always.'

He looked puzzled.

'I'd fling open the doors and punch my brothers in the face and tell them they were cheaters and that they weren't allowed to stand that long looking in at me without saying they were "hot" and so I'd win by default,' I said, closing my eyes.

'So you didn't win. Sinéad, that's not winning,' he said. 'They just let you away with this, that's really not winning ... They ever fight you on it?'

'What does it matter, Alex? We were kids. Technically I didn't win. You're correct, Alex,' I said, slowly, carefully. 'But they were decent, they didn't ... They could see my wet pants, they backed down, they didn't tell on me either.'

But we played it over and over. And it was always the same. I didn't dare tell Alex he was the only person who didn't always let me win, that this was a good thing. I didn't tell him that I wouldn't be punching out at anyone any more, but as with Father and shutting him the fuck up, I wasn't sure this was such a simple thing to stop.

'You feel cornered now?' Alex asked, as he held my gaze, which was woefully awkward, but as embarrassed as that made me, I didn't close my eyes or laugh or snort or curse like I usually would, like I always did when someone tried to see inside me. It was a simple question. To which there was only one answer. But I needed to appease him. He worked in simple. Explain. Explanations. Total simplicity.

'Yes. Yes, I do. I so do. I'm so … fucked.' I didn't want to hurt him. Or remind him of what a failure I was, what a failure my body was. What a failure I am. I didn't want him to start telling me about all my brilliant accomplishments that I knew meant nothing. I grabbed his shirt, pulling hard at the small buttons. 'Look, you have to get me out of here, you just have to …' I said, suddenly frantic. 'I can't take another weekend in here.'

'You sure?'

'I have to, I have to get out. I miss it,' I said, finally admitting some truths.

I missed walking through the Galway Market picking up crêpes filled with banana and chocolate, stepping upstairs into Sheridan's cheese shop, looking over the blue hues of the market vendors' tarpaulins below, sipping tasters, reds and browns and yellows and whites, before deciding we'd start with Prosecco, move along from there, a Gneiss Domaine de L'Ecu (no more clunky Chardonnay), or a crisp Gavi di Gavi, sharing a cheese board, Ardrahan and some hard-smoked English cheddar, with spongy orange apricot chutney, pick up wild salmon from Stefane at Gannet on the market, or instead, go to Aniar for eels and turnip, sea buckthorn, or Kai for hearty supper, monkfish with sea spaghetti and cockles in broth for me, him usually having something earthy, ox tongue and pumpkin jam, many whiskey sours. Finish in the Bierhaus or the Black Gate. Drunk. Row. Make up.

And I missed my sons. I missed them. So much of them.

'I will, look, I'll try my very best to get you … out,' he said, 'but we need to chat to the right people first though, see, you need an ambulance to come … home, they told me, they gave me a list …' he said, his eyes closed.

'Do not ... I'm fine, I don't want a fucking ambulance, not again. I'm not an invalid. I can't do another ambulance, either you sort something or I'll walk. Last time I came out of an ambulance I was starkers.'

'OK, I promise, really soon, I'm sorry, it's just that I don't want to ... you know, put you in ... danger.'

I looked over and saw Claire was fixed in an unusually sloppy pose.

'Would you look at herself asleep in the armchair?' I said, distracted. 'Look what Hospital does to ... us.'

'Hegs looks rough, what colour at all is he?' Alex said.

'Primrose.'

'Ah, he's more red-of-an-egg-yellow than yellow-yellow,' he replied.

It made me panic.

'It's yellow, the yolk of an egg is yellow. How come you don't know this? It's not red. It's not red. I've never seen a red yolk in an egg.'

Alex looked stunned.

'How can you raise children if you don't know the colour of the inside of an egg? A fucking egg? How can you get to mid-life almost without knowing what the fuck the inside of a fucking egg is called?'

Fuck.

'What's the white bit?' My voice caught.

'The white what?'

'The white of the egg? Egg white. What's the white of the egg called?'

'Please,' he said, gently, lifting up off the chair, 'stop. I don't like eggs. You know I don't even like eggs. Actually,' he paused, 'I think I might have an allergy to them.'

'What?' I said.

'I can Google it, if I need to.'

'Google, really? Google? Are you joking?'

'Well, if it's good enough for you to live your life ...' he said. 'Bet you told Google you were dying –' he paused – 'before me?'

Low. But accurate.

'You don't *chat* with Google ... it's not a chat. You don't just chit–chat with a fucking computer.' I was irritated.

'Did Google tell you that? G'wan ... did you? Did you Google it? Tell me.'

Fuck. We both went quiet.

He closed his eyes briefly. 'I actually do really think I'm allergic to them.'

'You don't have an egg allergy. You had a quiche last month. You're such a drama queen,' I said, rapidly.

My heart still pounded. The smell of paint and baling twine and a feathery bird, the eyes of it peering at me, a pheasant, it was a pheasant, little red and blue head on it. They'd locked the press door and I couldn't get out.

'What if you won't know when to search for things, important things?' I said. 'You'll just say it out, even lie about it, you'll just spit the thing out, and the kids will think it's the truth because they'll believe everything you tell them ... that's how parenting works.'

He was picking the quick at the edge of his thumb, making it bleed. 'I think you need a glass of water, love.'

'I don't need water. I need you, I need you ...' I searched. 'You need to be ... capable.'

'I am capable. Ah, here, that's not fair, Sinéad.'

'Capable. Right. Let's see. What's my middle name?'

'What?' his blue eyes widening.

'My middle name. What is it? What's my middle name? My star sign? What star sign am I? What star sign is Joshua? G'wan, all the boys? Dates of birth?'

Rapid inane questions fired at him.

'I wish you'd stop ... please, please, stop.'

'I can't find one of the blobfish ...' I sobbed. 'I'm stuck with a fucking loony, and another fucking loony and a dead fucking loony, and one of them put these ridiculous fluffy socks on me. Shane's dead, you know?' I yelled now. 'And we have every loony fucking visitor in from the west for herself here, and I want to get out,' I yelled again. Margaret Rose bit her lip. 'And you don't even know what the inside of a fucking egg is called, and you're supposed to take over? Take our family. Over. What the fuck? Right, last one. What day was I born on?' As an angry red blush rose up all over my chest, Alex looked totally bewildered, staring down at me, his face dotted in reddish-grey stubble, deep crow's feet pencilled about his eyes.

I was glad when he finally began to cry. I wanted him to cry.

Chapter 16|

Margaret Rose ran a facecloth under the tap at our communal sink and brought it to Alex, handed it to him, and caught his elbow, shoving it towards me. He placed it on my forehead, then he put his arm around the small of my back and he sobbed into me. I struggled to catch my breath, but I stayed still, like an animal in shock, or hit by a car bumper. I didn't want him to let go. I was afraid if I let go, he would too. I spat my tears out to the air and to the ward. Jane raised herself bolt upright, yellow mask in place, and leaped from her bed, incontinence pad stuck to her milky calf.

'Darlings,' she said, 'you're all here, how wonderful, how wonderful.' She began screaming. 'Well now, everyone is here, and oh, how wonderful. WOnderFUL.'

'Tuesday, TUESDAY,' Alex said, breathless, and lifting up his head, 'you were born on a Tuesday, ten-twenty, night-time, Labour ward five.' He smiled. 'Tuesday, you're a Tuesday girl, Fair, Tuesday's child is fair of mind, here, you were born here, here in this Hospital on a Tuesday.'

Jane hadn't stopped. I pushed my thumb into the soft green button and our bell rang out over the door. Flashing lights, but no one would come quickly, of this I was certain, but my certainty was not a victory, I rang again. I was wrong. Molly Zane rushed into the ward dabbing the corner of her mouth with a tissue. Pink bandana – check. Vintage pink matt lips – check.

'Hey, hey. What's going on? You OK?' she said, and looked at me. 'All OK?' Alex nodded.

Her eyes found Jane.

'Oh, absolutely WONDERful, you're here. The pretty one. With the cowboy scarf. How lovely.'

'Ah, Jane, come now. Let me grab that pad off your leg, darl,' Molly said.

Jane watched her closely, growing quieter now.

'You're in a tirrible fix, Jane,' Molly said, kindly, pressing another buzzer on the side of the bed that also went off outside the door.

Ted Baker arrived and he ignored Molly and Jane. Appeasing old ladies was not his brief.

'Miss Hegarty?' Claire nodded. 'Hi, hello, the nurses are telling me your father is bradycardic.' He looked rather puzzled and checked his chart and another and tapped Hegs with a long stick with a circular thing attached to its end. 'Could you perhaps, hmmm, maybe turn out this way, sir?' he asked, as he rotated Hegs until his legs dangled off the side of the bed.

'I'm really not sure this is entirely necessary ...' Claire offered.

In here, reflexes were everything. Well, next to bowels. Ms Claire was edgy.

'It's just so very strange ...' Ted Baker went on. 'Now I wonder, sir, if you could maybe get up and try and walk ... one foot in front of the other, like this.' He mimed the walk across to me, and back, keeping the glasses in place with a long white index finger. Heel. Toe. Heel. Toe. His coordination wasn't magnificent.

'Ah, here, no, no, stop this ... this really is not necessary. You can hardly do it yourself,' Claire said, insisting, and linked her father while he attempted to sit back on the bed.

'But there's really no reason for him to be so, so ... well ... lame. Or bradycardic.' Ted Baker was most puzzled.

And they went out to check again. They would check, and maybe if Claire would step out with them, until they checked.

As Hegs began to lie back down, Margaret Rose offered him reversing advice. 'Nather bit, bit more, good ... yar on the pillow naw, good man.'

He thanked her.

Alex squeezed my hand. 'Here, I'm going to head out for a little while, just to check your mother is OK, and give the kids clothes, settle them.'

'Yeah, yeah, of course,' I said, and waved my free arm over the nightstand contents. 'Will you take some of this?'

He grabbed a kidney dish and some plastic cups. 'I am so sorry,' I said. I toyed with the idea of telling him I didn't exactly *tell* Google I was dying, like he accused me, I more hinted at it, but I resisted.

'I know you are,' he said, rushing about, frantic to get out the door. 'I really need to get out of here though,' he said and kissed me hard.

'Albumen, the egg, the white,' he said as he walked out.

★

I tossed and turned for some time and eventually lifted Shane's thin laptop in my hands. Whirr. It was fully charged. Odd. On the home screen I could make out a bird, a long-legged goofy thing with black feathers, slick with a white stripe. I remembered seeing one like it before in a swampy field on the way from Orlando to Siesta Key on a trip some years back. We had headed for the coast to get away from the tacky theme parks. I'd bought some villas in Kissimmee the night before to market at home and rent out to Irish families. Alex had stayed in with the kids, watched some films. We hit the road early, despite the fact that I'd had a very late night. I hadn't slept at all. I'd crept in at around six a.m., after closing a deal in the Red Lobster with the builder, and we'd gone on to a party. He was from East Clare. That morning, after arriving home, I showered, and made pancakes for breakfast. Alex didn't care, or didn't seem to care about my tardiness. They ate the pancakes and we headed off.

After some time on the road, we cut off at a junction to head to a restaurant specialising in home baking, southern comfort foods. Feed the kids again. In the diner I drank iced lemon tea with gin. Through the window I was taken by the way these two birds fought, an arid dryness in my chest, these birds bickering, us silent amongst the billboards and the chains upon chains of same-food-place. Her feathers were raven black with a dirty white neck and a dipped beak. This one's feathers were raven black with a dirty white neck too.

There was one Word document on the home screen, one media clip and in the top right-hand corner, a Netflix icon and Spotify link. Cool Runnings was recommended, and he had some half-finished films. *American Psycho*, *Kill Bill*, *Blue Velvet*.

Things linger after you die.

FaceBook birthday wishes come in. Shopping vouchers arrive. Hospital appointments. Phone calls from old uni friends. Who don't know. TV licence people call. Text messages from your mother who often forgets you're dead. Cold callers from TV and Internet companies.

A text from Alex checking in to see if I need him to stop at the shop.

You are fair and born on a Tuesday.

Things that don't matter. Things that matter.

Father cried into his hands night after night, big fucken wailful cries, after my mother eventually left him, the night he sprinted up the stairs and kicked down the bathroom door. She'd escaped out into the night as he shouted after her, about her having put a spell on him, telling her everything she touched was fucked, that she brought badness, and that he'd burn the house to the ground and this time he (fucking) meant it. And no cross of reeds would save us. She kept running.

After. After. Always tears after.

Nothing matters after. It's too late. G'Luck.

Margaret Rose's phone rang. Dadadadadadadoom. Dadadadadadadoom. 'Hello, yeah, this is she. No, I'm Margaret Rose, no, hold on, I cannot speak up ... I'm not alone. No, no nono ... Ah, is that you, Jim? Yar in fair traffic ... Yar number is withheld ... What? When? Shit. Shitshit. Well, shit anyway.'

Silence. Pause. Quiet. Oh so Quiet.

'Fuck, where'd she go? Ah, Jim ... Christ above ... Ya had wan job. Wan ... OK, that's fair, ya had two. Oh, Christ, and no, she hasn't rang me since ... the clinic ... I only heard from her wan time and I didn'a think she

was in the best of form, but I thought 'twas natural ...
I'll try her in a minute ... Are you in Birmingham?
OK, shir of course ya can come back, come back, it's
fine. She's grown up now ... 'Tisn't yar fault ... ah,
sometimes she won'na listen ta any of us. Let's not worry
... yet.'

Grand we would all be with air, I thought, not the city
air outside the ugly windows, not the diseased Hospital
air, that germ-infested warm air that clings to the walls.
Real air, the air that would blow the cobwebs out of
you, could burst open some of our diseased pods and
empty them out to the Atlantic.

'Good, well, tell the boys ta hold off, that's OK, he's her
father ... no way ... he'll look after her. Watch.'

We could all go off in our knickers and jocks, Hegs,
Margaret Rose, Jane and me, and bomb-dive off Black-
rock Pier.

'Ah, she didn'a tell them ... silly girl. I'll get Mic to ring
her.' Pause. 'Yeah, I'd say so. Look, Jim, thanks ... and
love, just do yar best. But don't send in the boys if Nick
is in the house with Paddy and Bernie ... 'K? And my
guess is, that's where she is.'

I could feel cold salty water up my legs, stinging me.

Grabbing the laptop, I took myself up and out of my bed and I climbed on top of Shane's rubber mattress and closed the curtains around me. I lay back. Trying to imagine lying completely still. All. Of. The. Time. Shane's view, as near as it was to me, was so different. I clicked open the Word document.

Suggestions for My Wi-Fi Interceptor

Fuck.

Morto.

He had left me a kind of mix-tape, with links. Jesus.

1. Exit Music for a Film - Radiohead (OK Computer)

2. Gavin and Stacey Christmas Special

3. Sylvia Plath reads Daddy - YouTube

4. Links to Harry Potter and the Philosopher's Stone (For your kids)

5. Iron and Wine - Upward Over the Mountain (Early stuff's the best)

Really sorry we didn't chat or get to know each other better.

But happy to share my Wi-Fi. And here, have a bigger screen. That phone will screw up your eyes, at least that's what my mam used to say.

All very best, Shane x

Fuck fuck fuck.

Fuck.

I bawled.

Chapter 17|

For some hours, like with a text from a lover, I stimmed on the list.

Michaela Sherlock skittered onto the Ward, howling gently, face white with mottled red spots.

'Mammy, Mauuuummmmmy.'

Margaret Rose tried to move quickly, but she hadn't time to close across the curtains without making a scene. 'Sssshhhhh, ssshhhhh, Jesus, will you get a grip of yourself, Mic … Mic … ssshhhhnow, Christ, get a grip of yourself. Stop this now. This is no way to be behaving in a place … like this.'

'Nick's with that Bernie wan, Mammmmy,' she screamed, breathless.

'Yes ... yeah, I know. Did ya run the whole ways here?'

Michaela nodded. 'You knows about it? Why ja not tells us?'

'Why? Why would I tell you that? Would it have been a nice thing to do?'

'Nice?' Michaela said and threw her hands up in the air.

'Well, would it have helped you? Yar sister? No. So why? So why should I have gone and burdened ya both?'

'Well, just, it's a shock is all ...' Michaela looked softer at her mother.

'Look, Mic, ya have ta remember ... yar father made his own choices, and now Nick's making them too. That's life, love, and to be honest, I have nothing ta add. Ya canny make choices far others, ya can only control yarself.'

'What?' Michaela exclaimed, thinking on her mother's words.

'We can only wait. And hope she'll see sense.'

'I know, Mammy, but I'm so filled up with worry now.'

'Don'na worry ... see yar worrying now because ya know ... look ... Nick'll be back. She loves ya too much ... but you badly need to rub some cold water on yar face, and tidy yarself up ...' Margaret Rose urged her daughter towards composure as her own face danced with rage.

'Are ya all right, Mammy? Yar gone awful red?'

'I'm grand, I'm just worrying about yar sister too. Did ya manage ta talk ta her?'

'Yeah ... just Snapchat ... said ...' She baulked.

'What she say? Tell me out.' Margaret Rose was cross.

'She's swearing she won'na come back,' Michaela said, turning quickly to avoid her mother's hurt, then went to the loo to compose herself, but it was pointless and when Michaela Sherlock returned from the toilet she was still crying uncontrollably.

'Why is she crying? Stop her, we need to stop her crying,' said Jane, jumping off her mattress towards them.

'So, tell me about Nick ... she's ran off and left Jim. Right? She with yar father?' Margaret Rose asked.

Your father. Endgame talk.

'Yeah.'

'How is she?'

'Angry –' she paused, hesitant – 'with you.'

'What? Angry with me, why? What's she angry with me far? Shir, I did'na go off with Bernie, why's she angry wit me? Fuck this . . .'

Michaela lifted her shoulders and dropped them. 'Dunno. Just is.'

'Christ, she was so silly ta lave Manchester, she could of bled da death . . . She was'na fit ta be taking off like that. Will she ever learn? Well, did she say she got a fright or what? Jim's worried sick. There's no talking ta her.'

'Shir, why ya arsking me if Jim's telling ya everything?'

Michaela was hurt she'd been left out of the loop.

Jane was getting very agitated. 'No one can learn with you galloping off like this. You'll need to step out of this classroom at once,' she shouted. Michaela ignored her. 'Well now, aren't you an insolent young madam. You will step outside this door at once. You're too loud . . . far too loud.' She danced over to Michaela and stood in front of her, wagging her finger, then raised her arm. 'Is that what you are? A big-mouthed fishwife?'

Margaret Rose looked like she'd been stung by a racer wasp. She pursed her lips and stood out of bed. 'Now just hold on wan minute, Jane.' Insanity and old age would be no excuse for insulting her anguished daughter.

Jane grabbed Margaret Rose hard in a chest lock beside her nightstand. Margaret Rose was gentle, tried to coax Jane and move her backwards, unhook herself, but Jane held her hard and Margaret Rose was now doubled over. Jane reached out with her right hand and picked up the hairdryer, pretending first to shoot her in the head, mockingly, but then she waved it backwards, up and high, and whacked it hard and fast off the corner of Margaret Rose's temple and again, bangbangbang, on the eye socket. Wallop. And again. Wallop. Margaret Rose toppled sideways, landing over on her bed.

Claire's feet remained motionless behind the curtain.

'What the fuck?' Alex said, as he returned onto the Ward, just as I was getting out of bed, followed fast by two young girls in violet tops and hairnets from the kitchen. He leaned over Margaret Rose, calling out to her. More buzzers.

Jane cried to herself, being pulled back into her own bed by the kitchen girls and dragging her feet along the floors. When she was safely back in the bed, she drew the white sheet up under her chin, and whispered away to herself. 'Ann should never have come back ... I won't stop ... Stop yourself ... Why are you all leaving me here? They're all at me ...'

Michaela put a white facecloth under the running tap at the small sink, wrung it and gently placed it on her mother's forehead, then turned off her radio. Michaela then rang Niquita, hysterical. As Niquita asked questions, Michaela in turn relayed them to the cleaners, while covering the mouthpiece of the phone. The cleaners were having difficulty understanding the requests, and unable to give any solace or advice to the young woman. 'Look, they're not telling me nathing, these wans, all I knows is Mam's rall bad ... Just five minutes ago ... She was calling me names ... I canny remember ... Why ya arsking so many questions? Fuck, Nick, I dunno ...' Michaela had a hand on her hip as she stood over and looked down at her mam. 'And she knows yar with dad ... What ja mean, did I tell her? Jim did, yar bodyguard told her ... Ah, it's all a mess. What are ya doing ta her? Ya rally nade ta come back now ... Ah here, look, I'm gonna send ya a Snapchat ... Ya might believe me den ... And shir ...'

Michaela reached out her long thin arm and took a selfie with Margaret Rose passed out behind her. The white facecloth was dramatic, and Margaret Rose was as pale as the sheet that surrounded her. Michaela cursed the flash for working and then cursed it for not working and on the last click she pulled a duck face.

'Hello. Niquita? Ya. There. Look at that … Ya get it? Did ya see her?'

'Nick?'

Pause.

'Ja knows what, do what ya like.'

Margaret Rose finally had the facial trauma she required so badly. No more novocaine.

Michaela put a flashy neon hairband in her mother's hair and some glittery lip balm on her lips.

'Christ almighty,' Alex said, 'look at that bang, jeez.' A poppy bruise was growing on her temple.

'I need to get out of here, Alex,' I said, grabbing him desperately. 'You have to get me out, I can't, I just can't, you can't make me, and that girl needs to leave too, someone needs to get her out, this place isn't ...'

'It's just shock.' He tried to soothe me. But it was useless.

I didn't tell him about the mix-tape.

Chapter 18|

'You sure you OK?' Michal asked Molly as they sponged down Margaret Rose. 'You look so so tired.'

'Just wrecked darl. Too many shifts.'

Margaret Rose was stirring a little. Her face had fallen, but the machines said everything was perfectly fine. It was probably shock and she was sleeping off her pain relief.

'Can I bring the boys in tomorrow? It's Sunday, Sundays are boring and they'd love to see you?' Alex asked, softly.

'Who? The kids? Are you mad? Look at them all, Alex,' I said, 'look across at them, talking yesterday, unconscious today. I can't have the kids here. They're young, I don't want this to be ...' I said. 'They're too young to have to watch this. This is not OK, they shouldn't have to be here ...' I paused. 'To see this.'

I could see him thinking – about leaving it, pushing it – forming a sentence.

'I can't think straight in here,' I told him.

'But you're getting, so, so ...' He paused. 'Fast.'

'Fast?'

He left out Worse. Or Incontinent. Perhaps Unbearable. Or Thin.

'Alex, if you don't help me, I swear I will throw myself from the window.'

He looked aghast.

'Sinéad, please ... I'm trying.'

I attempted to change the subject.

'Michal's very fresh with Molly.'

'He's a player,' Alex said and laughed.

'Ah, he's not,' I said.

'He certainly is. And you're right, you are in that bed too long.'

'That's what I'm trying to convince you of, see you'd go mad yourself in here.'

'Right. Fancy a walk? I'll push if you sit. Deal?'

This was a test.

'Deal. But just to the loo?' I motioned, feeling queasy.

I could see he was ahead of me, plotting.

'I'm taking my wife to the corridor and we will stop off at the loo upon our return,' he said, formally. 'Now, isn't this like our good pub days? Me pushing you along in a shopping trolley?'

The corridor was apricot too. Nurses moved fast with clipboards and cans of Coke. Patients shuffled along, keeping close in to the walls, some were holding onto a railing with both hands. It was too busy, even for Alex, negotiating the chair. We came back past the loo.

'Please,' I said. 'Need to go …'

He opened the door inwards, and awkwardly dragged my chair in after him.

First he put down the toilet seat, and held my elbow as I lifted myself up and out, and crouched over the loo. I vomited, he held my hair back at the nape of my neck, cold and clammy, and when I was finished he wiped my face with those thick paper hand towels.

'Shit. Can I help?'

I gawked, and blew my nose.

'Sorry, but I still … I still need to … go.'

'Yeah … OK, right, sorry.'

He lifted me onto the loo.

I sat there and he tried to be discreet, checking out the mechanics of the showerhead and running his hand along the uneven grout and over the sink. Hhhhhmmm. He went. Then he hummed. Next he played with the SOS cord.

'Pull it.'

'No.'

We laughed.

But nothing.

Stranger fright. Performance anxiety.

'Run the tap,' I said.

'What? You finished?'

'No, just turn it on. The tap.'

And he did.

And finally, I peed. I told him a little about Father as I sat on the loo and someone else's hair emerged from the shower hole. He had always known, he said, all my ranting on and on and on in my sleep, well, it had given him many clues over the years as to my busy mind, busy, like an insect, but he felt that if we put our love out there towards each other, we'd at least get some of it back, and I told him I didn't purposely hold love back, but he knew that too, because he'd watched me for years, protecting myself, knocking all the things I loved, or should love the most, because then there's no expectation, not really, and he knew this too, really we both knew that and I said I was sorry about all the people throughout our life that I *met* (I'd usually just fucked them, but I didn't want to break us entirely apart). But that was the extent of it. I did want to tell him that builder guy from East Clare was the very last. That was the end. But I wasn't going to go into specifics because that's torture, giving someone specifics, a name, a face. Alex said he always knew, every time, but I didn't press him on it. I wasn't a masochist. And he said, of course it bothered him but also he sort of understood it. I asked him why he'd never left, and he said, he'd often thought about it, made plans, but that really it made him think of me as alive, like a grapefruit sliced open, and there was nothing better than thinking of someone alive, like the day I wrestled the Whooper swan, he said, and something about the boys and my father. I made it up off the loo without him having to help me, but collapsed into him. As he lifted me back to the chair, he said that it was his decision to stay, that was his responsibility, and that he had a fair grasp of the facts, and himself. But that he knew me most of all, and I suggested to him that if he came early tomorrow morning that I might shower alone and he might dry my hair and fix it, paint my nails again, now that we were sharing a bathroom space. He said he would. I thought a peppermint green would be nice and he thought fuchsia would be better (because he knew where the bottle was), but we settled on a glassy peach colour, because they sold it in the Hospital shop, and it would remind me of the walls and the floor and the scanner. I said it would probably be the last time that he painted my nails. And he said no, it wouldn't, and that he would race me back to the bed.

And he did, abandoning me in my chair, and he won.

So in the glow of his victory, I begged and I told him I can't be a prisoner. That is not who I am. And that a taxi driver can't be paid in red lipstick and blobfish slippers, that I am, for all accounts, entirely poor. Which is ironic. But devastating. Alex didn't commit one way or another. Stoic.

★

The ward was eerie as the late afternoon wind rattled the windows.

'You never told me,' he said as he was settling me back in to bed.

'What?' I said.

'What was on the laptop?' he said, eyes firm on the silver casing.

'Just games, you know.'

'Games?'

'Yeah, just things like, you know, the way kids stick gummy teeth in their mouths.'

It was all that would come to me.

'What ... the ... fuck?'

'Oh, nothing, just rubbish. Fail Army Stuff. I think they were all mixed up.'

His face froze.

'Kinky shit, like?'

I laughed.

'No. Not kinky.'

I laughed again.

'Kids love that game where you eat the doughnut but you can't lick your lips,' he said, forgetting.

'I don't know it.'

'You do, I play it all the time at the kids' birthday parties, you do, it's bloody impossible, and if you hit the jam squidgy centre, you're fucked entirely then.' He grabbed the machine. 'Gimme a look,' he said, teasing me.

'No, please, leave it, will you?'

I shut down the lid hard and he kissed the top of my head.

'You'd better wash my hair soon,' I groaned.

The window was rattling harder now, and started to bang.

'I need to leave. I wish you'd just …' I couldn't bring myself to push the word *respect* into my sentence.

'I need to get things for the house, to make everything comfortable, sorted.' He was awkward now.

'What do you mean sorted? We don't live in a cave, we have everything.'

'There's a few things we need. That's what they think …' He trailed off.

'Who the fuck are *they*, Alex?' I took a breath. 'I need to see the boys. But not here. Not like this. They are not to know, please, I really can't. I'll tell them … in my own way.'

324

'But you won't, Sinéad, you'll hint and shuffle and no one will know what you're on about.' He softened. I had to stop pushing him. 'Can we talk later? I'm exhausted?'

'Fuck, fuck, shit, ouch, OUCH.' The curtains rustled around Hegs and brown liquid poured out on the ground and across the middle of the Ward. Claire jerked the curtain back; hot chocolate had gone belly up on the floor beside her slipper socks. Alex sprang forward to help.

'No no, no no nono NO NO NO ...' Claire insisted. 'Just leave it.'

He came back and rolled his eyes, his patience waning.

'Look, it's Saturday, what would you think of getting a proper tea?' Alex said to me.

'Oh, Alex, I just ... I haven't the energy, or the clothes.'

'I'll run out for it, we can have it here.'

'Here?'

Claire mopped the chocolate liquid off the floor.

'Sure, sure,' I said, distracted. 'What you thinking of getting?'

'Takeout? Wine?'

It was adventurous for him. 'Or. Falafel maybe? Pizza? Indian?'

'Indian, yes, great! Not too hot.'

My stomach heaved, but it was progress. If he could get takeout, he could drive me home.

Jane was wearing a small navy vest top that Michaela had given her, all forgiven now we were reassured Margaret Rose was just sleeping and not dying.

'Thank you so much, my dear,' Jane said to Michaela, as she pulled at the string of the top. 'Quite the drapery you two lovely young ladies have going.' Michaela looked at me, and we smiled. Everything started to go infundibula and yellow and fuzzy and I could hear a whoosh in my head as I shook all over.

Jane came and pulled the curtain around me and I succumbed to her, lay back as she pulled my oxygen mask onto my face. I imagined her twisting the little copper nozzle on the oxygen tank and then Iron & Wine's banjos came through the headphones on the bed. Jane leaned her willowy frame over me and kissed me with her stained lips, sitting on my bed, like a parent tucking in their child. She rubbed my hair out of my face, kissing me again, gently, on my forehead.

'Now, that better?' Jane said, lifting the mask of my face.

I nodded, and she grabbed my hand.

'You OK? Why are you crying so much?'

I shook my head. Oxygen escaped.

'I know, I know, you see, your breath is going against you.'

I smiled.

'You're having a little attack. I get them all the time.'

Air passed a little further down now, my belly rose gently, small ball.

When Alex returned, I'd play What If. Show him I believed he was up to it. The job. The kids. What If, yes, I'd play that game with him. What If the house was on fire but Jacob was showing signs of meningitis and then Nathan fell and banged his head? What If the boys wanted to go to a disco and bring a naggin and sleep over in the house of a parent we didn't know? What If Joshua got *Grand Theft Auto* and you found Jacob playing it? I stopped the game. I couldn't answer the questions myself.

'Thanks, Jane.'

Head. Heart. Hands. Husband. Hold all. Home.

She sat at the end of the bed now and put her feet in under my chin, I threw the fuchsia hoody over them.

'You've lipstick all over your face, Jane.' I smiled.

'I have?'

'Yeah, look.' I passed her a little silver mirror.

'Ash, ash, hash, ta-da, ta-da, ya still have it, Jane,' she said, and smiled in at the mirror. 'What is this awful shade of red? Is this blood? Oh, my God, am I bleeding? Oh, my goodness, I'm dying? Aren't I?'

'No, no, no ... it's only lipstick, Jane, just some red lipstick. Look ... it's OK.' I showed her the tube and began twisting it up and down in an effort to rejig her memory, remind her.

'Oh, now, now, rub it off me, girl, it's a dangerous red, pillar-box red, red is a dangerous lipstick, polish up my skin, make it like your skin, polish it young for me like a good girl, you know Ann told me how very beautiful I am, do you know I have nine children and not one of them even met her?'

I pulled a baby wipe from a packet and began rubbing her face gently, attempting to remove the stains.

'Ah, thank you, much appreciated. Now, tell Jane, why are you crying? You see, life's too short for that, you know?' she said, rubbing my hand. We were like two ewes in April nibbling each other's wool after they'd taken our lambs away to slaughter.

'I'm not crying Jane, promise, it's only the air ... or the oxygen.' I took a deep breath. 'It's going against my eyes, and watering them,' I lied.

'You've only gone and reminded me ... I haven't watered my hanging baskets once this summer. Did you know I made a lovely job of my hanging baskets last year? Stuffed them full of pansies and lovely trailing ivy and lobelia. They were magnificent.'

'It's not summer yet, Jane ... Don't worry, you've plenty of time.'

'Isn't it? Isn't that a pity? Have I really? Plenty of time? Are you sure? Before summer. Is it really not summer? Feels so very hot in here, that's good though, for the flowers won't wilt and die without me! Aren't I very silly thinking it's summer, and do you know what, but that nurse looks just like summer, doesn't she?'

'She does,' I said, 'she's lovely.'

'No, she certainly is not lovely. Are you gone completely astray in the head?'

'She works hard, no?'

'Well now, doesn't everyone work hard? Isn't that only what you're supposed to do? She's so fresh that one, you should stay away from her, only bring you trouble, I'm telling you.'

'Ah, no, she's no ... no trouble, Jane.'

'I saw them,' she said, giggling. 'Both of them. Together. I just peered out of there like this,' she went on, and put up her gloved hands to her face and opened out the palm of red leather like a peacock. 'Ah, see, I did I did I did, ah, they were there, you know, all curled up like little field mice, yes, that's it, little field mice curled up in the cold. She'll end up like Ann if she's not careful. Did I ever tell you that Ann went and hung herself off a banister ...' she said, rocking. 'Did I tell you this?'

'Yes, yes, you did.'

'Lovely Ann. With a terribly narrow cord, yes, wrapped all tight.' She squeezed the hands around her neck. 'I put those bitches of nuns in their place, look –' she nodded over at Margaret Rose – 'I think I killed this one with the barrel of a gun. That summer nurse needs to be careful. No good will come of her and she all curled up with him and up to all sorts.'

'You didn't kill her, Jane, that's Margaret Rose, she's your friend. You like her. It was just a hairdryer. But you did hit her hard with it ... she's a lovely woman,' I said, slowly, and she lifted her hand to her mouth about to cry. 'Margaret Rose is a good woman, she's your friend.'

'Oh, feck it, is she? Oh, no.' She lifted her leathered hand to her mouth. I wasn't sure I had been fair to the old woman, perhaps I should have played along. 'Did I upset her?'

'No, no, she's fine. She's just tired,' I said, having gone too far.

She was silent a minute.

'Have you ever told Tom?' I asked.

'About the summer nurse all curled up like a little dog with the Polish boy? No, no, sure, I haven't seen Tom, with my holidays, you know, he needed to stay home, cows calving.'

'No,' I said, rubbing her back, 'did you tell him about Ann?' I couldn't imagine Molly and Michal. Not then. I distracted myself.

'Of course. Jane Lohan does not like secrets.' She swatted my hand down, crossing her heart and hoping to die. 'Just before our wedding, oh, now, you see, it was so very early on the morning that we were married, that was the way things were done, early morning, up to the altar when the cock crew. I called out to him, to his house, out to his home place. It was about six in the morning,' she said, tracing her finger around an imaginary clock, 'I couldn't sleep for days with the big secret, and I knocked on their front door. Big house. His mother answered and she wasn't going to let me in, bitch of a mother, you see, imagine, a morning breakfast celebration? That's the way we did things,' she said, distracted, and caressed my neck. 'I couldn't keep it from him any more. I hardly knew him, but I was in love with Ann, I always would be, despite all that happened, and I was not in a good place to be marrying anyone. I told him all about her, Ann, how he'd never be as good as her. And that I probably couldn't . . .'

'Oh, God. How'd he take that?'

'Him? Oh, now, he took it very badly, not good if you must know. For he went as quiet as a mouse, you see, and didn't utter a word back to me. But we had to marry, you know?'

And she curved her hands in front of her.

'Oh, he marched off out of the short hallway like a lunatic, and went into a bedroom and slammed out the door. Cursing. I had to leave, the mother was shouting all sorts at me, and told me I better be at that altar by nine, or she'd let everyone know . . . she was wild and angry. I did what I was told, went home, and readied myself. I got dressed, it was just a light pink jacket and skirt, we didn't go in for much fancy nonsense then, and I went along and met him at the altar, an hour later. He was terribly white. Wouldn't look at me, or link me. I pulled the wedding band on myself in the end.'

'Did it help?' I said, unsure of why she exposed herself like this. 'Telling him?'

'You can be so silly,' she said, 'really, a most incredible fool sometimes, I think you're such a clever girl, and then you're not that smart at all.'

She smiled, showing only her bottom teeth.

'It was the worst thing I could have done. He held it against me my whole life. He went absolutely crazy. Mad crazy ... and he knew I would never love him, but I do, you see, I do love him ... he would just never accept it ...' She stretched and wriggled. I let go of her foot. 'Just after the wedding breakfast, we took our leave and went on to a guest house, that's what you did then, different times now, and he dropped me at the front door, big green door, with a brass knocker, but said he couldn't bear to come up with me or be near me and sped off out the gravel. He didn't want to check in with me maybe, in case people knew. Or have to lift me up going through the door, like we did back then. I was watching for him out the window of the guest house, and I didn't hear him come in after me, and I was waiting at the window. He snuck up behind me –' she placed her hand to her forehead – 'so I had no idea he was still so angry. Indeed, maybe I was a stupid girl, I was, so very naive, a bit like yourself, and when he came into the room behind me, before I had a minute to turn, he grabbed both my hands and twisted my arms up behind my back and shoved me hard into the window frame.'

She pointed to her forehead, to the long narrow line, the shiny snail-like track that ran from the crown of her head to the bridge of her nose. I had thought it was a deep furrow line, from ageing or squinting. 'Yeah,' she sighed heavily, 'the blood gushed from me, he said I was a dirty rotten cunt,' she coughed, 'pardon me,' she coughed gently into her hand, 'and that he'd knock all of that dirty American slut, Ann Hegarty, out of me, that's the way he said it, now pardon me again,' she said, coughing gently again as she blessed herself. 'You see, I'd never heard those kind of words before, and then he turned fully on me, and said that I drove her to it, Ann, that I drove her to the banister, and the cord, he was roaring then, all bothered about what he had gotten himself into at all at all, and that he'd heard about women like us. Dykes. But he hadn't been crazy enough to believe it, because women like us were worse than witches, fucking dirty rotten devil whores.'

'Oh, Jane, it's OK,' I said. 'There's no need to go back over this.'

'Oh, I can assure you I spoke up,' she said, sensing my apprehension, perhaps not wanting sympathy, 'but it got me nothing, nowhere. I tried to defend myself. I shouted back at him, for I think I was braver then, that's what being young does, "Well, Goodman Tom Lohan with all the big horrible words," but he roared out and I was so afraid everyone in the guest house would hear, which I am sure they did, even though I tried to keep him quiet, and the more I shhhh'd him, the angrier he got, he was mad with himself for going ahead with it, the wedding maybe, I don't know, he said nothing else but took the paisley neck tie off from around his neck and twisted it around mine.' She stretched again as I gently wiped the rest of the lipstick off her face.

'I thought I'd go the same way as her, as Ann. But that was not good. For as bad as the longing was upon me to see her, I'd go to the fires of hell with her, because that's what he said would happen, a devil like me. I wanted to die. But sure we'd never have met again. I knew I needed to repent before I could meet God, and of course, who knew if poor Ann had gone to God at all?'

Her back was soaked in sweat. I offered her a drink.

Margaret Rose woke and began touching her bruised eye socket and poppy temple.

'Eventually, I must have passed out,' she said, sobbing.

'Jesus, Jane.'

'I came around in the dispensary. You see, frightened with what he did, he had taken me to a doctor. I was so glad and I thought it was for some stitches in my head. But they paid no heed to my head, as Tom blurted out the whole tale, the doctor gave me an injection into my arm as he held me again, tight, and told Tom to bring me in every day for a week. We were only staying at the guest house for a night, but Tom booked me in for the entire week, brought me every morning, then back to the guest house, put me to bed. I slept for most of that week. I don't remember much. It made me sleep all the time. And after the week of injections he gave me tablets to take home, back to the house I'd live at, a big country house, with his mother, until she died. I said I wasn't taking them, but Tom said he'd crush them down my throat if I didn't and the doctor agreed, and he'd help Tom if needs be. Tom said it was OK, he'd make sure his mother gave them to me, if the need arose.'

'Oh, Jane,' I said.

'They were friends, you see, himself and the doctor, and he knew the guest house owners, they were all the one parish, and sure I hadn't a friend left, they were friends from primary school, and I never went to the doctor ever again without Tom by my side. Everyone in the parish knew. I wasn't allowed to visit a doctor alone, they said. It was about trust. And I took the tablets. For ever. For here,' she said, pointing her ring finger at her head, 'but I've been his wife, you know, in that way a woman can be a wife, and I've taken them every day since, but now sometimes I forget. Sometimes I'm always forgetting, you know. Did I tell you that they told me if I didn't take the tablets I couldn't be around my children? I've nine, you know. That it would allow me to be ... allow the children to be near me.'

'Ah, Jane. Jane ... sorry.'

Margaret Rose was awake now, with the flannel on her forehead and a huge bruise around her eye.

Alex was always so gentle.

Something about him not having written down the food order and reading it back to me was new. And unnerving.

And if he never arrived back on the Ward, I would never blame him.

Chapter 19|

Jane had fallen asleep beside me, and was eventually put back to her own bed and remained quiet for the evening.

'How're ya feeling?' Margaret Rose asked me.

'Nice to see you up and about,' I said. 'Shit, nasty bang though.'

'Only a bang sure. Poor Jane. What'd she hit me with?'

'Your hairdryer,' I said and Margaret Rose laughed, and then coughed gently, moving towards my bed.

'Look, Sinéad ... loveen –' she was awkwardly hovering – 'OK if I ...?' I patted the bed and she sat. 'I'm so sorry about, ya know, yar scan and all. Maybe ya need ta tell

me ta mind my own business, but it's just, ya hear everything in here. But I'm rally sorry.'

'Thanks,' I said. 'I know it's impossible not to hear. This
place.'

We both rolled our eyes.

'It's vary unfair, and yar young family. I'm so sad far ya.
I knows yar not a praying woman. I wish I could do
something more. But please, ya canny be keeping news
like this ta yarself, ya need people around ya ... yar
mother, someone ta help.'

'Thanks,' I said again. Utterly lost for words.

'They find your husband?' I asked.

'Ah, that lad, he's never lost, not rally. Just disappears.
He's off with another woman. State of them.'

'I know, I'm so sorry.'

'Ah, I'm used ta it. But ya know yarself. It's so shameful.
I've a plan ... of sorts.'

'Good.'

'What are ya going ta do? You canny just lie in here like this, hope it'll all go away, because it won'na, ya know?'

'Not much I can do, really,' I said.

'Well, that's not true.' She leaned over me, talking faster. 'They said ya cud do something ta give ya longer, ya should think about it, rally. Yar kids'll need time with ya, 'tis a terrible shock on everyone. Look, love, I have not a right ta interfere, but yar in shock ... yar not thinking straight, love. Ya need ta think long and hard about the choices yar making.'

'I know,' I said, 'I just can't think straight. It's too much.'

She stared at me, fidgeting with the bed sheet, took a sharp breath. 'I think 'tis afraid of living ya are. No?'

'What? That's unfair,' I said, uncomfortable now.

'Is it?' she said, lowering her chin and lifting up her eyes.

'You don't know anything about me.'

'Maybe,' she said. 'But tell ya what I think ...'

'What?'

'I think ya need ta get down off the cross and use the wood. Come on, yar poor boys, and that lovely husband. Ya have it all really. Ja know that? And ya shouting at him about eggs. It's not right, shouting at him ...'

I groaned.

'Look. I knows things can be very tough. And the past never laves us in much peace. I rally do know. Look, life is life. And while ya have it, ya canny be messing with it. It's not a game.'

She hugged me tight and I grabbed her, desperate.

★

Alex returned later that evening, wearing a denim shirt and black jacket, carrying a plastic bag of takeout and two bottles of Tempranillo. Lamb.

'Supper.' And he smiled widely.

I pushed off the bedclothes.

'Anything exciting since I left?'

'Don't ask ...' I lifted my legs out and felt for the tiled floor.

'Shit, what're you doing?' Alex said.

'Ah, here, I can't go to a restaurant without doing myself up a little. I'm showering.'

'No need, it's just me, and this ...' he pleaded, lifting up the pink–and–blue striped plastic bag and looking about him. The bottles of wine were rolling along on the bed.

'Please,' I said, 'please leave it, just let me.' I smiled again, at him. 'But you can help. Grab the black skinny Levi's in here –' I motioned to under the bed. 'There's a white shirt too, the one with the triangle diamonds on the front.'

Nothing was going to upset my focused mood. I would have a meal. Nicely dressed.

'But the food will go cold ...'

'We can microwave it at the Nurses' Station.'

"K. Wear this,' he said, lifting a pretty turquoise bra from the bag and hanging it on his wrist. I had forgotten I had it. I felt a surge of guilt for Jane and the Wonder-bra. A dark red ribbon weaved through the cups and the straps had a muted cream trim.

343

'Oh!' I said.

Alex handed me his suit jacket. 'This any good to you?'

'Great,' I said, 'I can be like Madonna or Diane Keaton in that movie, what was that movie?'

'*Manhattan*?'

'No, not that one, the other one . . .'

'*Annie Hall*?'

'Yes, her. Tonight . . . Matthew Kelly . . . I will be Annie Hall . . . mwah . . . mwah.'

I would prove to Alex I could make it home. I'd eat all the food, whatever it was, saag and almonds and something with garlic, a garlic and coriander naan maybe.

'You can dry my hair after,' I said, as he linked me to the loo.

'I'm not so sure this is a good idea. Please, just . . . just let me come in.'

But I eventually locked the door behind me, locking him out.

Alone.

I placed the toilet bag and the bundle of clothes on a large towel on the ground. I laid out a razor, purple shampoo, and conditioner. I turned on the shower and I sat down on the white-yellowed plastic seat, the long red cord waved back and forth, it made me feel safe and terrified. I wondered how many others had sat on the chair, taken a shower, died. At first it made me fainty, the thought of bare arses before me, and thinking of how their thigh skin caught in the dodgy edge, as the water got hotter and hotter. I closed my eyes and drank from the faucet. I let it run on my hair and down over my breasts.

The heat of the water burned me. I wanted it to burn me. I wanted it to hurt. *Fuck You All* the water said, I am alive. I am alive. I am. And I will stay alive. But I knew it was no use, water, oxygen, pills, blahdeblah, all of it, none of it was any use, but maybe would I give them all more hope if I just sat with a mask on my face and stayed in Hospital and pretended to fight it? I dried my body off with a towel too fluffy to be useful, another gift from Margaret Rose, and I let it fall to the wet ground. I stood in front of the narrow shaving mirror. I thought about her advice.

I touched my damp shoulders. I felt my hot earlobes. I touched my gums, ran my finger across all of my teeth.

I squirted blobs of pink body cream onto my hands and I touched my shinbones. I touched my breasts, empty and saggy. I felt between my legs. I held my head and dropped it forward. It made me dizzy. I bent my wrists and then rotated them. All these parts of me, that somehow made me, all these odd bits, that sometimes looked nice and more often didn't, when I pieced them all together, even if I didn't feel connected to them, they were essentially me. I breathed in as fully and as deeply as my lungs would allow, in through my nose, out again, square breaths, don't collapse, in – hold and out – hold. Don't cry. Do not cry. Do not cry. You are only made of air and water. You will not survive. No one will and you are OK. You have survived till now. I ran a list of all my achievements through my head. I was an OK mother. I was trying to accept this. I made Alex laugh sometimes. I didn't have a big gang of friends, or a wild network of people. I was a dutiful daughter for the most part. Do not cry. I loved my mother. He won't stay another night if you cry. I sponged some make-up onto my face and blended it in under my chin. I drew my eyebrows in. But nothing would stick. It was too hot. I was too wet.

Fuck achievements.

You are OK. You have definition now.

I had three little ripples where my stomach turned over on itself and standing up or lying flat made them disappear. Some wiry black hairs sprouted from my right breast.

★

I returned from the bathroom, slowly, feeling more Michael Keaton in *Batman*, but Alex and Molly and Margaret Rose and Michal had grouped together and they clapped. And I winked with both eyes.

'Ah, darl, nice to see ya up,' Molly said, leaning forward and linking me to Alex's chair. I sat on it. Weak. Alex began brushing my hair and rough-drying it.

'Proper boutique we have here, now,' Jane said, looking out the window. 'Great set-up.'

'I want them, y'naw, kids?' Molly said to Alex, as she shouted over the sound of the dryer. 'But I couldn't do it without a lot of encouragement, and I don't know, Bobby just feels it's time, but I think we're too young.'

'Well, we're mad about our scuts,' Alex offered, tapping my shoulder. 'They're great, well, they're grand, you know . . . they're there, I guess,' he said as he reduced our children to ornaments.

'I guess,' she smiled, and left. Alex turned off the dryer and put some mousse in the roots of my hair, massaging my head with the tips of his fingers.

'I so wanted you to ask how they were thinking of doing it?' I whispered when Molly walked off.

'How what?' He looked at me, mousse bottle in his hands.

'How they are thinking of trying to have the kid, you know, like how they'll do it?'

'Do it?' he asked, alarmed.

'Conceive the baby, ya twat?'

'Oh, oh God, oh, that's none of our business.' He waved the bottle in front of me. He was a useless gossip. He'd never survive the Ward, Hospital.

'Now don't you look just gorgeous?' he said, and laughed, neither of us convinced, but I took his word for it. He tidied up and I stayed sitting out on the chair. It was a pleasant break. The feeling of clean hair was unworldly. Someone came in and reattached my leads and the telemetry monitor and complained how the shower had fucked it all up on them, but I didn't care. It was glorious to be clean.

I grabbed on to Alex with my two hands. 'Look, no one would know I'm a patient now, would they?' I waved my hands over my Batmanesque costume.

'Maybe?' he said, doubtful. 'But they'd certainly think you were fucking crazy.'

'If you love me … you'd kidnap me.'

'That's blackmail,' Alex said. But he didn't say no. I was about to explain that people don't blackmail for their own kidnapping, not usually, when Jim arrived on the Ward.

Chapter 20|

'Well, Mags, so gud ta see ya,' Jim Maughan said, arriving nervously back on the Ward, and greeting his anxious sister, gauging her reaction.

'Jim,' Margaret Rose said, quietly.

He leaned in slowly over her and kissed her cheek, gently. 'And look, Michaela's here too. Hi, how're you, love? Lovely ta see ye both.' And he kissed his niece in turn. 'Now look ...' he said to Margaret Rose. 'I came as fast as I could ...'

'Right,' Margaret Rose said, eyeballing him. 'What's wrong, Jim? What's happened?'

'It didn't go so ... so smoothly ... sorry.' Jim nodded at her phone.

Margaret Rose knew it was all gone belly up with Niquita's absconding.

'Is there more, Jim? Tell me.'

Jim opened up the top button of his shirt, and spread across the collar with his large hand. He shoved his wheelie case into the corner. 'Now, plays, don'na be alarmed.'

'What? What is it?' Margaret Rose said nervously, and grabbed Michaela by the shoulders.

'Well, we managed ta bring them back, but he's, they've ... well, they've followed me ...' he said, breathless, playing with the collar, 'here ... I asked them not ta, but he won'na listen. Now ... are ya up ta it?'

It was a warning more than a question.

Paddy Sherlock was returned.

'Have I a chaice?' Margaret Rose said.

'Well. No, not really,' he said, shooting his eyes downwards towards the bed, 'but be ... warned. He's like a fucking lunatic.'

Michaela Sherlock grabbed her mother's black rosary beads.

'Well ... well ... well, now, would ya look here? Rosary beads. Rosary-fucking-beads. Well, I've seen it all now.' The shout was rather ineffective, something uncertain about the way the man landed himself into our space, but land Paddy Sherlock did, banging his hip off the bin. Then he focused without blinking on his wife. 'I canny fucking believe ya, Margaret Rose Sherlock.' Michaela sat up straight on the bed, and played with the caviar balls of the rosary beads, clacking them inside and outside of her fingers, quickly.

'Look at ye all praying with the saints?' he said, eyeing up the Ward's elaborate grotto of religious knick-knacks. He glanced at Alex and then me and looked somewhat disappointed. Taking a long in-breath, Paddy Sherlock then turned his attention back to his wife. 'I canny believe what yar after doing to our Niquita ... ya know something? Yar nothing but a bitch. How ja think ya could keep me away from helping her just like that? I have rights, ya know?'

'I rang ya ...' Margaret Rose offered, quietly. 'Many times.'

His large belly was housed in a blue Adidas zip top. He bent over and rubbed down the front of his shiny black slacks, a strange time for vanity. Niquita appeared behind him, banging into the bin also, and then helping Paddy upright as he groaned and rubbed his lower back. Jim put his head in his hands. The defeated. 'Well, Mammy,' Niquita said, cheekily, as she fawned over her father, rubbing down his arm, and thrusting herself about this way and that, giddily.

'Nick, ah, love, it's good ta see ya, don'na be like this,' Margaret Rose pleaded; she remained motionless all the while, like a queen on a chessboard, taking her time, considerate or considering.

'I tells ya what ... yar an absolute thundering bitch, Margaret Rose, an absolute wan,' Paddy said, '... and I'm, I'm disgraced to death with ... ye all. All da cousins in Glan knows what she did too.' He put his large head into his hands and ran them back along his hair.

Margaret Rose shot Niquita a wounded look.

'What ya looking at her far? Bit late like ... shir, she's only gone and blabbed it to everywan she saw yesterday, and she came ta me and tells me all about it and how sorry she was,' Paddy said.

'How ja get to Birmingham from Manchester, Nick?' Margaret asked her daughter calmly, her voice deadly serious.

Jim began to pace the length of the bed.

'I like left da hotel and took a bus, like. What's ja take me far? A fool? That's all – a bus. Don'na be cross at me just because you got a bad slap.'

'How ja let this happen?' Margaret Rose asked Jim.

And the entire matter landed on Jim, who neither caused it nor fixed it.

'Killing a child. Well, that's murder, I hope ye all know that?' Paddy said. 'Since ye all know so much 'bout everything.'

'I'm so sorry, Mags ...' Jim nodded apologetically in his sister's direction.

'I'll tell you, Mrs High and Mighty Morals, you've reached a new low now, ya have. Ta tells ya da truth, I'm awful shamed yar m'wife, I really am. Like ... if things were different, I'd lave ya here. Disown ya.' Paddy was shouting now, more certain of himself, darting his wild eyes around the Ward.

Michaela played with the beads and didn't look at her sister, unsure of how this should play out, in the short term, and longer. Unsure of whose side she was on. Or whose side she should be on. She was buying time. Niquita moved and slowly lay back, naturally, with her mother. Margaret Rose put her arm around her daughter, gently kissing the top of her head and with both daughters lounging on her bed, she hissed back at her husband, 'Disown me, disown me always, whenever ya like, 'cause, Paddy, yar a good-far-nathing bastard, ja hear me?' Margaret Rose said. 'And I tells you this, it was a sorry day I married ya. And all da time ya were off with Bernie Kelly. All these years –' she stood up out of bed, moving Michaela with her like a small tide – 'ya brought nathing ta dis family … but work. But you listen well ta me now …'

Margaret Rose began counting out on her fingers, starting with her thumb.

Thumb – 'I was a good wife.'

She spoke rapidly now.

Finger one – 'I did well by m'family and by yars –' finger two – 'and yar people.'

Ring finger – 'I was a good mother, and I loved m'boys and girls.'

Pinkie – 'I tried my best with you and I kept our place nice in far tougher times than now. And that's enough.

I never split myself with loving or running foolish around after any other man ...'

'Ah, would ya listen ... who'd have ya?' Paddy said.

Both girls cried out.

The Queen can move in any direction. Forward – back\ diagonal/all moves, fast.

King moves slowly. Awkwardly. A step at a time.

'Ah, now, that's a low blow ... even far you, Paddy. And only far ma brother –' she motioned to Jim – 'ya'd have ruined us, so don'na come in here and give me lip about my girls. They're my girls, and they certainly don'na deserve Jonathan O'Keefe laughing at them, or taking his dirty way with them. Ya know what, 'tis an awful pity you didn't you come in here and demand his number far getting fresh with her? And do something useful ... like a father should.'

'Ah, stop, they're well able ta look after themselves, that pair,' Paddy said, glancing at the two girls, '... and signs on yarself that yar not dying neither? Big hoax, I suppose?'

He was correct.

But there was nothing behind his words now, everyone knew it, and he couldn't seem to withstand the pain of his bruised leg, rubbing at it constantly. Margaret Rose did not shut her mouth and Margaret Rose would not stop until she had made her point clearly, and knocked the King over.

Checkmate.

'All them times you were off getting Bernie to open her legs for ya ... I stayed.'

Paddy muttered something.

'I did my best and I'll continue ta stay and I will do my very best by them, but ya'll listen ta me now, don'na ya dare come in here, Paddy Sherlock, claiming all sorts about murder and yar girls, when 'tis not you that'll pick up the pieces ... and yar own morals are out of kilter.'

'Ya finished, are ya? Morals? What are ya spouting about?' he shouted, spitting his words slowly now; standing down was not a trait of their union, either of them. But the fight was dying.

She lay back.

'I am. I'm well finished. Finally ...' she said, looking up at the ceiling. 'And if 'tis shame yar afraid of, ya've given us plenty of it. Michaela and Niquita will marry whomever they wants. Jim'll look after us, you won'na see us wronged, Jim?' Margaret Rose looked at her brother.

'No, no, I promise, no,' Jim said, uncomfortable at being dragged back into the row.

'Well, I knows you won't, ya pansy,' Paddy shouted at Jim.

'Ya need ta watch yar mouth. Ya'll only love wan of us, I've had it now,' Margaret Rose said loudly, sitting up again, wagging the finger at him, 'and Bernie hasn't a penny, so g'wan off with ya, g'luck with that.' She waved him off with her two hands like a sweeping-pan brush.

Up. Down. Dismissed. But he was a dismissed man with nowhere to go.

Not in the short term.

He softened, and began explaining that he couldn't love just one of them, and wasn't that why all the bother began in the first place. And if he could, then none of this would have happened.

'Look … it's just … Mags, 'twas my grandchild, that's all,' he finished, gently.

'Sweet Jesus,' she said on a sharp in-breath, 'ya have others, some ya never see. Evan fell a few weeks ago, but you wouldn't know, yar never here.'

'Ah, fuck this. I love them children as me own. I canny be listening to this —' he looked at Niquita, hopeful — 'is there someone to fix my tea?' They both shook their heads. He looked around at us all, eyeing our takeout, 'Anyone?'

No one answered. He didn't push it. Not today. Paddy turned awkwardly and before he left, he put out his hand to shake his wife's, but she refused it, looked away. Paddy blessed himself and began to mumble prayers that he couldn't finish; so, rather embarrassed, he turned and left the Ward.

'Wasn't even a baby,' Michaela shouted out after him, far enough out of earshot, but conscious of her mother's hurt. Niquita kissed her mother and said, 'I'm so sorry, Mammy, I just taut he'd help us, I was just sad for the baby being gone ... and,' she paused, '... well, I missed him.'

'I know, love, but try ta put it out of yar head now, ya need ta get on with life. I know that's easier said than done, but Jonathan O'Keefe is a bad sort, didn't I promise you this? Ya should'a kept your mouth closed like I begged. See, it might be harder on ye both now, but it'll be OK, yar father never solved any problem, you should know that, love. He only made them.'

They opened some Kimberley biscuits, the ones individually wrapped that you get at Christmas, with the thick chocolate, and slowly peeled the black-and-purple wrappers off. Michaela came over offering me one and I smiled with my lips pursed tightly, like you'd do at a funeral. I'm-sorry pursing. I took a chocolate biscuit, as it would have been impolite and awkward not to. She took my wrapper off for me, and unpeeled one for Alex too, and she shared one with Jane by lobbing it on her bed, unopened, afraid to go too close.

Mammy was awake again, and that was all that mattered.

I held the chocolate biscuit until it melted in my hand.

'I'm just going to head and heat this up,' Alex said, quietly, carrying the takeout bag away.

Chapter 21|

'Shit, you OK?' I said. Margaret Rose was combing her hair when all her visitors had left for chips.

'Ah, look, loveen, these things happens, I'll be fine.'

'Sure?'

'Ah. I've been through worse. I'm just glad really he's back, and ... in one piece. Look it, what can I say ... sure yar husband is yar husband and as well him as another, or so they say. I canny remember who said that, but there's a lot of truth in it.'

I nodded, though she didn't seem convinced, or seemed desperate to convince herself.

'I'll always take Paddy back, because he's mine, ya know?' she said. 'And ...' she hesitated, 'I made a solemn promise in front of God.'

'Yes,' Jane said, thumbing the wrapper, trying to open her biscuit. 'Yes, you did. Promise in front of God. Like me.'

It was bleak. But true. True to them both.

Margaret Rose got up out of bed, and rummaged underneath. She lifted a large Tesco bag for life and came over to me, dropping it on my bed.

'Just a few things, tide ya over. Got wan of me own lads ta sort it far ya. My boys are good, ya know?'

'I know,' I said.

Maybe it made her a little more comforted, at my isolation, perhaps. My self-imposed isolation. Two jars of apple drops, three naggins of vodka, because, though not a drinker herself, she couldn't say the same about me from the amount of times I went on about it.

'Ya could keep wan handy under yar pillow.'

We laughed.

Some *Take a Break*s, pink fluffy pyjamas that said 'Sweet Dreams' with matching socks that had little moons on the soles. She placed it on the ground and handed me an envelope. A mass card for the sick with Mary on the front holding out her hands and looking upwards to the sky, with the most ridiculously thin nose.

'God is good,' she said, watching me stare at the card. I patted my bed, and she sat. 'I'm sorry, maybe 'twas the wrong things ta get ya ...'

'It was so kind, specially the vodka ...'

'But ya know what I meant,' Margaret Rose said, eyeing the card. 'It's just, everyone sick should have wan or two masses said far them. They might bring ya some good. Well, I suppose, they canny do ya any harm at the very least.'

We laughed again.

Jane opened up all our curtains wide to let the *Good Lord* in and upon seeing the Hegartys who were sleeping, she crept slowly over towards them. 'Little lambs,' she said, sneaking up to them, flicking water from a white plastic cup onto Claire and Hegs, waking both of them. 'What are you doing?' Claire shouted at Jane, rubbing her nose. 'Go away. Go back to your bed. No one wants you here.' She swatted at the old woman but Jane wasn't moving back.

'Ah, bless the little ones. And you poor thing here, here with her,' she said to Hegs, nodding at his daughter. He was just opening his eyes and Jane climbed up onto his bed, looking down over him.

'Please,' Claire said, coming around to the right-hand side of the bed. 'Don't. Please just leave him. Please, not here ... this isn't the place.'

'She was beautiful, longest eyelashes I ever saw,' Jane said, and she began to rub down his eyelids, as Hegs groaned out. 'You are ... just like her. Just like her, oh, Ann. Oh, my God, I am so sorry, I love you. I do, I really do.'

Margaret Rose moved from me, and attempted to coax Jane back to bed.

'Come on now, good woman, he needs ta sleep.'

'You, well, you are nothing like her,' Jane hissed at Claire. 'Not one part of you.'

Hegs was awake now.

'Please, Mrs Lohan, please, no, leave him be.'

'I love you, Ann, it's so sad to see you in here ... like this. I am so sorry. And your hair, it's all gone.'

Hegs didn't flinch.

She blessed him again with her fingers, crying now, as Margaret Rose linked her and began stepping her gently back to her own bed.

A text from my mother.

… How are you feeling? Any more word from the docs? I'd really like to see you. x (Emoji of a doctor with a pair of glasses and yellow hair)

Good, hope to get out today or tomorrow. Miss you.

Delete Miss You. I Love You. All the best.

Hoping to get out soon, miss you, c u later. (Double heart emoji, pink, swish)

Return message about how cold it had turned and a freezing-blue face with ice hanging out of his mouth. And then a clapping hands. She'd hit a wrong key.

… I'll leave in some food, tell Alex to be careful on the roads, it's to freeze later. Xz

Thanks. X

'Michal and Molly up a tree k-i-s-s-i-n-g,' Jane sang.

'Shush now, good woman, and lift your leg now . . .' said Margaret Rose.

'FIRST COMES MARRIAGE AND THEN BABY IN A CARRIAGE.' Jane pointed at Shane's empty bed. 'I saw them, you see, all curled up together like two little field mice. Field rats. Field rats.'

First do no harm.

Claire hit Hegs's buzzer.

Molly ran onto the Ward, stirring a drink for Jane which splashed over the rim and down onto the tiles.

'Now, now, what's wrong, hun?' She smiled at Margaret Rose. 'Thank you, darl, I'll take her from here. Drink a little now, that's it, and open . . .'

'I don't want it . . . I don't like it, you're trying to poison me,' Jane said to Molly. 'I don't want it and I won't take it and you cannot make me. I'm not drinking it, I won't and you can't make me, you haven't even told me how Tom is, and my dog, you see, do you know I have a bit of a burger for my dog, you'd better not have taken it.'

366

'Hey,' Alex said, returning with the bag, steaming saag and coriander.

'You'll have ta lie still, hun, come on Jane, now, now,' Molly said.

'I know you, oh, now, I know you ...' Jane said. 'I most certainly do, from somewhere, don't I, my dear?' she asked. She pulled open Molly's lips and shoved her thin small index finger in, then pulled out her tongue. Molly turned her head downwards, her hands too occupied to defend herself.

'You really have the most beautiful teeth, has anyone ever told you that? You are, in actual fact ...' Jane announced, 'beautiful,' and with a loud cackle she banged her foot on the steel side grille of the bed. 'A little pretty mouse curled up with your Polish man.'

Molly turned and placed the drink on Jane's nightstand, then ever so gently, began trying to fix the covers around her, but it was no use, Jane was up again.

'Caw,' Jane screamed. 'I do know you, ah, I know you now, caw, ca-caw.' Jane began pulling clothing from herself, and stepping out of the navy top. She was entirely naked as she waltzed over towards the empty bed and began pirouetting. 'Full up of ghosts there, full of dead

ghosts and I don't like you, not one bit,' she said to
Molly. 'I know what you've done. See, I have you now,
oh, you silly girl. Not a place to be up to your
business.'

'Jane, come back to bed, g'lady, you'd be more comfortable if ya just ...' She took Jane gently by the arm. 'We
need to git you dressed now, girl. Have you knickers
under here?'

'Oh, I surely do, have them, knickers, but we can buy a
pair here in any case, lovely boutique this, but I surely
do, was I making a nuisance of myself? I hope not, I like
shopping here, and I hope to return. Mother says if I
make a nuisance or a pest out of myself, I won't be
allowed, you know, return.'

'Knickers?' Molly repeated, distracted.

'Try da purple bag,' Margaret Rose said.

After she had searched in the holdall, Molly lifted Jane's
legs by the ankles, like a blacksmith would shoe a mare,
and tried to coax each foot into the knickers. Jane stood
on her two flat feet with the knickers around her ankles.

And she sang

And she sang

Michal and Molly up a tree, k-i-s-s-i-n-g

'Here and there and everywhere, here and there and everywhere,' to the tune of 'God Save the Queen'. Jane then leaned in and hugged Molly Zane so ferociously that Jane tumbled forwards up and off her bed, knocking Molly off balance, both of them falling hard onto the windowsill, Molly first, but she held Jane tight like a rugby ball. Wallop. The sheet of glass fell out from its putty and dropped to the ground, smashing and shattering into bright confetti. The two women clung to one another.

Chapter 22|

It was pitch dark outside. It took ninety seconds to move everything from the Ward under the big lights. Except Hegs and Jane. He was too unstable to move anywhere, and she was being sedated. There was a hollowing wind coming in through the open pane. The Ward was finally officially deadly dangerous.

I don't remember who packed my bags. I don't remember who swarmed in to move us all. I don't remember if by then, I looked more like the guy from The White Stripes or Patti Smith or still Michael Keaton. I resolved not to look in mirrors any more.

Off in a tiny side room, Alex wasn't giving up, as he tried to serve out the hot food with a spatula thing and pour red wine into plastic cups. I wasn't sure of the timing, but it was impulsive and this excited me.

'Fucking hell, it's not safe here.' Alex was flustered, his eyes darting around the tiny room. 'What the fuck's a colposcopy?' he said as he read the health posters and warnings on the wall. His hands were shaking and he drank from the cup.

'You don't want to know ...' I muttered.

'Christ. That window,' he said, interrupting me. 'It was so clearly ...' he trailed off, agitated. 'Rattling,' he decided on, his eyes fixed on the soap dispenser that was poorly attached to the wall, lopsided, hairy rawlplugs sticking out.

I had escaped a little, just a little.

'You look lovely,' he said, suddenly staring at me. 'Really lovely.'

'Here, take this off me.'

We unclipped the wires from the telemetry machine they had brought out with me, Big Brother, and freed the little clips from each of the steel nipples.

'Are you actually sitting on a commode?' Alex asked as he circled me for attachments.

'Yeah,' I said. 'Bon appetit!'

We laughed as he started to crunch a poppadum. Then he lifted the bottle of wine, throttled it by the neck and drank straight from it. 'Ah, here, I can't do it, Sinéad, I just can't,' he said, taking another fast swig. 'We're not, well, to be fair, we're not organised, I'm not that kind of person, you know, that would know what to do ... it's terrifying ... and I need to get you that special bed.'

'I'm on a commode. I'm living on a toilet – we don't need a special bed. Besides. We have a special bed.' I tried to wink.

He guffawed, knowing my winking was bullshit.

'OK, maybe we can manage without the bed, but I need to get you oxygen, I'm supposed to get this number, and then ring it,' he said, trailing off. 'Hospice, I was supposed to be given a Hospice link, or number or woman or something,' he said, swigging again, and talking more loudly. 'Molly, Molly has it for me, shit, shit ... The number, it was Molly who ... Her legs, Molly's, they were shaking ... Poor women, that was some fright.'

'Calm down, it's grand, drink your wine. You need to stop panicking. You've had a bit of a shock, we all have ...'

And he did drink.

'Hear me out,' I squared with him. 'Please. I'm a good wife, right?'

We both made faces as though the food we were about to eat had gone off.

'OK, I'm an OK mother, right, can we agree on this?'

He nodded. 'Come on, Sinéad, you're a great mother, you've always been great.'

'I've been absent, you know, and look what I've gone and done. I should have told you. I'm so sorry. I really meant to, you know, I wanted to, I just, I really couldn't.'

'You were absent,' he said, swallowing the wine.

'I know, I really can't go back ...'

'But we are all absent,' he went on, interrupting, 'even when we're there. I've been absent too. I've regrets, the way I've been, and distant, afraid to make a decision, take a chance, taken you for granted. I always knew who you were, you know, you didn't change that much, Ms Sinéad Hynes. You were always a terrific dose, but buyer beware. See, I love you, you were a big gamble ...'

'Lovely, an outsider?' I said.

'No, you're getting me wrong, I loved that about you. And me, that I'd take a chance on you. And they love you, the kids, you make us all laugh, even when you weren't there.'

'With me or at me?'

'At you.'

He put the bottle down.

'They love you so much.'

'Really?'

'Oh, Sinéad –' he cupped my face in his hands – 'you're so hard on yourself. Please don't, it's fine, you're a human being. Fine. A Fine one. We're just humans, chance encounter, trying.'

'Everything OK in here?' Molly slipped her head in.

'Yeah,' I said, quietly.

'You been drinking, hun?'

'No, no, it's blood,' he lied, rubbing down the wine stains on his shirt.

I held up the empty bottle of wine and she laughed.

'Got any lift? Jeez, I need some.'

''Fraid not,' Alex said.

But then he remembered the second bottle and handed it to Molly and she twisted off the cap with her teeth, placed a chair beneath me, and left the commode out on the corridor.

'So sorry, so gross,' she said.

She poured into two plastic cups. 'Cheers, darl,' she said, handing me one, and let her glass down to me.

'Sláinte!'

She was still shaking.

'We'll git you moved, we're going to move you to ICU shortly now. Gawd, some night, huh?' she said.

I nodded.

'ICU'll be the best place for you, hun.'

'Please,' I said, 'let me go, please, Molly. I can't spend another night in here. Tell him.'

Molly leaned forward and kissed me on the side of the face. She downed her wine in one big gulp and threw the empty cup in a needles bin.

'Naw, ya can't,' she said. 'Naw one could. Or should.'

And just like that I was free. But I was always free. Alex just needed approval and inebriation. Molly instructed Alex to ring her when he needed to, and told me it was really great to have met, then she told Alex that a husband should always do what his wife says, darl/hun, and walked out. He was wild-eyed and daft but he had an order now, from someone else.

He plonked me back on the commode after convincing security to let him onto the Ward for one last time, and grabbed my things – headphones, books, Santa's grotto, care package, kidney dish – and stuffed it all in a large green refuse bag. He pushed me along the corridor as I drank from the second bottle of wine. And he hurled the bag over his shoulder.

Claire Hegarty came along the corridor and stopped abruptly when she saw me. 'Why are ye all out here? Have they not sorted you another room yet? Dreadful,' she said, eyeing the large sack. 'Where did you get the wine? Am I missing a party? Awful what happened the window. Very worrying, but did I not say something would happen, did I not say it? Luckily, I was flat out, I'd have gotten a terrible fright. Daddy's still asleep down there. They're waiting to move him, but there's something up with ... a machine. He's not —' she broke off — 'stable. To be honest, the whole thing is making me all anxious. I hate leaving him in there ... alone.'

'Hegs is still on the Ward?' I said, concerned.

'Oh, yes, sure this is twenty-first century Ireland. Disgraceful.'

Her energy was frightening.

'Well, we're going to head on,' Alex said, slurring a little. He began pushing the commode along the corridor; we didn't need to listen to Claire Hegarty in the real world, and she sensed it, then tottered along beside us.

We all waited, awkwardly, for the ping of the lift.

'You know, Daddy just wants to get out.'

'Right,' Alex said, bewildered, but Claire was staring directly at me.

I shot my eyes to hers. 'Right,' I said.

'Well, goodbye then,' she said, with a little wave.

'Bye.'

'Bye,' Alex said. 'All the best to your dad, with the elections and all, hope he pulls out ... round. Ground, please,' he said to a man in green scrubs with a white coat and white shoes, mask around his neck.

'Hold,' someone yelled and the man put his white plastic shoe to the door and we all squeezed up, Alex dragging the commode over to allow a young porter with Manchester United arm tattoos, push in his trolley.

'Thanks, man,' he said, as we accommodated a young kid, fresh from theatre.

His mother's panicked face softened and she smiled down at me. 'Celebrating?' she asked, desperate for a distraction.

'Kind of,' I said. 'I'm going Home.'

'Ah, that's great to hear. Hear that, Mark? You'll be out next, see, everyone gets better.' She smiled down at the child on the small trolley. 'Great to be getting out of here. Best of luck.'

We watched as they all took leave of the lift.

Alex then wheeled me out and round the corner past the public toilets, past the entry to Accident and Emergency where a man sat crying as a child bounced beside him with a bar of chocolate. We went on out past the café with long queues for the deli counter. I didn't speak. I didn't dare open my mouth. Truthfully, we were both a bit pissed, and afraid of getting caught. Alex didn't usually drive under the influence, but he was too astray in the head to stop now.

He didn't stop at the café; he didn't change his mind when the air hit back at us through the revolving doors. I felt light and giddy as we went out towards the night.

Under the street light some magpies swarmed over the roof of the Volvo. White plumage, neon orange lamps. Fluttering. Circling.

One for sorrow.

Two for joy.

Three for a girl.

Four for a boy.

Five for silver.

Six for gold.

Seven for a story never to be told.

I saluted seven times.

Chapter 23|

Shortly after returning home, we decided, together, that I should go for treatment and we decided, together, for better or worse, not to prepare the children yet, or speak much of it, not directly. Not in a sit-down way, for they were all of such different characters; especially Nathan who I worried about the most, how much like me he was, how he'd retreat, disconnect.

We took long slow walks. My mother visited every day, and in her way, and she avoided all conversations around my sickness, though I heard much about other people's misfortunes. Language failed her, though she stayed for hours, often past teatime, just there, in our company, in a new comfortable silence, or pottering about. I grew less and less impatient with her, as she sat on the couch watching *The Chase*, or helping the boys with their routine.

Summer came early and we sat out in the back garden for much of it, the boys jumping into the large paddle pool, except Nathan who didn't like sun or water, and sat under a tree with a Stephen King book. The yellow rosebuds were coming out, and the black spots were challenging them. Alex had littered pots here and there, terracotta ones, with bright daisies and sunflower seeds, all potential. Until they got eaten by slugs.

I picked up my laptop once, and closed up some deals. I read some books, lots of books.

Time slowed.

The tooth fairy came and three legged-races were lost. Matches were played and mostly lost, dinosaurs were renamed, teeth were left unbrushed, jocks were left for pick-up, and fights broke out. Someone on the bus told Jacob that he was a pansy. And I told the little shit that I'd break his fucking scrawny legs if he hassled my son again. And I taught Jacob how to say it, loud, and not to be afraid. It took a long time to get him to scream out. He kept giggling, and covering his mouth with his little fat hands – no, Mammy.

Piano grade one, violin grade three and a row with Joshua about giving up music altogether. We compromised and he switched to electric guitar. I instructed

Alex to burn all school reports, for no news is good news, because we should be valued in neither our successes nor our failures, but in our endurance.

We redecorated every room with colour.

★

One Monday, Margaret Rose came around for lunch. She arrived at the front door and when I opened it she looked unusual, somewhat uncomfortable in her clothes. She had a fussy peach-and-gold scarf about her neck, and her hair had been blow-dried and back-combed; her face looked strange, somehow more stern or lined, with dark foundation and black eye kohl and lashings of blue mascara. In the kitchen she fussed with her large orange handbag and after much coaxing, eventually sat on a high stool at the kitchen island, constantly checking behind her. Hegs had passed away some hours after the glass fell from the window, she told me – it was the shock – but he went very fast, and looked younger as a corpse than he had ever looked in life. She always went to removals, it's the right thing to do, she said.

Things were not so good with Paddy. He was missing again, but the girls were doing OK, it was hard keeping them away from trouble. My boys hadn't reached this age, she said, and quickly apologised and blessed herself.

But just wait until they do. Then apologised again and blessed herself, and a final apology for blessing herself. We laughed and she relaxed a little. We had tea and a slice each from an apple tart after lunch, which she'd brought; I was embarrassed I hadn't baked anything, and she told me life was too short to worry about baking. That she'd only come to see me, to talk to me, because in truth, she missed me. She'd sent Jane a care package, every month since, you know, they moved her to, well, you know, she wasn't comfortable with where they had moved Jane and so I didn't press her; she chatted about the care package, just things, photos of Clifden, Dog's Bay, boats at Roundstone, some soap, handcream, magazines, a few loose tops and nice trousers, some bras, knickers and a lipstick. But she was refused entry to see her. Only family.

I thanked her for coming and said I hadn't been sure she would.

We hugged, in that awkward way misplaced people do, and neither of us knew when to let go. So we stood for a long time, my face in her fussy scarf.

Byebyebyebyebye.

Bye.

Margaret Rose dipped her finger into the hole at the foot of Jesus. She then walked out the front door backwards, blessing herself.

'He's a finer, right?' I said, nodding at my mother's gift.

'Not funny, Sinéad,' she said, laughing. 'Jaysus, God be good ta ya,' leaving the way she arrived, to leave luck in our home.

★

Later that evening the boys were in their PJs. Except Joshua, who no longer wore PJs and was walking around the house in a pair of jocks and a black hoody, the hood permanently up on his round head. We lay under duvets that Nathan had placed down in the sitting room, coaxing us all to watch *Harry Potter and the Philosopher's Stone*. Getting everyone off personal screens was almost impossible, but Nathan worked hard at family gatherings. Joshua complained, wanting to play Xbox, and Alex plucked down his hood and tossed his hair – fuck sake, Dad – and Joshua quickly put it up again. Alex then told him to put on pants, and he grunted, fuck sake, Dad, pants, really? And saying he'd watch the dumb film only if he could stay on his phone, but Alex pleaded, no phones rule, remember, and Nathan kept repeating, Alex went on, you know the rules, you do, and Joshua told him the film was full of inaccuracies, but also said it was all dumb fiction in any case. Alex pleaded again, put-on-pants, get-off-phone, stop-cursing, and though he continued revealing spoilers, Joshua did what he was told, eventually, and took the hood down, telling Nathan and Jacob that it was all about Harry's dead parents, which, he felt very strongly, was a stupid way to begin anything, but Nathan disagreed, saying, look what Harry had achieved, all alone, and Alex said that when someone loves us, like properly loves us, we bring that love for ever, and ever. Nathan agreed, and Jacob looked wide-eyed and interested in how a kid like Harry could do so much with a wand, until Joshua said they were all just silly posh kids, and Harry Potter didn't exist anyway, so it was all a big waste of time. Jacob said he was real and had curly glasses. And we all laughed, except the teenager who watched it with one eye on his phone, and one on the TV screen.

★

I was shearing a ewe and she was wrathful, for she was an old ewe, the oldest ewe we had, and we had kept her from when she was a pet lamb, fed her by the bottle, for her mother had died moments after birthing her, and left a white mound, heaped out on our scraggy hill, just down from the yard, where she lay among the yellow ferns and tall thistles, so when she was a young lamb, all her memory came from touch, our early touches of the bottle towards her mouth, her wool hard and coarse, and as she grew, her sensory memory was alive, and now, she'd had enough of her wool being taken, stripped off her, she kept hopping and leaping at the back of the holding pen, late May, flocked with all the other sheep, ready, she darted this way and that, head down, for the old ewe was too old to be meat, as she scrambled back into the corner, her feet skidding out from under her, desperate to stay heavy with her coat, for maybe her memory knew that November was cruel, but nothing to the March winds that would come again, with hail and wicked frosts, and that utter cruelty of April, trying to kill off what it has spawned, spiting itself, when the early growth would flourish in earnest, and this old ewe had birthed lamb after lamb, clean and fast, each spring, early to drop, always one of the first, giving us Easter meat, and every summer we'd grab her by the neck in the pen, and straddle her between our thighs, my younger brother holding down her body, I'd knock her sideways, gently, and he'd kneel softly upon her warm coarse wool to pin her, as I'd snip at her with an old blade shears, as her coat flocked back on itself into folds, wings of buttery yellow, damp, it became one rug, and we'd skirt it, roll it, helping her up, as her frightened eyes watched for my brother to lift up the blue metal clasp of the gate, and when he'd swing it back open, she'd dart out, rushing up the steps of the pen, shitting nervously, and run back down towards the scraggy hill, unused to the lightness of her body now, two or three fresh red wounds in my wake, and I'd berate myself as I was falling to sleep that night, tossing and turning, for the clumsy sharp cuts I left on her, that she didn't deserve, that would sting, I'd felt woeful, embarrassed at her exhaustion, at her body's benightedness, her terrified dark eye staring at me, and my hands, wet from sweat, sticking to the small shards of paint on the old royal-blue shears, the paint chipping off to reveal a rusty dirty brown, like the ewe's particle knowledge, in pieces, how to lie still, play dead, hide, show yourself, hide again, when to jump up and run, and run, running fast away from us, giving her last birth out on the hill, the old ewe is *down,* the ewe is *sick,* hunt her in, grunting, hunt her out, bleating, leave her to the sun, the wind, the rain, spray her, dip her, copper injections, toss her, watch her, count her, until she dies, until we rolled up her last wool coat, the last offering, and we gathered it, twined it neatly, it was warm and comfortable, and I let her go, as she skittered out through my hands, running on past the open gate, out to join the herd, though this time, she slowed to a walk, uncertain up against the strong breeze on the hill, her shorn beating skin stayed throbbing under my nervous hands as she, at last, put her head down and grazed a little, and until eventually, I could no longer feel her body under mine, as my own blood roused through me now, coursing, hot, alive, just, then rushing, whooshing, whooshing, until I no longer felt pain, just a gentle gushing in my ears, warm, goodbye, I have known you, I have known the way of you, now as you were, and I thanked her for all she had given us.

Acknowledgements|

Many thanks to my first readers, Aoibheann McCann, Saoirse McCann-Callanan, James Martyn Joyce, Alan McMonagle, Lisa McInerney, Caroline Moran, Claire-Louise Bennett, Nicole Flattery, Mike McCormack and Conor O' Callaghan.

Very special thanks to my mum, Catherine Feeney, who introduced me to books, understood their significance in a world where a woman's voice was often unheard, and for her close reading of each draft.

Unconditional love and gratitude to my husband, Ray Glasheen, and to our sons, Jack and Finn.

This book would not exist without Sinéad Gleeson, who is utterly selfless in her promotion of other writers, particularly women, and has done Trojan work to recover and uncover women's voices in print.

To my kind and lovely agent, Peter Straus, who loves poetry as much as I do, and to all at Rogers, Coleridge and White, especially Matt Turner, Eliza Plowden and Laurence Laluyaux.

Thank you to all at Harvill Secker, Vintage and Penguin Random House Ireland who worked on any part of this book. In particular, many thanks to Mia Quibell-Smith, Aimée Johnston, and to Rosie Palmer for her bold and brilliant jacket design. It was a dream come true to feature work by the incredible artist Daisy Patton on the North American cover. I am indebted to Zoe Norvell for her daring design, and to Natalie Olsen for the beautiful rendering of the hardcover. A huge thank you to Dan Wells, Vanessa Stauffer, Michaela Stephen, and all the team at Biblioasis who were a dream to work with on all aspects of this edition.

And finally, to Kate Harvey, my editor and friend. For her patience and dedication with this novel, and her love of its characters. Here's to the great mad journey we went on! x